NOW THEN

NOW THEN

a novel

MORGAN RADFORD

AMISTAD

An Imprint of HarperCollins*Publishers*

HarperCollins books may be purchased for educational, business, or sales promotional use. For information, please email the Special Markets Department at SPsales@harpercollins.com.

hc.com

FIRST EDITION

Designed by Yvonne Chan

Library of Congress Cataloging-in-Publication Data has been applied for.

ISBN 978-0-06-345783-6

Printed in the United States of America

26 27 28 29 30 LBC 5 4 3 2 1

To Adelana, the conduit by which good things have—and continue to—come.

PART ONE

CHAPTER 1

Lily

Cambridge, Massachusetts
September 3, 1991

My body jolted forward, stopped only by the nylon seatbelt strapped across my chest.

"*Oyeeee!*" my mother shouted. "Kem, watch where you're going! You almost hit that kid, *pobrecito*."

"Take a breath, Mari," my father replied.

My mother was always like this when she was nervous: short-tempered, less patient. She'd been tense ever since we left the Elk River exit off I-81N, fists clenched, eyes darting across the road as if a semitruck were waiting for just the right moment to wipe us off the map.

"Mami, it's okay," I assured her, reaching toward the front passenger seat to put my hand on her shoulder. "I think those are the dorms there, just beyond the gate."

Johnston Gate.

I recognized it immediately from the brochure: the imposing black iron rods flanked by walls of deep red brick.

The portal to access and privilege.

Less than a year ago, Mami had slid that brochure tentatively across our kitchen table, eyes peering over the steaming plate of *vaca frita* she had whisked off the stove.

"*Querida*, just take a look," she said, handing me a metal fork from the creakiest drawer in our kitchen cabinet. Her hair was still in the bright orange head wrap from the night before, a few wiry curls escaping from beneath the cloth; her cinnamon face, round and eager.

My mother tapped twice on the pamphlet, forcing me to look at the photos of smiling multicultural students, their arms slung loosely around one another as they posed for the camera.

Mami had been pleading with me for months to apply to a university. I was just starting my senior year at Western Piedmont High, the dilapidated public high school at the bottom of the Appalachian mountain we called home. I spent my days with five hundred other teenagers, moving together as one huddled mass between classes, a single organism under the microscope of overworked, underpaid teachers.

There, I bided my time, unchallenged and uninspired.

I had already applied to Elk River Junior College, planning to get a serviceable degree from their English department. Sure, it wasn't anyone's dream destination; I'd be enrolled alongside the meth addicts I would soon graduate with, sent there pityingly in the final stop of their two-step diversion program. The crumbling limestone was not the place of dreams, but rather a receptacle of broken promises—the exclamation point to our failing public education system. Surrounded by a rusted chain-link fence, the college looked more like a prison than a school.

For many of us, this was our final stop.

And our last hope.

Which was why I knew I needed to stick around. My aging parents, despite their pride and independence, were not cut out for this life alone. Mountain life is quiet and hard, physical and consuming. It's not meant to be lived in isolation.

As if reading my thoughts, my mother cleared her throat, leaned across the table, and touched my arm. The dime-size medallion she always wore around her neck glinted in the light from the window.

"We will be fine without you, *querida*. This is a parent's job—and a parent's dream. There, you will be competing with the sons and daughters of princes and presidents. You, the daughter of these mountains. The daughter of an immigrant."

"Where?" I asked not registering the name on the front of the brochure.

"Harvard," she answered simply.

I blanched.

"Huh?"

My mother picked up her fork and started eating, as if she hadn't just named the most prestigious university in the world.

And yet, seven months later . . . here I was.

"Pull over!" my mother shouted, pointing to a small parking space left by a departing station wagon.

My father glided off the uneven cobblestone street, maneuvering our beat-up blue minivan between the compact white lines.

"Ready, Pickle?" he asked, using the nickname he had started calling me as a child, back when he said my head was the shape of a small cucumber. I was looking out the window but could feel his eyes staring at me from the rearview mirror.

"As ready as I'll ever be," I sighed nervously, grabbing my backpack before unlocking the door. I saw my father reach over the console to give my mother's hand a squeeze.

"It's going to be okay, Mari," he whispered quietly in her ear. "Everything has its season."

He leaned over and kissed my mother on her cheek as she pressed her head against the headrest, her eyes closed.

Eager to stretch my legs after the fourteen-hour drive, I climbed out of the back seat and spun around to close the door.

That's when I saw it.

All of it.

Vines of deep green ivy snaking their way up old Georgian brick buildings; students, hair unkempt, plodding across manicured lawns with backpacks bouncing to the rhythm of their steps. The leaves were still green, clinging on to their final days of summer and framing the campus as if it were a painting brought to life.

Where the hell was I?

This didn't look like anything I'd ever seen, and certainly no place I belonged.

My father walked around the car and lifted the door to the trunk, handing me a small duffel bag sandwiched between my suitcase and a leaning stack of brown boxes.

A neon Frisbee whirred by me, its sender a blonde, floppy-haired coed wearing a Bob Marley T-shirt.

"Looks way better than the photos, huh?" my father marveled, taking in the action.

"Yeah," I mumbled, looking down, suddenly conscious of my scuffed Chuck Taylor sneakers, the laces shredded and gray.

My father carefully took down the single suitcase filled with gently worn sweaters and the winter coat we'd pulled from the donations bin at church.

"Let's go ahead and get your things inside," I heard my mother say from the sidewalk, having finally emerged from the passenger seat.

Beads of sweat dripped from my hairline as my parents and I carried our flimsy taped cardboard across the lawn to the entryway of the building. I read somewhere that Harvard called all of its dorms "houses" to create a sense of *familial cohesion*.

Others might call it elitism.

"Welcome!" A voice chimed over my left shoulder as a middle-aged woman with tight auburn curls came bouncing toward us.

"I'm Dean Grant! You must be Miss Walker?"

"I am," I smiled, wondering how she knew my name.

"We have a photo list of faces to look for on move-in day," she said tugging at the lanyard hanging across her neck, answering my unspoken question. "Helps us spot the first years."

First year.

The beginning.

A *new* beginning.

I stared at the cracked red brick beneath my feet.

"You're going to be in C-twenty-two," Dean Grant continued. "I think your roommate has already moved in—Hana Kang. I met her parents about an hour ago."

Hearing the word *parents*, my mother stepped forward as if released from a trance. "I'm Marisol," she said, emphasizing the short "o" in her name as she extended her hand. Mami's accent was always thicker and more pronounced when she was nervous, as if out of sheer exhaustion she had given up trying to hide the swaying vowels of her youth.

"We'll take good care of your daughter, Marisol," Dean Grant assured her.

My mother gave her best smile and clasped her hands together in an expression of gratitude. Still, I could feel the nervousness radiating off her. She had barely said anything the last three hours of the trip.

My parents and I walked across the courtyard and left what we couldn't carry beneath the curved arch of the entryway. Together, we made our way up the chipped marble stairs to the third floor, my father lifting the largest box while my mother and I balanced the small suitcase and duffel bag.

C-22.

The door was open.

Inside, a petite girl was organizing her books along the wide base of a light brown bookshelf, her back to the door.

"Knock, knock," I said hesitantly, tapping my knuckles against the weathered wood.

The girl turned with a start.

"Oh hi!" she beamed. "You must be Lily. I'm Hana. Nice to finally meet you!"

I could feel my face turn red.

She was stunning. Asian. Petite with a crop top and loose-fitting jeans, this girl looked like she had taken a quick detour from her summer vacation in Greece to casually enroll in school. Her bangs, cut bluntly across her forehead, were the perfect frame for her almond gray eyes. Freckles lightly scattered across her nose and cheeks, pouty lips any Hollywood actress would die for. We'd had one brief, long-distance phone call after the house leader sent us a packet with our room assignments, talking for all of three minutes and collectively deciding if there was any furniture we needed to bring. Her voice, low and resonant that day, didn't conjure the image of the diminutive woman standing in front of me.

"It's so great to meet you," I said, immediately regretting my choice of ripped jeans and oversize Frida Kahlo T-shirt. "This is my mom Marisol, and my dad Kem Walker. We're arriving from a pretty long car ride, so we're all just getting settled . . ." I trailed off, trying to offer an excuse for my poor appearance.

Or, for just being poor.

"Of course! Let me get out of your way. I put my things on the bottom bunk since I'm so short. Judging from your height, I made the right call!" she said, her friendly laughter escaping like a wind chime in the breeze.

Standing five feet, ten inches, I'm hard to miss, having inherited my father's height. Still, I'm convinced my stature is not what people actually react to when they see me: it is the mountain of curls I inherited from my mother, the ones that add at least another six inches of height and spill wild and unruly just past my shoulders. The white kids at school used to call me "Brilly Lily," comparing my hair to a coarse yellow Brillo pad used for cleaning. They would pluck out single strands to see if I could feel them snap, silent tears falling down my cheeks as I faced the teacher's chalkboard. I sat unflinching, praying they would eventually get bored and move on.

They never did.

"The top bunk is fine by me," I answered, tossing my backpack onto the stiff mattress.

Mami squeezed my arm, a signal for us to get the rest of my boxes. I excused myself and followed her back down the marble steps. There, we waited while my father went to the car to check for anything we'd left behind, jogging across the lawn like a twenty-year-old himself. As I bent over to grab one of the smaller crates, my mother held out her arm to stop me.

"*¿Qué te pasa, Mami?*" I asked. "You okay?"

Her face was drained of color.

"Listen, *querida,* we said we couldn't stay long, remember? Just long enough to make sure you got safely inside."

"There's no rush, Mami. We can set things up and—"

She interrupted me.

"No. We need to get back. It will be too expensive to find a hotel here tonight. But listen, there's something I want to tell you."

I set the box I was balancing back down.

My mother unzipped her faded army green cargo jacket and pulled a white envelope out of the inside pocket. She put one hand on my shoulder, and with the other, pressed the creased paper into my palm.

"What is this? I don't need any money . . ."

My parents had already given me a wad of five hundred dollars to pack in my suitcase before we left. I knew coming up with that amount wasn't easy for them, but they insisted I have something for emergencies, enough for a one-way train ticket back home.

"It's just a letter," she whispered, pausing as she saw my dad approaching.

"But Mami, I don't understand . . ."

"You don't have to understand right now, *querida*. But you will. Just trust me this once, okay?"

This once.

Hadn't I always done what she asked, trust aside? She never gave the full picture, always stopped just shy of sharing anything personal that might expose even a crumb of vulnerability. And yet, time and again, I followed her blindly. Call it respect, call it duty, call it the occupational hazard of being the only child of an immigrant. Obey, but don't ask. Why wouldn't she give me credit for all those times? I could feel my frustration rising, her lack of acknowledgment aggravating the tiny lacerations in our relationship.

I slid the letter into my back jean pocket, my mother and I watching in silence as my father went up and down the stairs one final time.

"Welp," he said, standing with his hands on his hips, feet shoulder-width apart, "that's the last of it."

My father looked up at me slowly, wiping the thin layer of sweat from his forehead. I could tell he was trying not to cry.

"Let's go before it gets late, *mi amor,*" my mother nudged, just as my father reached out to tousle my crown of curls.

It was all happening so fast.

"You sure you don't want to stay and find somewhere to eat?" I struggled, feeling my throat close in my attempt to delay the inevitable.

"No," my mother interjected firmly before my father could answer. "We should get going before it gets dark."

The sun was just beginning to set, its reflection bouncing off the freshly scrubbed glass of the dormitory windows.

"We love you, my darling," my father said softly, leaning in for a hug.

In that moment, his arms felt like the safest place in the world.

I took a deep breath, inhaling the familiar scent of his laundry detergent.

Our laundry detergent.

One of the millions of micro-decisions we silently made as a family.

At least, until now.

My mother looked away.

When my father let go, she, too, gathered me in her arms, the tip of her head landing beneath my chin. Standing this close, I was reminded of how small she was. I could feel her tears through my T-shirt.

"Lee la carta," she whispered so that only I could hear.

Read the letter.

She pulled away and grabbed my father's hand, reversing the steps they had taken just moments before. My mother wrapped her arm around my father's waist, squeezing firmly as his body released a small shudder that could have only come from crying. As I watched their figures grow smaller in the distance, a memory of my mother clutching that brochure at our kitchen table flashed through my mind.

That tiny piece of paper had carried both a future and a promise: a promise that the life she envisioned for me could be bigger than the one I'd imagined for myself.

But now, standing alone in front of the redbrick dorm—the shadow of the towering gate behind me—I was adrift and untethered.

Perhaps my mother's faith was enough to get me here, but it wasn't enough to help me survive.

CHAPTER 2

I picked up my weathered suitcase and scaled the stairs to C-22, stepping over crumpled boxes and discarded books to get to my new bedroom, sparse with only the set of bunk beds, a tiny wooden desk, and a dimly lit floor lamp. Not hearing any signs of my roommate, I closed the door behind me and crawled up the narrow ladder to my twin mattress, burying my face in the palms of my hands.

What the hell had I done?

I could feel the pinprick of fresh tears burning my eyes. Here I was in a barren room with chipping paint—the only place in the world to call my own—and it wasn't even mine. I had to share it with a girl I didn't know while my father worked an overnight double shift and my mom scrubbed floors just to afford the Goodwill clothes on my back.

My heart sunk as I pictured my parents on the car ride home, too afraid to speak for fear of falling apart, each one trying to be strong for the other.

I leaned back against the wall and carefully slipped my mother's letter out of my back pocket, the envelope crackling as I split it open with the edge of my nail. Inside were three sheets of lined paper that looked like they had been torn from a notebook, folded over twice to form a neat square. My mother's graceful, looping Spanish stared back at me.

Lily,

They say that no immigrant parent tells their children the full story of how they came to be, living the second act of our lives in a foreign country that—no matter how hard we try—will never truly be our own. We are a tribe of dreamers and seekers: we pack secrets like we packed our belongings, making an impossible calculation of risk—is the life that we want worth wagering the life that we know? How do we choose what to bring and what to leave behind?

I know you know the basics: I came here from Cuba, I met your father, and our lives changed beautifully and irreversibly when we had you.

But you, my child—who silently shoulders so many burdens of this world on your own must know that you are neither the first, nor the only, to experience the pain of solitude.

Watching you pack your suitcase, stacking your notebooks and snapping your pens into place, I am reminded of a girl I once knew—many moons ago—who also embarked on a journey alone, hoping to change her stars.

It was so long ago that when I look in the mirror, I barely recognize her.

I, too, went to university.

I can still smell the must of the boarding house that I stumbled into when I arrived, just blocks away from the sea. Those walls, holding the secrets of other girls like me—girls who no longer had a home—who left behind the life they knew for the life they wanted.

There I stood, just like you, staring out into the city that had become my choice: a choice that changed my life in ways that were beyond the foresight of my youth.

It is time for you to know my story, the true story of how I came to be. I am sorry I wasn't able to share more sooner.

Maybe one day you will understand why.

For now, I simply want you to know that you are not alone.

When you look up at the stars thinking of home, and hopefully of me, remember that you are part of a larger history that has conspired to bring you here.

And as you grasp your future with both hands, please remember that you too have a story to tell . . .

I put the letter down in disbelief.

Mami had gone to university? She cleaned houses for a living. I had always assumed she didn't have the opportunity, or perhaps, as much as I hated to admit it, the will.

But this—all of this—was *her* dream.

I stared up at the blank walls, frozen, until I was startled by a knock on the door.

Hana tapped twice more before peeking through the narrow crack.

"Heineken?" she asked, widening the opening just enough to show me the cold glass bottle, small droplets of water sliding down the front. She must've seen the surprise on my face.

"What? You think we all just drink *soju*?" she laughed.

"No, it's just . . . where did you even get that?" I asked. "And what is *soju*?"

Alcohol on the first day in an underage dorm was a bold move. And the truth was, I never really drank that much, except for a few times with Eric, my best friend back home. He would sneak a dusty bottle of gin from his grandmother's cupboard, the same ones my mother cleaned every day for work. Together, we'd sit by the bleachers at dusk, sipping slowly from our plastic water bottles with the labels ripped off, watching the track stars or football players run laps.

That's all we *could* do.

Watch.

We lived in their world, but not in their society.

We were different.

"It's basically Korean vodka," Hana continued, sensing my hesitation. Her wide smile matched the twinkle in her eye. "I got all the girls at my boarding school obsessed with it. There's a stash in the mini fridge. Want to try?"

"I'm okay for now," I declined, hoping I didn't sound like a prig. "Save me one for later?"

"Only if you take me up on it," Hana quipped, prying off the silver bottle cap. "Hey, where were you before this?" she asked, plopping down on the dirty white carpet to face me. "Some preppy Southern school in the 'burbs?"

I rested my back on the wall and pulled my feet up to my chest, sensing I wasn't about to escape this conversation anytime soon.

"Hardly," I laughed. "But I guess that's why I wanted to try something new . . . a change of scenery."

"I hear you," Hana said. "I actually love L.A., but I left to get away from my dad, mostly. He runs this massive skincare company and wanted me to be the perfect image—and the perfect prototype—for his business. Turns out, I wasn't. I was too curvy, too artistic, too unfocused, and basically everything he had promised himself I wouldn't become once we moved to America. He was constantly trying to tweak me as if I were one of his mannequins: 'I know a great surgeon in Seoul for that new eye surgery,'" Hana imitated in a deep male voice. "'Oh, and we just introduced a new skin lightening cream coming out next month!'" she added with a smirk. "He never understood that I didn't *want* any of that bullshit. I just wanted to be free. So he sent me to a rich boarding school that's basically like an Ivy League farm and I applied here as a compromise: he gets bragging rights and I get distance."

I was stunned by her candor. How was she able to get so personal . . . so quickly? She had only just met me. My mother always taught me to keep "family business" private and to never reveal anything that could leave room for public judgment.

"I get it," I said, wanting to sound compassionate, even though I didn't get any of it at all. Skin bleaching cream? Eye surgery?

"Well listen, if you ever want to try some *soju*, you're welcome to join us for some fresh air and massholery." She paused for dramatic effect, hoping her sarcasm would land. "A few of the kids who made it here from my high school are going to Minos Bar once everyone makes it to campus."

"That'd be great," I conceded, stretching out on my bed for the first time. "Count me in."

CHAPTER 3

Marisol

Elk River, North Carolina
September 17, 1991

Marisol twisted the rag in her palm with both hands, squeezing until her knuckles turned white. The gray water filled with dust, dripping steadily into the bucket below.

It had been two weeks since she and Kem dropped Lily off at college, her mind wandering back to the last time she saw her only daughter.

Had she made friends? Was she lonely? Did she miss home?

Marisol hurried as she took her last circular strokes along the porcelain backsplash, a cascade of blue and gold mosaic. The clock read 1:42 p.m., an hour and a half until the Mitchell kids would return home from school. Annie was six and Ben almost eight, both with boundless energy and very little patience. Marisol savored the few hours in the afternoon when she got to work in peace, only the echoes of her cleaning bouncing off the walls of the imposing mansion.

Marisol picked up the rag and wiped the kitchen counter once more for good measure. Taking off her apron, she folded it neatly before placing it in the tiny drawer at the bottom of the cabinet that Miss Eva, the heiress of the Mitchell estate, allowed her to use. There, hidden in the corner, was Marisol's notepad and old fountain pen. Since that first letter to her daughter, Marisol had begun writing again, hand hovering over the notepad, trying to force herself to say the harder things—*write* the harder things—the parts of her story that were too difficult to share in person.

Marisol stared at the blotches of navy blue ink splattered across the cover, bent and misshapen. Had Lily read the first letter? Would she? Was the truth she'd begun to unravel in those pages too much of a burden to place on a young girl just beginning her own journey into adulthood?

With every baseboard washed, every window cleaned, and every hard-earned vowel she learned to say without accent, raising Lily had been Marisol's redemption, the clean slate she wasn't sure she deserved. Marisol had worked invisibly and tirelessly to forget the trauma that first led her to this country, knees cracked and body bleeding as she stumbled onto its shores.

From that moment, she knew she had to erase everything she was before.

Especially once her belly was full with child.

But staring at the blank page before her, Marisol now realized the severity of the price she'd paid: she, too, had lost a piece of her daughter. For every effort she had made to protect Lily—to keep her from the ghosts that chased her to these shores—Marisol had sealed off a piece of herself, cauterizing the softest parts of her that Lily needed as safe landing. Marisol yearned to reach out across the expanse of time, to share some shard of truth that would tether her to her daughter once and for all. But each time she tried to close the abyss of misunderstanding between them, the flood of her own memories choked her with fear before the words could leave her mouth.

At first, Marisol felt she could barely muster up more than simple pleasantries when she first tried to put those words to paper.

She pressed the edges of her memories—tested the bounds of her own vulnerability—hoping to build some common understanding with the person she wanted to love her most in this world.

The only job of a mother, she had believed, was to protect her child and to comfort her. And yet, this was the central role at which she felt most inept.

Marisol knew there was no recovering the pieces of connection she had lost, the ability to feel that she had suppressed in order to survive. But, she thought, if one day Lily could hear her story, then perhaps she would understand.

Maybe, even, forgive her.

Which was more, Marisol knew, than she could ask for in person.

She also knew, as she stared down at the blank page in her notebook, that if she didn't try now, her daughter might be lost to her forever.

Havana, Cuba
August 23, 1956

The bus left me with a whir, its wheels spinning against the broken asphalt.

I stood there in a puddle, the water seeping into the thin soles of my leather shoes. It was the rainy season and the late afternoon shower was finally tapering off. The skies would soon open up again, pouring out their anger.

Or perhaps their disappointment.

I stared down at my dress, my mother's hand-sewn tulips already discolored, a large dark spot spreading across the seat of the fabric.

Maybe the house mistress would think it was rain?

There were no bathroom stops on the twenty-three-hour journey from Camagüey.

I stood soiled and alone and, as my father would say, getting what I deserved.

"Silly ideas are for silly people," he'd cautioned, warning me against the perils of Havana and reminding me that I should be grateful for the chance to finish high school. My place, he explained, was back in Camagüey, building a life and a family next to his.

I tried to tell him that things were changing, that I had run into Caridad Acosta at the market who told me all about her adventures in the city.

She left last year for Havana to become a doctor.

When I asked my teacher about the possibility of studying at university like Caridad, Señora García said my grades were good enough to warrant review from the registrar.

But that still wasn't enough for my father.

When the day finally came, Señora García was the only person waving proudly as the bus pulled away from its dusty stop, my father having refused to allow my mother or brother to see me off.

Now, more than five hundred kilometers away, I held up the handwritten note Señora Garcia had shoved into my hand before that final boarding call. I squinted as I struggled to read the numbers scrawled onto the paper, small droplets of water falling from my ringlets of curls. The rusted brass symbols on the outside of the two-story building dangled against the façade.

Was this it?

¿Número 152 Calle 19? La Bombonera Boarding House for Girls?

I walked up the tilted staircase, splotches of gray concrete peeking through the peeling paint.

I knocked twice.

No answer.

Gently, I pressed the door open as it creaked on its hinges. There was no one at the front desk, bare with a telephone and blank calendar hanging by the wall. Despite the empty foyer, I could hear a buzz coming from the back salon.

"¿Buenas tardes?" I called out, inching into the doorframe until the door latched behind me. Still hearing no response, I threw my cloth knapsack over my shoulder and walked down the hallway toward the low hum of voices. Pictures of women old enough to be my grandmother were framed on either side of the corridor, plaques of their professional achievements listed beneath each photo: *scientist, doctor, lawyer.*

The final plaque showed the photo of a sleek, bespectacled older woman with dark hair pulled into a chignon, staring openly into the distance.

Isabel M. Collado, writer.

As if on cue, the woman from the final frame came to life, her tall figure blocking the warm light that filled the room behind her. I peered just beyond her shoulder, watching in awe as more than a dozen women passed plates piled high with steaming food across one long wooden table.

"Buenas noches," the older woman greeted me mirthlessly. "I didn't hear the door ring. Are you in the right place?" She took in my tattered clothes and frayed knapsack, the small puddles of liquid pooling around my ankles.

"Sí, Señora. I was told to come here for room and board. My teacher, Señora Elena García in Camagüey, said she contacted Señora Collado for a spare room?"

"Ah yes, García's girl. Marisol, is it?"

Before I could answer, the woman turned toward a younger coed with curly red hair and chubby cheeks. "Mirta! *Ven!* Show this girl the sleeping quarters."

The young woman scrambled off the dining bench as the older woman turned back to face me.

"*I* am Señora Collado. This is a house for unwed women pursuing higher education. There is no room for gallivanting, entertaining members of the opposite sex, or engaging in overtly political activity. Any infraction and you will see yourself out. Understood?"

Staring at the stern, bony woman in front of me, I thought of my mother instantly: her plump cheeks and soft eyes, everything this woman was not.

I fought back tears.

Why had I ever thought any of *this*, was worth losing all of *that*?

"*Hola*," the young woman from the table beamed, bouncing over to extend her hand. "*Soy* Mirta. You'll be on the first floor with us."

I followed her past the stairs and farther down the narrow hallway, leading to a small, drafty room with two rows of neatly stacked beds.

"This is where we sleep," she said, "and only sleep. Señora Collado demands we spend our waking hours studying or at the university. Which is fine by me," she added with a snort, "anything here is better than Las Tunas!"

"Las Tunas," I exclaimed, the first smile escaping my lips since I'd left home. "I'm from Camagüey. Did you come here by yourself?"

"We all did," she answered quickly, the light suddenly draining from her eyes. "My parents said if this was my choice, then I couldn't come back."

I imagined there was a story—all too similar, and all too sad—for many of these women.

But I didn't want to pry.

Instead, I offered an admission of my own.

"My father said whatever happens next will be my fault."

I looked down at my shoes, now dark with both rain and urine.

My mind flashed to the night I told my father I had been admitted to the university. He was unlacing his boots by the door, his nailbeds still black and tacky from the sugar cane.

"*Me aceptaron, Papá.*" I looked at him nervously.

He refused to meet my gaze.

"Why fantasize about what you can't have?" he asked distractedly. "The pain of failure only makes the torment worse."

He placed each boot neatly beside the door, turning his back to me as he walked to the kitchen.

For as long as I could remember, my father spent his entire days in relentless heat, the sun beating down on his bare back. As if driven by some physical memory lodged deep in his bones, he worked the fields, his dark arms bearing the lashes of his machete. He once told me his own father had taught him how to cut cane when he was just a boy, having emigrated from Jamaica like so many others in the Eastern provinces who had come from nearby islands, hoping for better luck in the Cuban soil.

Now, he teaches my brother Mateo those same powerful strokes, the bedrock of his trade.

All summer I watched the two of them from my window, wiping their faces with damp towels, their bodies weary. Once, I heard my father tell Mateo that there was no greater nobility for a man than working with his hands, staying close to God's earth.

But did he believe that?

And is that what my brother wanted? Mateo, who rushed home before sundown to feverishly read ripped textbooks from the neighborhood schoolhouse?

Or was my father simply protecting his only son from the failure of a dream unrealized, collapsing it before it could launch?

At least I knew what was expected of me.

All I had to do was look at my mother.

She prepared our meals every day and lifted sacks of burlap filled with coffee beans to ship to the Americans, bringing in a few extra pesos for us to buy meat on Sundays. Watching her was like seeing a premonition of the life I was condemned to if I didn't break its cycle, drastically and decisively.

I just hadn't realized it would cost so much.

Mirta looked at me, as if seeing the images that flashed behind my eyes.

“I’ll show you the way to the university tomorrow,” she promised reassuringly, nodding toward my small bag of damp clothes.

Mirta put one hand on my shoulder before reaching for the brass doorknob. “Get some rest,” she whispered, turning back one final time. “It only gets harder.”

With that, Mirta stepped out of the room, the heavy door slamming behind her.

Alone once again, I stared at the stacked row of barren bunks. Each one belonged to a girl just like me, scared and searching for more.

CHAPTER 4

Lily

Cambridge, Massachusetts
September 20, 1991

Students zipped across the manicured lawn, crossing paths with bedraggled professors, their papers spilling from old leather briefcases. I adjusted the straps of my Jansport backpack, shifting my weight from one foot to the other.

I still couldn't believe I was here.

I'd spent the last few days rushing between classes, lost inside the labyrinth of buildings older than the country, hiding in corners of dusty libraries with books older than me. These initial two weeks following orientation were called Shopping Period. We got to sample classes without commitment—no strings, no grades—just the freedom to learn.

It was one of the many perks I'd discovered in the crash course on privilege since I'd arrived: rarely did the bounds of commitment or the burden of duty apply to this world of the elite. They always kept their freedom to choose. In fact, there seemed to be an entire series of "off menu" items in their universe, items that the rest of us plebeians never even knew existed.

Don't like your table at a restaurant? Ask to be seated closer to the door.

Don't have enough money for that fancy internship? Quietly write to the director.

Don't like your teacher? Publish a bad review in the student journal.

No consequences? No problem.

These kids had such agency. Or entitlement? Perhaps both. And I wasn't sure that was such a bad thing. If the kids in my high school had any fraction of the same, we would have known we deserved new books and fresh desks without drawings of penises carved into them.

We would have demanded better.

Hell, maybe we would have even succeeded.

I readjusted my backpack one final time and prepared to step onto the grassy knoll. After narrowing down most of my classes to the Social Studies department—a mix of government and philosophy courses—I headed to the one class I was taking just for fun: Conversational French 101.

A few students were already seated as I walked inside, pulling erasers and pencil sharpeners from the deep pockets of their backpacks. I made my way toward the edge of the classroom, choosing a seat just beneath the window, the sun shining brightly through panes of scratched glass. Taking a quick look around, I felt the buzz of chatter; faces, diverse and different, filled every chair.

Suddenly, the double doors swung open with a bang and the professor came stumbling in.

The famed Madame Carole.

I'd heard other students describe her as gloriously eccentric and lovably loopy, a Parisian woman in her seventies who constantly lamented the "*rapidité*" and "*vulgarité*" of all things American.

"*Bonjour, tout le monde!*" she shouted to no one in particular, spreading her arms widely as a silk shawl dangled from her shoulders.

Just as the professor began her introduction, a tall, bespectacled boy busted through the doors in a frenzy, the last student to arrive.

"Crickey! So sorry. Err, *desolé*. Is that right? Just got turned around is all. Is this Conversational French 101?"

"Seulement Français dans cette classe, monsieur," Madame Carole gently scolded. "French only!"

"Oh yes! Yes, of course. Doh!" he said, slapping his forehead with his open palm. "Err . . . *Bien sûre! Tout de suite!"*

Giggles rippled through the classroom. He sounded British.

"Have a seat, *monsieur*. There's one by *la fenêtre,*" Madame Carole said, drawing out the last syllable for effect.

More giggles.

Wait.

La fenêtre?

Didn't that mean *window*?

I looked down, suddenly feeling my cheeks get hot. *I* was by the window. Sure enough, before I had a chance to look up, I heard a thud.

The mystery student plopped down beside me.

"Bon," resumed Madame Carole, "since we've already welcomed our final colleague, let's begin. Please give us your name, your concentration, and one fun fact."

I immediately felt nauseous: the dreaded "fun fact." Why did every teacher think this exercise did anything besides make students sweat with embarrassment?

I rummaged through my brain for something even slightly interesting as I listened to my classmates, eager to impress. They each cited competitive black diamond snowboarding skills, dizzying Guinness Book of World Records feats (this was Harvard, after all), and self-deprecating asides about successful missions to save starving orphans in developing countries.

Finally, it was my turn.

"Umm, well, *je suis* Lily. Short for Liliana. I'm from a town you've never heard of in North Carolina. I'm concentrating in Social Studies, which is just a fancy way of saying I'm paying too much for a degree that my parents still refuse to tell their friends about, since they think I'm studying fourth grade geography."

A ripple of laughter.

My seatmate turned, smiling. What was that look in his eye? He leaned over.

"Immigrant parents?" he whispered.

"Nailed it," I answered, laughing softly.

"*Alors!*" Madame said sharply, bringing the attention back to the syllabus. "Let us begin, *n'est-ce pas?*"

After exercises in introductory phrases and a refresher in present tense verb conjugations, a soft timer beside the professor's desk buzzed, signaling the conclusion of our first class. I gathered my backpack while the students around me thrust loose pages into overstuffed binders.

Just as I was leaving, I heard a voice over my shoulder.

"*Ciao!*" the mystery student called, staring straight at me.

"Oh," I mustered awkwardly, "*au revoir*. See you soon."

"Looking forward to it," he said, sliding the last of his books into his black messenger bag.

I gave a crooked smile and angled my body sideways, slipping out of the narrow doors and into the sea of students making their way through Sever Hall.

By the time I made it back to my dorm I was sweaty and out of breath. The summer heat hadn't quite dissipated, producing a stifling humidity that was even more vengeful than the one back home.

"How was it?" Hana asked, looking up from her physics book when she heard my key turn the lock.

"Uneventful," I answered.

Hana and I had developed a nice rhythm over the past few weeks. She had told me about life back in Los Angeles, and before that, Seoul. Through her, I'd learned about staples of Korean culture and even mastered a few words to impress the *ajummas*, or "aunties," who worked in some of the dining halls around campus. For two girls born a world apart, Hana and I discovered we actually had a lot in common.

"Chris and I are going to Minos tonight. Wanna come? He's bringing some of the guys he plays pickup soccer with," Hana offered, crossing her legs on the bottom bunk.

"No thanks," I sighed reluctantly, pulling the books from my backpack and stacking them on the bed. "I have a diagnostic for my Intro to Social Studies class on Monday. I heard it's a killer and separates the stars for the thesis track."

"Oh come on, Lilz," Hana moaned, tossing her frilly pink pillow from her bunk, hitting me softly in the head where I was standing. "This is *literally* what college is for."

I immediately thought back to my mother.

We hadn't spoken about her letter since she dropped me off. I knew that to bring it up directly would make her blush with embarrassment; the tenderness of the act—her inability to say those words in person—would undoubtedly leave her feeling exposed. But when I called her at the end of my first week, she'd made a point to say, "*Hay que disfrutar, querida.* You only get this opportunity once." Her advice surprised me, since my entire childhood had instead been defined by her constant string of warnings: *Think before you speak. Always be first to listen. Don't share your secrets, you can't take back what people know.*

But this time was different.

"Half of this opportunity is getting to know yourself, the other half is getting to know your peers," she said just before hanging up the phone. "This is your world now. You deserve to enjoy it."

Maybe she was right.

I looked at Hana, realizing in that moment, that even though she was my roommate, I still needed to prioritize getting to know her. After all, wasn't *she* a success story? Hana was already forming a tight group of friends and was a member of an elite Asian women's organization. She had even started dating a senior on the Crimson soccer team named Chris. She told me she met him our very first week of school when a student slammed into her coming out of Lamont Library, sending her flying onto the concrete. Chris had rushed to the base of the steps to help scoop up her books and apparently picked up her heart along the way. They'd been sneaking off to see each other every night since; she thought I didn't hear the door creak when she crawled into bed long after she assumed I'd fallen asleep. According to Hana, Chris was the most handsome guy she'd ever met.

"Come out with us tonight," she insisted again, staring back at me with those big almond eyes. "You've got to finally meet him. He's soooooo *exotic*! Like, *gorgeous*! His dad is from Côte d'Ivoire and his mom is from Belgium. Did I mention Chris is team captain?" she added, spinning in a dramatic circle before falling back onto her bed.

"Exotic?" I repeated. "Hana, that's a word used for rugs and rare birds—not people."

"Always so politically correct! You know what I mean, Lily. He's hot!"

"Fine," I relented, pretending to be exasperated. "I'll come out with you guys."

"I knew it!" Hana squealed. "You can't resist me!"

I couldn't help but smile.

"Put on those jeans with the rip at the knee. And wear some good earrings. No heels! You may intimidate them since you're so tall."

Ah, Hana. Only she could turn a barely-there compliment into a criticism.

"Yes, captain." I gave her a mock salute. "I'll meet you there after I get back from the gym," I promised, grabbing my keys from the recycled mason jar we used as a coin dish.

"Don't be late!" Hana yelled.

But I was already out the door.

CHAPTER 5

Tossing my gym bag over my shoulder, I laced up my sneakers and started the long walk along the Charles River toward the football field.

It was dusk.

This was my routine twice per week, running through the concrete seats of the athletic stadium after lifting weights at the gym. The curved walls of the Roman-style coliseum, large and imposing, felt like they had been left behind from another era.

After scaling all twenty-six rows, I climbed to the final step and sat along its deep concrete edge, still trying to catch my breath. At this hour, I typically had the entire place to myself. I opened my gym bag and pulled out the thick envelope that had arrived in the mailroom yesterday, the second letter I'd received with my name scrawled across the front in my mother's handwriting.

I had written my mother one letter since I'd arrived, telling her about my classes and Hana's fascination with college nightlife. Each letter, in some sense, felt like our first real bid for intimacy with each other. I felt nervous tearing open the seams of this latest envelope, unsure of what she'd say or what admission awaited me inside.

I wanted to know her better.

I always had.

And yet, something had always seemed to cause us to just

miss each other: two well-navigated, well-intentioned ships that slipped past each other in the night. I could never put my finger on the source of the gulf that stood between us. Still, that didn't stop me from yearning, from wanting the type of mother-daughter relationship the girls at school seemed to have as they pulled up in their station wagons, giggling in unison when their mothers dropped them off.

And I suspected my mother wanted it, too.

I had always chalked up our inability to reach that level of ease to her sternness, her cool, emotional distance. I could always hear my mother's voice in my head, "*No hagas eso,* Lily," or "*Ten cuidado con esto.*" Her communication was a string of warnings, steering me from whatever invisible cascade of social or physical danger she saw barreling toward me. It only made me feel chastised, corrected, evaluated—even when I hadn't done anything wrong.

I tore open the seam of the envelope with my two-dollar BIC pen, the cold Cambridge air whipping the loose strands that had escaped my ponytail. Inside were four single-spaced pages written on the same notebook paper as before. As I peeled apart the first page, I saw Mami's familiar handwriting, the accents over the "i"s and occasional "e" written in the one language that had always bonded us, our one shared secret.

Mi querida Lily,

By now, I am sure you are making your way.

I imagine the new friends, classes, and homework might be challenging, but please remember one simple truth: you belong there.

I've been thinking about you a lot lately . . . and about time.

I think as we get older we finally begin to appreciate the power of having a true purpose, a reason to wake up in the morning—a destination that guides our steps.

That is what you have there at university and what I miss

most about my youth: the infinity of days in front of me, the momentum of being part of something bigger.

My own father didn't want me to go to college. He believed girls were meant to be wives and mothers—nothing more. Participation in our larger society, in the changing winds of a country on the brink of revolution, was a man's work, he decreed.

But I wanted to record history, especially as that history was sweeping me into the eye of its storm.

I wanted to become a journalist.

Like you, I craved more than the land I was born onto, and the station I was born into.

And I got close—very close—to making it possible.

The letter nearly fell from my limp hands. Mami, a journalist? During a revolution?

When I told my mother in high school that I wanted to write for the school newspaper, she had simply smiled. At the time, I figured she had stopped listening, likely distracted by her grocery list or the new bus schedule she needed to take to get to the Mitchells.

Now, staring out onto the starry skyline of ivory towers and yellow streetlights, I realized that my mother's look that day had meant something else entirely.

This was her dream.

This was what *she* had always wanted, back when she had been someone else entirely—back before she was mine.

CHAPTER 6

Marisol

Havana, Cuba
October 1, 1956

This place feels like the center of the universe.

The streets are packed, people going everywhere and nowhere in a hurry.

And yet here I am, rudderless and adrift, spinning as everyone breezes past me in their haste.

Even Mirta.

Mirta spends hours in the library searching for information about some satellite the Soviets are building called *Sputnik*, claiming the United States is putting together an entire agency just to go to outer space.

"*Camarón que se duerme se lo lleva la corriente*," she reminded me this morning, rising from her cot early to begin the fifteen-minute walk to the university. "Soon there will be a race for every country to explore the universe, and I want to be first when they do."

I sighed and rolled over, the coils from my mattress poking the flesh beneath my rib cage.

The truth was, I wish I had Mirta's vision.

After risking everything to get here, I had made no other friends besides her and I still hadn't found a paying job. Even worse, in a few short months I wasn't sure any of this would even matter.

Protests had erupted shortly after classes began, small crowds of students gathering with makeshift posters outside the bursar's towering double doors.

"Abajo la dictadura," they chanted, the familiar anti-government rallying cries now a mantra around campus.

At first, Mirta told me to look straight ahead, to ignore the flyers in their outstretched hands, a red "X" tearing through the image of a tattered Cuban flag. But soon, the crowd was too large to ignore, swelling as the weeks went on, two dozen students turning into hundreds.

Our country's president, Fulgencio Batista, even threatened to shut the university down if the protests didn't stop. The college had become a hotbed of defiance. Rumors were spreading that a group of students was working to remove Batista from power, which is why men in beige shirts had infiltrated our classes, posing as students for the last three months. They were the president's men, spies who lurked in the hallways of our department and spent hours hovering by the pastry stand, hoping to pick up any morsels of information about the Resistance. Those students not wise enough to keep their dissatisfaction quiet had disappeared, rumored to be hidden in Batista's jail just outside the city.

That's why last week, the university called an emergency government meeting; some two thousand undergraduates gathering to address the crisis at the base of the grand staircase at the heart of campus. The students had become restless, and in their disillusionment, the vast majority believed that a revolution was the only alternative, their only hope at a dignified future.

I pushed through a sea of sweaty bodies the day the meeting was held, maneuvering through angry protesters as the back of my shirt stuck to my skin with sweat. Just as I reached up to wipe the beads trickling down my neck, I looked up to see a dark-haired boy in a crisp collared shirt and blue worker pants striding deliberately across the stage.

"*¡Manzanita!*" the students began to chant, their shouts rising as he reached for the microphone.

José Antonio Echeverría.

He was the president of the *Federación Estudiantil Universitaria,* our student government.

A rising star throughout Havana and a bonafide hero on campus, every local newspaper bore his face on the front page, clean-shaven with piercing hazel eyes. He had skin the color of toasted coconut, his thick dark hair parted neatly on the side.

José was an architecture student from Matanzas who the papers said was quietly building a small but growing coalition of opposition against Batista. Rumors were that he had also formed a more militant group called the *Directorio Revolucionario*. None of us knew the details of how the group operated, but Mirta said she heard a crew of students from his department warn that "something big" was coming.

"*Compañeros,*" José roared into the microphone, turning every head in his direction. "*Este momento es el nuestro*. We are starting the revolution from within. The heroes of this country—its future leaders—are already among us, standing here beside you, capable and willing."

José leaned forward, placing both hands on the podium as he locked eyes with the crowd, pausing just long enough for the echo of their cheers to fade.

I squinted between the shoulders of the students in front of me, balancing unevenly on the tips of my toes.

"José Martí . . . Antonio Maceo . . . Máximo Gómez—they would have never stood for this tyranny! Batista has desecrated our Constitution and we must show him the price of ignoring us!" José paced back and forth across the stage, the beaded bracelets he wore on his wrists rattling with each step. "It's time to close your stores and close your wallets. No patronage, no work for one week!"

The crowd exploded in response to his call to action, roiling anger that had finally found a place to go. José threw his fist in the air, chest heaving as he exited the stage, flanked by six men carrying the Cuban flag who hoisted him high above their heads.

"*¡Man-za-ni-ta! ¡Man-za-ni-ta!*" the students shouted with pride, his spell cast over their open, eager faces.

I stood transfixed.

Never had I seen anyone filled with so much passion. This man had more vision—more direction—in his few words than I had in my entire body.

I had been searching for that same fire, and had only come close to finding it once, for just a fleeting moment.

It happened when I first visited *Radio Reloj*, one of the largest radio stations in Havana. A few weeks into the semester, I'd seen a bulletin in the humanities department saying the radio was in search of an assistant. As soon as my first history class ended the next day, I walked to the sprawling *Radiocentro* CMQ building complex just blocks away with the flyer in hand. The station's manager opened the door to a wood-paneled room filled with thick black cables and long microphones. He stared at the crumpled flyer and asked if I was currently an enrolled student. He wanted daily reports of "revolutionary activity" on campus, and said if I took detailed notes, the apprenticeship was mine.

Twice a week, I sat in the station's newsroom until my fingers were sore, hunched over a fat typewriter transcribing my observations. The manager said I worked faster than any typist he'd seen, and soon, he let me try my hand at writing one of the bulletins for Emilio de Guevarra, the radio's lead reporter. It wasn't a formal job, but it was a taste of the life I could have—and the one I wanted—if I managed to graduate with a degree.

That is, of course, if I still had a university to graduate from.

Perhaps that is why it felt like fate when I was leaving the station a week later and saw José walking along the Malecón, carrying a stack of books in his arms, his burlap bag slung over his shoulder.

I jogged across the street to catch up, gently tapping his shoulder from behind.

"*Permiso* . . ." I began nervously, surprising him as much as I had myself with my boldness.

"*¿Sí?*" José answered politely as he turned to face me.

I paused sheepishly, suddenly realizing I had no plans of what to say. I was distracted by the glistening sheen of sweat forming along his brow, framing eyes that burned with a fire that stunned or frightened.

A smile played across his lips as he watched me struggle under the weight of my nervousness.

"I . . . I . . . I'm Marisol," I finally managed, "a first year at the university. If you ever need a hand with student government, I could help you after class. I have a small internship at *Radio Reloj*, but I'm usually done around four . . ."

"*¡Claro!*" José interrupted enthusiastically, his eyes landing on my tousled curls, a red flower pinned above my ear. "You work at the station? Well, we can always use more hands in the fight against tyranny. *Además*"—he paused, shifting his weight as he swung his bag across his body—"sometimes a beautiful smile is more effective than even the sharpest machete."

My face flushed.

I looked down at the wrinkled red skirt I had sewn myself, a loose thread escaping from the seam.

"When do I start?"

"Tomorrow night. Six p.m. There's a meeting on *Calle 19* between C and D. I hope to see you there, Marisol."

José extended his hand.

"See you then," I promised. My palm felt warm inside his.

I took off in the direction of my boarding house, waiting several seconds before gathering enough courage to steal a look over my shoulder.

When I finally turned around, there José was, staring right back at me.

CHAPTER 7

Lily

September 20, 1991
Cambridge, Massachusetts

I wiggled into the black bandage dress I bought at Filene's Basement. Flinging aside my wedged shoes in frustration, I accidentally knocked over the glass of water teetering on the edge of our mini refrigerator. Hana had made me promise not to wear heels, but how else could I make this nine-dollar dress from the discount pile not look like . . . well, just that?

I settled on some white Keds I had tucked in the corner of our closet, pairing them with the big gold hoops I bought with the money I'd saved scooping ice cream at Baskin-Robbins last summer. When I was done, I stood in front of the mirror and figured the final look wasn't half bad.

Grabbing my purse from the desk that I shared with Hana, I noticed the red blinking light on the telephone.

A voicemail.

Eric had been trying to reach me since he got to New York, starting his first classes at Parsons School of Design. He had finally convinced his mother to let him go, telling her that his eye for design was more than just a "hobby" and that he wanted to focus on textiles. Ms. Mitchell had long lamented the prospects of Eric getting a "Yankee education" from the uncivilized perpetrators of the War of Northern Aggression, as she constantly reminded him, but I suspected somewhere deep down she knew that our mountain town would not be fulfilling or welcoming for a man of her son's talent.

Or preferences.

I planned to call Eric back, but now wasn't the time.

We needed a longer window and less pressure to talk.

He deserved that from me.

But tonight I was distracted.

Anxious, even.

What the hell was I getting myself into? Who were Hana's other friends? Her boyfriend? And who did *I* need to be to stay on her roster? For her to want to include me again?

I adjusted my dress and ran down the stairs two at a time until I felt my sneakers hit the lawn. Walking the two blocks down Mass Ave., I took a right on Plympton Street before stumbling upon the entrance to Minos Bar. Through the window, I could see groups of students sitting at tall tables, colorful pitchers of mixed drinks perched between them.

The place was packed.

I made my way through a crowd of people, angling my body toward two empty stools shoved beneath a lacquered wooden counter.

"What're ya havin'?" A middle-aged bartender shouted in a deep Boston accent.

"Gin and tonic?" I replied, more of a question than answer. It was the first thing that came to mind, the only thing I'd grown accustomed to in my bootleg Friday-night bottles with Eric. Luckily here, I could sip my drink slowly and openly since the bar didn't ask for ID.

"Comin' right up," the bartender obliged, removing the white rag resting on his shoulder and pulling a clear glass down from the shelf behind him.

As I reached into my purse in search of a few loose dollars, my eye caught a tall guy at the end of the bar, staring up at a TV mounted in the corner. A soccer game was on, the bright colors of two African flags billowing across the screen. The man stood completely still, the strong angles of his jawline almost aquiline, even more pronounced as the uneven light from the field reflected off his face. He had high cheekbones that framed thick black eyebrows knit together in concentration. His skin was too dark to be considered olive, too light to be the color of coffee. To use Hana's word, this guy was *exotic*. I wondered how Chris would compare.

Suddenly, the bartender slammed my drink down. "Looks like we've got another fan here, mate," he shouted, motioning toward me with a nod of his head.

I jumped.

The bartender had caught me staring, thinking I was staring at the game, not the man watching it.

"Is that so?" the mystery man asked, breaking his trance and turning to face me. "Super Eagles or Black Stars?"

"N-neither, really," I stammered, fumbling for the closure of my chain-link purse. "I guess it all depends on who could beat Bafana Bafana?" It was the only thing I could think to say, reaching into the recesses of my brain to the article I'd come across about South Africa's competition for the Africa Cup of Nations.

The stranger's eyebrows lifted in genuine surprise. "The Land of Springboks and *fufuzelas*? Not many South Africans in these parts," he smiled, revealing a set of perfectly white teeth and small crinkles around his eyes. "You're from there?"

"Hardly," I smiled, trying to regain my composure. "Just a fan, I guess you could say. Hoping for an internship there this summer. You?"

I motioned toward the screen.

"Hmmm," the stranger paused. "I'd have to say Super Eagles. It's all about the best *jollof*," he grinned. "Say, are you—"

"Six bucks," the bartender interrupted, tapping the counter where he had just placed my drink. "I'm going on break."

Feeling suddenly chastised in front of this stranger, I quickly pulled out the few crumpled ones I'd found in my purse, just as a flock of frat brothers piled onto the stools beside me blocking my view. I slid over to create some space, covering my ear as their laughter rose to whooping cheers. As soon as I put the bills down on the counter, I felt a hand on my left shoulder.

"There you are!" Hana squealed. "Just in time!"

"For what?" I smiled seeing her appear, alive and in her element.

"Shots!" Hana clapped her hands twice to hurry me along. "We just ordered some for the table. Come meet the team!"

Hana grabbed my arm and pulled me through the crowd, leading me to a corner table by the window where several players, still in their cleats, stood in mid-conversation.

"No mate, that's bloody impossible. Man United will *never* win the Champions League," I heard one of them say, the voice sounding vaguely familiar.

"Boys," Hana called over the clamor, "come meet Lily, my roommate." A few of them turned around, the conversation pausing for just a moment.

"Hey there," I said, startled by my own Southern drawl. It was always more pronounced when I was nervous. I stared down at my drink, hoping Hana would say something to divert the attention.

"These gentlemen play soccer on Chris's pickup team on the weekends," she started, seeming to read my mind.

Just then, one of the players who was facing the window turned around and smiled.

It was the guy from French class, the voice I'd heard.

He walked over and raised his glass.

"Cheers!" he beamed. "Or should I say, *santé*?"

"Lily, this is Vikram," Hana offered politely, standing between us. "He's finishing up his post-doc in the engineering school, but his biggest accomplishment is that he and Chris play pickup soccer Saturday mornings at Ohiri Field."

"Ah yes. I left that crowning achievement off my list of 'fun facts' for Madame Carole. You'll have to forgive me, Lily," he added with a wink.

"Who is Carole?" Hana asked.

"She's our French teacher," I answered, finally finding my voice. "We're in the same class. Nice to see you again, Vikram."

"What a small world! Let me get Chris. He won't believe this!" Hana disappeared toward the bar in a rush of excitement.

"Now then . . ." Vikram took a step closer, filling the space where Hana just stood. "Where are they from?"

I looked up, confused. "Beg your pardon?"

"Your parents. You said in French class they were immigrants?"

"Oh," I could feel my face blush. "My mom. She's from Cuba. You?"

"India, by way of England. Featherstone to be specific. A town that only the five thousand of us who live there can actually find on a map. But who knows, maybe your geography degree may come in handy after all . . ."

I let out a sharp laugh. "Ouch."

"What does one hope to do with a Social Studies degree, anyway?" he asked.

"I want to be a journalist, but since there's no journalism program . . ." I paused, gesturing to the campus around us. "Social Studies it is. It's the closest thing I could get to applied government and history."

"That's pretty cool!" Vikram grabbed his glass and held it like a microphone. "'This is Liliana, reporting live, from the border of Sarajevo . . .'"

My full name. He had remembered.

I couldn't help but smile.

"Well, there's still a long road ahead," I said sheepishly, taking a sip of my gin. "What about you? What're you in for?"

"Applied Mathematics post-doctoral fellowship. Far less exciting. But like a good immigrant boy who failed his parents by not becoming a doctor, I had to give them a consolation prize. I'll probably end up at some stodgy consulting firm to pay the bills."

"Well, *my* math is trash, but if I remember correctly, the Applied Math program here has like a 0.01 percent acceptance rate, so you must be pretty good at it."

"0.001 percent, to be exact," he teased. "But a wise woman once told me, 'There's still a long road ahead.'"

I smiled, taking another swig of my drink. It was surprisingly light; I could barely taste the alcohol.

"Finally!" Hana said, bounding toward us, leading someone else by the hand. "The two pillars of my life, here together at last!"

As Hana stepped aside, a tall figure behind her emerged. It was the guy from the bar, the one I'd seen watching the soccer game.

"Wonderful to finally meet you . . . properly," I said.

"You too, Lily." Chris extended his hand, his voice surprisingly deep, now that I could hear it over the buzz of drunken coeds. "Hana says you're from Carolina? Which one?"

"The best one," I answered playfully.

A smile crept across his face. "I'm gonna have to go with . . . *North* Carolina? I've played a few games down there. The people were always really nice."

"Nailed it," I said, looking over the rim of my drink with a dramatic pause. "Although, I've never had anyone get it wrong. I was worried you'd be the first."

All four of us laughed.

With Chris standing so close, I was able to get a better look at the face that before I could only see in profile. Hana had mentioned he was tall, but he was actually a lot taller than I'd expected, towering at least six inches over me. Something about him also felt older, more mature. There was an intensity to the way that he listened, fully and wholly. Good for Hana, I thought. This relationship would ground her.

"Can you believe these two already knew each other?" Hana interrupted, pulling in Vikram by the shoulder. "They're in the same French class!"

"Is that so?" Chris asked, raising his eyebrow.

"Indeed," Vikram confirmed with a smile. "Lily, can I get you something from the bar?"

"Sure," I answered in surprise. I looked down, the last of my drink gone. I guess I had enjoyed it more than I thought.

Vikram and I walked over to the counter, leaving Hana and Chris at the table with their friends. I ordered another gin and tonic; Vikram, an old-fashioned.

"Now then," Vikram began again, pulling out a stool for me. "Where were we?"

He slid onto the chair beside mine, close enough for me to smell the cologne on his neck.

"It's funny, the way you say that," I said, readjusting my weight to get comfortable.

"The way I say what, exactly?"

"'Now then,'" I answered, smiling. "Is that, like, a fancy way of saying, 'hello'?"

Vikram chuckled quietly, averting his eyes. "I s'pose I do say that, don't I?" he asked rhetorically, suddenly self-conscious. "Perhaps it is a slightly posh, British thing. And yes, it is a way of picking up where we left off."

He paused, looking back up at me.

"For me, personally, I guess it's a reminder that this thing we do as humans—this way we engage with each other—is all just a constant conversation. It has no end. It has no real beginning. It just . . . *is*. At least," he added, leaning in and lowering his voice, “for the people with whom you *want* to be in constant conversation.”

Our eyes locked. Who was this guy? He was alluring in an unassuming way, like the bumbling protagonist in a classic movie. Think Cary Grant in *Bringing Up Baby*—instinctively, and surprisingly, seductive. That much was undeniable.

“I like it. I might even steal it,” I teased.

Vikram smiled sheepishly.

“Well, if you’re impressed now, just wait until I take you to dinner.”

I flushed immediately.

I’d only been hit on maybe once before. My mind flashed back to prom night four months ago, sitting by the window in that awful pink gown, waiting for Todd Milhaven to pick me up.

Todd had asked me to be his date two weeks prior, and I couldn’t tell if it had simply taken him that long to find the courage to ask, or if he had just run out of options. Either way, I had never had a date to prom. Or to anything for that matter. I had learned long before that night that I wasn’t what the boys in my school were looking for: not blonde enough, not petite enough, not white enough.

Todd said he would be there at eight. But when the clock struck nine that night, I never thought I’d still be sitting stiffly by the front door, flower wilting and hair swelling in the humidity. As the minutes turned to hours, the sick realization of what was happening settled like a rock in the pit of my stomach: Todd wasn’t coming.

My mother began tidying the house nervously. I could feel her staring at me from the corner of her eye, trying to assess the scale of my disappointment. My father opened a can of beer on the back porch, hoping to avoid the emotional storm that was brewing; the thought of his baby girl in pain, too difficult to bear.

I was being stood up.

Todd didn’t have the courage to take me to prom. What would his family think, after all? Their All-American football player showing up with the high school "negress," as one homeroom mom had called me.

I took off the corsage that Mami had insisted we buy at the grocery store earlier that afternoon, placing it on the splintered black console by our front door. I dragged my legs up the narrow, carpeted staircase and headed for my room, not daring to look over my shoulder to see my parents' horrified faces. My mom rushed to the base of the stairs and tried to give me a hug, words failing her. But I refused to let anyone see my tears, too hot was the shame burning inside me. I simply wanted to close the door and bury myself underneath the covers.

And yet here I was, four months later, sitting beside a man this handsome and seemingly self-possessed, asking me to dinner. Or was he? I didn't want to make the same mistake twice.

Just as I was poised to respond, Hana came stumbling over, a green drink with a miniature umbrella sloshing in her hand. "Lilz! Let's head over to the Kong," she said with a subtle slur. "They're having a seventies night tonight. Ends in an hour. Vikram, you coming?"

"I'm not, I'm afraid," he declined politely, placing his empty glass on the bar. "As delightful as that sounds, I have an early study group tomorrow. The engineering fellows have a presentation next week."

I didn't want to go, either.

This quiet moment with this charming Brit was far more enjoyable than the insanity that inevitably awaited us. But this was Hana's night and she had invited me. I needed to prove I deserved access to her world, to be the sidekick she required.

"Then I suppose I'll see you Monday, *Monsieur* Vikram?" I asked, holding my glass up to meet his.

"You can count on it, *Mademoiselle* Lily. I'll be reporting live from our French bureau," he smiled, sliding gingerly off his stool.

"I look forward to it," I echoed, securing my purse strap over my shoulder.

CHAPTER 8

I stumbled out of bed, accidentally scraping my hip against the desk as I awkwardly climbed down from the top bunk. I kicked aside my Keds, clearing them from the base of the ladder. My dress from the night before lay crumpled on the floor, reeking of alcohol.

One more night out with Hana was going to kill me.

As if on cue, Hana barged into the room, a cup of coffee in her hand.

"So? What did you think?"

"Of what?" I asked, accepting the brown Styrofoam tumbler as I blew the steam rising from the top.

"Don't be coy," Hana teased, taking a seat on the bottom bunk. "I saw you huddled at the bar with Vikram last night."

"Yeah, he seems cool," I answered nonchalantly, hoping to move on.

"That's so crazy you two had already met," Hana pressed, not skipping a beat. "Maybe you can be study buddies, if you get my drift."

She let out a boisterous laugh.

"Shit, Hana."

"Yeah? What's wrong?"

"I actually do need his information. My French homework. I have no idea where I put the instructions."

"Sure you don't," Hana said playfully.

My head was throbbing. Somewhere in the madness of Shopping Period I had misplaced the assignment, which I hadn't realized until Hana mentioned it.

"I don't have Vikram's telephone number," Hana said, registering my confusion. "But you could probably look it up in the student directory."

She pointed to the red handbook on the corner of the desk.

"If not, Chris will have it. I can ask him when I see him later."

"That's okay. Do you know Vikram's last name?"

"Desai. Vikram Desai."

"Thanks, I'll find it. Are you headed out?"

"Yeah, going over to Ohiri Field. The guys are having a friendly scrimmage this afternoon."

"Seriously? After last night? How can they even stand?"

"You'd be surprised what those boys will do in the name of soccer," Hana laughed. "But I happen to know that Vikram won't be there since this game is just for undergrads. So maybe you can catch him," she said, tossing her keys gently in the air before tucking them into the pocket of her oversize jeans.

As soon as the door closed, I reached for the red directory, flipping to the tab for the engineering school. I scrolled through last names arranged alphabetically on the thick paper.

"C" . . . "D" . . .

Bingo.

Vikram Desai, Applied Mathematics, Division of Engineering and Applied Sciences. That must be him. I ran my index finger across the ten digits listed beside his name and picked up the receiver of the phone, its thick plastic base nestled beneath the windowsill.

6 . . . 1 . . . 7 . . .

I waited for three long seconds as the static crackled in my ear, each second feeling longer than the last. Just as I was about to hang up, a muffled voice broke through the line.

"Hello!" an unmistakably British accent answered.

"Hi, um, Vikram? This is Lily Walker . . ."

"Oh, Lily! Hi! Made it back safely last night, I presume?"

I flushed. This was him. Definitely him.

"Indeed," I smiled, bringing the thick handle of the phone closer to my cheek. "But somehow I misplaced my French assignment between last week's class and last night's tequila shots. Do you happen to have the worksheet?"

"I do, in fact!" he sang, his seemingly inextinguishable cheeriness coming through the speaker. "Why don't you meet me for tea tomorrow and we'll give it a go? I'll bring the assignment and we can conjugate our way through it together?"

My face flushed with excitement. Or were those nerves?

"Where should we meet?"

"The Cambridge 'T' Shop at 12 p.m.?"

"See you there."

"Cheers!"

I closed the student directory, placing it gently inside the drawer.

When I looked up, I caught a glimpse of myself in the cracked mirror above the desk, a faint smile still plastered across my face.

CHAPTER 9

Marisol

Havana, Cuba

November 30, 1956

Mirta was right.

Things have only gotten harder.

Much harder.

After only three months of classes, the school administration announced today that the university is shutting down, saying the protests have created an "unsafe environment incompatible with learning."

The entire university has been ripped to shreds: chains on the doors, locks on the gate, police sirens piercing whatever peace was left. Graffiti coats every inch of campus.

Now, only hollowed out classrooms and deferred dreams remain.

José had warned us it could come to this.

He knew that the university—the most powerful tool of the Batista regime—would soon become collateral damage.

Perhaps I should have seen this coming, too, if I'd only paid attention to the disgruntled whispers from the teachers pulling up in their beat-up cars, mumbling about their paychecks being late or not coming at all; or the students who spent all day lingering by the base of the *escalinata,* those who had just graduated but had too much time and too little money. They still hadn't found jobs.

Everyone was unhappy and, because of it, change was imminent.

The question was, who would deliver it?

José zipped the black duffel bag on the table in front of him, turning his back to me.

"What's in there?" I asked, straining for a peek at the contents inside.

His body became a shield.

"No te procupes, mi amor," he smiled, wiping away the hair that had fallen into his face.

José and I had begun dating in October, barely spending a day apart since the day we met along the Malecón. Our courtship—born of long walks and fresh *saoco*—often ended in rooms like this, with groups of current students and recent graduates arguing about the future of the country.

José was like fire in all these meetings, instantly becoming the center of gravity, captivating with his charisma and plans for change.

I, too, was mesmerized. I found myself slowly peeling back the layers to his world and, eventually, invited into his most sacred spaces.

Every Monday at sunset, José led a small group of his most loyal followers into the damp cellar of an apartment building on *Calle 19* in Vedado. There, beneath the broken lights of one of the city's most crowded neighborhoods, we passed small *coladas* to one another in the dimly lit basement, the sweetness of the brown sugar making our lips pucker.

José sat atop a stack of three empty crates, a blueprint of the city spread open on the metal table in front of him. He had been "preparing" for months, getting ready for some secret mission with his *Directorio Revolucionario*, a mission that he still wouldn't tell me much about. The group had emerged as one of the most powerful groups of the Resistance, with "action cells" planted throughout the city, underground apartments where they planned their strikes against the Batista regime. There were even whispers that the group was behind the murder at Montmarte nightclub back in October, where Colonel Antonio Blanco Rico, Batista's chief of the Bureau of Investigations, was shot and killed.

José unfurled the roll of parchment paper on the table in front of him.

"Fidel is almost back and he's ready to make a move," he announced, taking a sip of his coffee. "When I met him in Mexico City, he said he had the weapons and the infrastructure to make a real offensive strike."

Two of the most recent graduates, young men in their late twenties, exchanged looks in silence.

José was talking about Fidel Alejandro Castro Ruz, a lawyer who had graduated from the University of Havana a few years earlier. He had since been exiled to Mexico after serving time in prison for attacking Batista's military barracks out east.

Castro's stature had reached an almost mythical status, with campus organizers posting clippings of national newspapers along *la escalinata* with his photo. Castro was a symbol of the Resistance beyond Havana's urban walls, his haggard beard and piercing brown eyes, vacant and inscrutable.

Even before I left Camagüey, I had heard his name rumble down from the mountaintops, whispers of a young lawyer from the *oriente* calling for "change." Castro had represented himself in his own trial after the military attack, delivering a blistering speech in which he famously said that history would "absolve" him.

Papi was the first to tell me about Castro, handing me a smuggled pamphlet he'd finished reading of excerpts from that speech.

"Ese chamaquito nos va a salvar," he promised, barely looking at me as he slammed his rum glass on the table.

Papi believed Castro would topple Batista's corrupt government, finally giving a chance to Cubans like him—Black Cubans who tilled the earth for a few cents a day and who relied on the export of Cuban goods to feed their families. My father toiled through unforgiving seasons, extracting resources from land he had cultivated for decades . . . but didn't own.

Couldn't own.

"He'll make us proud again," he said, taking another sip of his rum. "Finally a chance to operate our own sugar mills, not cowering to a corrupt government mob that hoards the spoils *we* worked for."

In Castro, Papi saw a vision of equality.

But was he the only one who could deliver it?

I inched closer from where I stood in the back of the room, hoping to get a better look at José's face.

"Fidel and I agree on the essential goals of this Revolution, but we do not agree on the strategy."

José took another slow sip from the miniature glass cup steaming with coffee.

"Fidel wants a general strike, a work stoppage that will shut down the country. But I believe we must kill a fish from its head: We must dismantle the regime from the top."

José pointed to the map on the desk in front of him as the crowd grew quiet.

José was flirting with danger—and he knew it.

Several of the students rustled their backpacks, unsure of whether to stay. They knew whatever José said next could land them in jail.

"Before we can achieve any of the things we want—low bus fares, electricity in the rural provinces, a basic restoration of the constitution we already had—the fundamental conditions of democracy must be met. And to do that, we must get rid of Batista."

Students began to nod their heads in agreement, a restless energy swelling in the room.

"March 13 is our day," José announced. He pointed to the map of the presidential palace in front of him, his finger sliding down quadrants drawn in straight lines. "The plan is simple: we will surround the palace, force Batista to step down, and restore power to the Cuban people. This country will be ours again."

The crowd erupted with cheers, pubescent men raising their fists in victory, supportive women applauding feverishly beside them.

"While the first group storms the palace, the other will tell the world what we have done, announcing a successful coup on the airwaves."

José pointed to a small circle in the corner of the diagram and drew an "X" through the depiction of a modest building several avenues away.

My mouth fell open in shock.

I recognized it immediately.

It was the CMQ Building.

Suddenly, I understood the gravity of what José had just revealed.

He was targeting *Radio Reloj*—and I was part of his plan.

CHAPTER 10

Lily

Cambridge, Massachusetts
September 22, 1991

I adjusted my cardigan and rushed out of the dorm just in time to meet Vikram at the Cambridge "T" shop, its name a play on Boston's infamous and poorly routed subway system. As I approached, I could see him seated through the window, fidgeting with the collar of his light blue button-down shirt, a formal choice for a Sunday.

"Now then . . ." he said, sliding out of the booth to greet me. "A pleasure to see you again, *Mademoiselle* Lily."

"And you, *Monsieur* Desai," I said in my best attempt at a British accent.

"Not bad," he smiled, "but I'll spare you my best Southern accent in return."

I blushed.

I always felt slightly embarrassed when people acknowledged that they could hear my roots on my tongue. I wasn't embarrassed about *being* Southern, but I was mindful of the details that I hadn't yet decided to share. That was one of them. I couldn't tell if the other students thought my accent was a function of geography or a function of class. After all, there seemed to be fewer Southerners on campus than exchange students from tiny Eastern European countries. I felt like a novelty item.

"So sorry to bother you about all this," I began, unzipping my backpack and placing it on the empty chair between us. "I have no idea where I put the assignment. I could have sworn I slipped the worksheet into my notebook but . . ."

"Don't be silly! I'm afraid you would have never called me otherwise," Vikram smiled, looking up at me as he pulled his binder out of his black messenger bag. "What would I do if I had to wait until Monday to see you again?"

I met his gaze. Was he serious? Had he actually thought about me since we left that bar? My mind had wandered back to him more than a few times, but it never occurred to me that his might have, too.

"Well God bless a lost assignment and some fruity loose-leaf tea for bringing us back together," I quipped nervously. "Should we get in line?"

Together we walked to the counter, staring at the laminated menu with options like "Blue Line Berry" and "Copley Craze."

I could feel Vikram's shoulder slightly touching mine as we scanned our choices.

"I'll have the Central Square Pear," I told the cashier, a student clearly working her part-time job.

"I'll do the same," Vikram seconded, pulling out a heap of cash from his wallet.

"Thank you," I smiled, relieved and grateful for the treat. I had already dipped into my parents' "emergency fund" while waiting to hear back from part-time campus jobs.

Vikram and I returned to our table beneath the window, hands full with sugary flavored water, the afternoon sun warm through the glass.

"Where shall we begin?" he asked.

"I suppose . . . the assignment?" I smiled tentatively in return.

"Right, well." Vikram looked down sheepishly. "I had a peek before I got here, and since this is Conversational French 101, you'll see here that Madame Carole has asked us to deliver the answer to these three questions orally in front of the class." Vikram pointed to a set of bolded instructions.

"The entire class?" I asked, panic pulsing through my veins. I hated speaking in front of groups.

"Yes, but Madame says if we answer five questions total then we can do it in pairs. Shall we?"

"Let's see what the questions are first."

"Numéro un," Vikram read from the paper in his best French accent, "if you could go anywhere in the world, where would it be?"

"That's a good one." I paused. "I guess I would say South Africa?"

"Et porquoi, Madamoiselle?"

"I really want to get an internship there this summer. It just seems . . . I don't know. Like there's still work to be done? It's only been a year since they set Nelson Mandela free. It's insane to believe he's been locked up all this time for trying to end apartheid, basically the same segregation we had here just three decades ago. Essentially, right when my parents got together—before they had me."

"Oh really? Are your parents . . . different?" Vikram ventured politely.

"Not really." I shrugged, unsure of how to answer. "My mom is from Cuba. Back there, she's what you'd call *mulata,* a mix of African and Spanish ancestry. But where I'm from in the South, the 'one-drop rule' still applies: any drop of African blood and you're considered Black. The same is true for my dad. His mom was white but he never met her. She abandoned him when he was a baby."

"That's wild," Vikram said, his eyes wide. "Were they able to get married? You mentioned the laws . . ."

"Yes, in the end they were. When my mom came to America

in the fifties they didn't know how to classify her, so they marked her as 'negro' on her driver's license. That's when she first learned she was Black. They did the same for my father, since his father was the one to register him for his birth certificate. Fast-forward thirty-some years, since they were both technically within the same race, my parents could get married."

"Is that why you want to go to South Africa?" he asked, blowing on the steam rising from the still-warm mug in his hand.

"In a sense, yes. From everything I've read, South Africa seems to be grappling with a lot of the same questions that we dealt with here in the sixties—race, class, equality. I feel like if I could understand things over there—see things unfolding in real time—then maybe I could better understand things here. Sort of stop the clock, if you will."

"Don't they have elections soon? In South Africa?" Vikram asked.

"Yeah, they're saying Mandela's going to run for president. Can you imagine what that would be like? To watch him go from prisoner to president? That's why I want the internship. The application is due to the Office of Career Services pretty soon since they have to earmark the funding. Apparently, a wealthy South African alum is sponsoring three whole months in-country, and the university is partnering with a human rights organization based in Durban that has room and board."

"That would be incredible," Vikram marveled. "We have quite a few South Africans who've come to England in the past few years. I met some of them at university and they say the country has really been a mess."

"I guess it depends on who you ask," I wondered aloud. "What about you? Where would you go?"

"I'd go back to India. A bit practical, I suppose, but the truth. My brother is set to get married there next year. My whole family has been crazed preparing for it. This is basically my mum's World

Cup," he added with a laugh. "It would be kind of nice to sneak in and just hang out for a bit."

"Preparing a year in advance? How many guests?"

"About three hundred."

I nearly spit out my drink.

Vikram smiled. "Well Indian weddings are almost always enormous, and this is the first marriage for both of our families. Plus, my father isn't doing well, so my mum wants to make it memorable . . ." he trailed off.

"I'm sorry to hear that," I said, stirring my tea. "Do you miss him? Being so far away?"

"Who?" Vikram asked, looking puzzled.

"Your dad."

"Oh, I mean . . ." he stumbled, seemingly shocked by my candor. Back home, Eric always said my questions were blunt on impact, soft on intention—whatever that meant.

"Yes, I suppose I do," Vikram answered after a long pause. "It's just . . ."

"Just what?" I asked.

"We have a bit of a difficult dynamic. He wants me to come back and run his company, but I want nothing to do with it. I've seen the problems it has caused him both personally and professionally, and yet still, he's insistent. Now that he's got congestive heart failure, he's passing that urgency on to us. Or at least, on to me. My brother is safe, having already matched with the Indian bride of my parents' dreams."

"Matched?"

"Yeah, it's a long-standing tradition in a lot of Indian cultures, many of us have arranged marriages. My parents are Hindu from Gujarat and they got matched by an elder in their village before they even met. My brother essentially did the same thing, although he met Shivani twice before they decided to court seriously. I consider theirs more of an 'assisted' marriage."

"Fascinating," I said. "Are you going to . . ."

"Have an arranged marriage?" Vikram interrupted, knowing what was coming next. "I can't say it's completely off the table. I know it sounds dated to most Westerners, since out here we're sold fairytales of love and 'ever after.' But out East, we believe marriage is also a choice, a daily decision to commit, regardless of lust. It's a dedication to an agreed outcome despite temporary changes—emotional or otherwise. There's something to it, I think. A purpose. An order. It's lasted for centuries for a reason."

"So then you've never been in love?"

"Well . . . I didn't say that, *Mademoiselle* Lily." He looked down at the last of his drink, a smile playing across his lips. "But maybe that's another tale for when our French homework is complete."

I suddenly felt embarrassed. I had led us completely off course with my endless questions. Too personal, I'm sure. Maybe that's what Eric was talking about.

"Perhaps we can finish over dinner?" Vikram asked, holding his now-empty mug. "We could go to the Thai place around the corner?"

"Yes! Yes, of course. I'd love that," I mustered, trying to conceal my excitement as I zipped my backpack, the stitched Nirvana patch on the outer pocket fraying at the seam. My chair screeched against the checkered tile as I slid away from the table, ready to leave for the restaurant.

"Shall we?" Vikram smiled, slinging his messenger bag over his shoulder.

The bright white pages of our French notebook sat idly on the table between us, untouched and unfinished.

CHAPTER 11

Marisol

Havana, Cuba
November 30, 1956

"Seguimos pronto, compañeros."

José dismissed the group with a wave of his hand, rising from the pile of crates and rolling the blueprint in front of him into a tight cylinder.

The students cleared their plates, small flakes of crispy *pastelitos* falling to the floor.

José waited for the last student to leave before collecting his duffel bag and motioning toward the door.

"Was this your plan all along?" I turned to face him, my cheeks flushed with rage as we entered the street. "You wanted to use me to take over the radio station?"

"Of course not, Mari," José pleaded, taking my hand in his. "Don't you see? This was fate. When I saw you that day on the Malecón, I knew you were mine. And then, when you mentioned the radio, everything else fell into place. It was confirmation that you were the missing link to my plan . . . and to my life. This country—and our future—depends on a Cuba without Batista. Together, we have a chance to finally make that happen."

José drew me closer and kissed me slowly, as if trying to press the truth of his words onto my lips. When he finally pulled away, I stood there motionless, watching as the moonlight bounced off the waves.

"My boarding house is just there." He pointed to a tall blue building three blocks from the boardwalk. "Come back with me. Let me explain everything."

I had never seen José's home before. I knew he had stayed in a series of rented rooms since he moved from Matanzas, but we had never had the privacy—or the opportunity—to be alone.

I thought of my own curfew quickly approaching.

"*No sé, José . . .*" I considered aloud.

"Come with me, Mari. Let me explain the plan to you," he pleaded. He squeezed my hand and I could feel the resolve leave my body. I smiled. Seeing my resignation, José led me silently toward the weathered blue building with chipping paint, a warm light shining through the front window.

I followed him up the stairs, pushing through a creaking splintered door that deposited us into a tiny room off the second-floor balcony. There, in a cramped room that smelled of salt water and books, I saw the contents of his life in the hours he spent without me. His university papers were covered in black ink, hand-written notes scribbled across every blank space on the page; books from the library stacked above a wooden desk, a solitary lamp resting on its edge.

I looked down at his neatly made bed, the mattress sitting directly on the floor.

Together, we stood in silence, awkward and unsure of what to do with the sudden intensity of our privacy.

We smiled shyly at each other, José once again reaching for my hand, the tips of his fingers finding their way inside mine.

Before long, we were seated on top of the narrow mattress, shoulder to shoulder, talking about our plans for the future.

He told me about the palace, the radio station, and his hope for the Revolution.

"Batista just has to step down peacefully, Mari. It is the only way."

José rubbed my back as he spoke, his voice soothing and clear.

After hours of close whispers, animated plans, and shared kisses, José stared into my eyes.

"You're different, Marisol. *This* . . . is different."

I kissed him slowly.

"I love you, José," I mustered, swallowing my fears and pulling him down toward the bed.

I kissed him again, this time with purpose—a signal that I wanted more.

Sensing a shift, José asked if I was ready.

I nodded.

José took his time, waiting patiently for my body's instructions. Slowly he entered me, the first pains shooting through me suddenly and without warning.

My mind went blank.

I was filled with a feeling so warm and intense, I knew I was where I was meant to be.

This was freedom.

My freedom.

And he was my choice.

When we were done, José twirled my hair, pulling at a single coil only to watch it spring back to life. His bright eyes, deep pools of amber with flecks of green, stared down at my naked breasts.

"It doesn't matter what happens at the radio station, Marisol," he murmured, running his index finger down the slope of my waist. "I've already won the battle. I have you."

José leaned forward and kissed me slowly, one hand cupping the base of my neck.

I stared at the tiny scar below his left ear, the jagged "v" etched in flesh: a proverbial fork in the road.

An omen of our decision.

"You are already a part of me, Marisol," José whispered, sliding his hand down to my waist. "I would wait for you in every lifetime, and if I couldn't, I would die a thousand times just to come back and find you."

CHAPTER 12

Lily

Cambridge, Massachusetts
November 20, 1991

I sat at a large oak desk in the corner of Widener Library, tucked between rows of books stacked high in every color. A printed application from the Office of Career Services sat idly in my hands. The deadline for Ubuntu Leadership—the social justice nonprofit based in Durban, South Africa—was approaching in ten days, and I had to write three essays about why I wanted to work there.

I had been thinking about the essays for weeks.

Fall semester hadn't even ended yet and everyone else in the Social Studies department already seemed to have a summer internship: the associate's program at Goldman Sachs or Lehman Brothers, the early development rotation at Boston Consulting Group, or a competitive fellowship at a federal courthouse.

If I didn't land something soon, it would be one more reason for the moms on the Elk River school board to say I'd only gotten into Harvard because of affirmative action.

I needed proof that they were wrong.

"Hey there, mate!" Vikram chirped over my shoulder, appearing beside a shelf of neatly alphabetized philosophy books.

"What are you doing here?" I blushed.

Vikram placed his messenger bag on the dark wood table between us, straightening his collar as he ran his fingers through his jet-black hair. It was always ruffled in that effortlessly cool way that only movie stars—and somehow he—managed to achieve.

I set the pen down in front of me.

Since that first dinner over pad thai, Vikram and I had become inseparable, finding each other like two homing devices after class, heads bent over our French notebook, or any book for that matter. We'd spent the last few months exploring new libraries—the law school, the medical school, even MIT. Sometimes we'd take a stroll through Boston Commons just to venture into the city, almost always ending the day at our favorite tea shop.

Vikram walked over, rustling my curls playfully as he plopped down in the open chair beside me.

He had never touched my hair before.

I liked it.

"Just finished my Fourier Analysis class and figured you'd still be here. Want me to walk you home?"

I stared down at the application in my hand, the ink on the pages slightly smudged by the sweat on my palms.

"Yes, that'd be great. I don't think there's much left to say here anyway . . ."

"Are these the South Africa essays? Did you finish?" he asked, helping me gather my books and stack them in the return pile. "What did you say?"

"I basically explained why I think nonprofit work and mission-driven journalism could be powerful allies, since one helps a community tell its own story, and the other gives that community the opportunity to see itself reflected as its own protagonist."

"My my," Vikram smiled, "now I see why you're Elk River's finest."

I laughed, sliding the stapled pages into a manila envelope, the prepaid postage stamp already on the corner.

"Do you think you'll get it?" Vikram asked, taking my backpack and placing it over his shoulder as we stood to leave.

"I doubt it. But what other choice do I have? It's not like I could land an internship at the *New York Times* or the *Boston Globe*. They each want years of 'professional experience' that Elk River certainly doesn't offer. It just feels like, I don't know . . . I'm not quite sure how to describe it."

I struggled to find words, the fear of failure closing my throat.

"Like the system is rigged?" Vikram offered, holding open the library's massive double doors.

"Yes," I replied simply, turning to face him.

How did he do this? How was he always able to take the words right out of my mouth, right off my heart? Did he know me that well? Or did he simply know the world, and was able to name its heartbreak and its beauty, just as I saw it?

We walked down the same expansive marble steps I'd first seen in the admissions brochure, a thin layer of snow coating the grass in front of us.

"Do you know what it feels like," I continued, "to know that no matter how hard you try, you can't find a break in the fence? It's like the whole system is designed to keep you exactly in the same spot—in the same station—right where you started. Even if I *did* get one of those internships, I wouldn't have the money to pay for an apartment in New York or Boston for the summer. I'd need a scholarship."

We walked along the winding, red-brick pavement toward Harvard Yard.

"It's really no different in the U.K., Lily," Vikram sighed, slowing his pace beside me. "It's all a massive racket, this culture of 'elitism.' They tell you that all these things are accessible—the sweet nectar of the 'American Dream'—if only you just try." He pointed to the tall steeple of Memorial Church, the imposing columns of Widener Library. "That way, if you fail, the onus is yours. But what they never tell you, *Mademoiselle* Lily, is that the system was never designed to grant access. It is designed to protect power. Or else it wouldn't be exclusive. That's the allure of the American, or British, or whatever first-world Dream: it is the pursuit of riches that power and protect the ruling class. No one *wants* to break that cycle. They simply make exceptions."

I looked at his profile, the bare branches in the distance framing his silhouette.

This is precisely what I had grown to love about Vikram.

He saw the world in its glory and in its deception.

And he saw me.

"Don't let the assholes win, Lily," he said, taking my backpack off his shoulder and placing it gently on the grass in front of us.

"You are too bright, and too beautiful," he added sheepishly, "to let anyone make you doubt yourself. You are here for a reason. You are here because you belong." He looked at me with soft, brown eyes.

"Plus," he motioned again to the campus around us, "you've already found the break in the fence. And I have no doubt that you will make room for many others."

I pressed the snow-covered patch of brick between us with the toe of my boot, unsure of what to say next.

The truth is, I wanted to say it all—to say everything all at once:

Do you like me, Vikram?

Are we a couple?

Because I think I'm in love with you.

"Listen . . ." I began, my heart pounding, trying to muster the courage to end the stalemate that had plagued us for months. We spent every day together, but Vikram had never so much as held my hand.

"Vikram, I guess what I'm trying to say is . . ."

He looked at me inscrutably, the ornate iron bars of Johnston Gate looming in the background. Then, suddenly, as if responding to an invisible jolt, Vikram took two steps backward, away from me.

"It's getting late," he said abruptly, picking up his messenger bag and tucking it under his arm. "I'll come find you tomorrow."

I stared down at the keys in my hand, unsure of what to do next.

"Sure. See you later," I offered weakly, my heart falling silently onto the concrete as I watched him walk away.

I had come so close to saying the words.

What had stopped me?

Why did *he* stop me?

I thought back to all the false starts I'd had before Vikram, all the boys in high school I had just wanted to notice me.

To make me feel like I was normal.

Or pretty.

I had only been kissed once before, months before prom. Todd Milhaven caught my eye on his way to the locker room, right after our football team won the regional championship. He pointed behind the fence as a signal for me to meet him beneath the bleachers.

"Lily! We did it!" he jumped up excitedly, cupping my face between his calloused hands. "We're going to the state championship!"

I smiled at his unbridled, boyish pride as I reached up to hug him.

But instead, he kissed me.

There, with the rain seeping through the cold metal benches above our heads, I felt like Ione Skye in a scene from *Say Anything*, heavy droplets sliding down our eyelashes as our noses touched, my hands resting tentatively on the small of his back.

I lingered there full of hope, staring into Todd's icy blue eyes like small, round glaciers.

Was he . . . *choosing* me? Would he tell those girls—blonde and primped as they paraded past me in sky-high heels toward the homecoming line—that I was his?

Todd smiled softly as he wiped aside the hair that was plastered against my forehead. For just a moment, we stood entranced in a world of our own making. Those few seconds felt like an unbroken eternity, until we heard the first whooping cheers of victory as his teammates headed toward the bleachers.

Todd froze.

"I've got to go," he said abruptly. "I'll see you around, Lily."

He pinched my cheeks between his fingers, suddenly replacing the burning chemistry we'd shared moments before with a childlike playfulness. Then, just as quickly as he'd appeared, Todd jutted out from beneath the metal seats to join his teammates, squeezing his padded shoulders through the small opening in the stands. He tossed me a wave over his shoulder, a wobbly goodbye as he jogged back onto the field to celebrate.

Alone and left behind, I stood there silently as the rain soaked through the new Abercrombie & Fitch shirt I'd bought just for the occasion.

I realized then that what Todd was offering wasn't romance.

I had let myself be tucked away like some private fantasy, good enough for underneath the bleachers but not worthy of holding my hand in public.

Eric had warned me about this.

"They'll take you to coffee but not to dinner. They don't want us, Lily. Not when it comes with a cost."

Eric had known what it was to be hidden and forbidden.

The boys who had loved him hadn't felt safe enough—or brave enough—to love him in the light. He knew the pain of silent dismissal and averted eyes in the hallway when the object of his desire passed his locker without so much as a glance in his direction.

Is this what that was?

Maybe Vikram was no different from Todd, or any of the boys back in Elk River. Maybe he *wanted* to like me—*did* like me, even—but I didn't fit the image of what he thought he could bring home. I likely wasn't the trophy his parents wanted, their symbol of success at the end of immigration, hopeful assimilation and educational investment.

I was still too different.

Unlacing my boots, I walked inside my dorm and flipped on the lights.

The common room was empty.

Hana was spending the night with Chris . . . again.

Why *was* it so hard for me to find that? And why didn't Vikram want it with me?

I wanted those same stolen kisses, high off adrenaline and teenage hormones.

I wanted to be chosen.

But perhaps I was asking for too much.

I had never received romantic attention before, so why the despair now? The truth was, I was happy to have Vikram's companionship, even if that was all it was going to be. He was something—and someone—I had never encountered before.

CHAPTER 13

Marisol

Havana, Cuba
March 13, 1957

Just fold it down the center," I instructed Mirta, pointing to the poster in her hand, its red paint still wet and dripping from the edges. Thick, sticky heat wafted through the single open window, its bars covered with rough black net to keep the mosquitos away.

Mirta stood there, her big brown eyes unsure and afraid.

Mirta was everything I was not: measured where I was impulsive, demure where I was fiery. We were the opposites that attracted, a sisterhood borne of circumstance and isolation.

Which is why she was helping me prepare for a mutiny she wanted nothing to do with.

"Remind me why we have to do this?" Mirta asked, nervously running her fingers along the edge of the crisp cardboard. "Why can't we just let José and his crew do the heavy lifting and tell us about it in the morning?"

"¡Mirta, *ya*!" I sighed, exasperated and trying to sound more confident than I was. "There won't *be* another chance if we don't go through with this tonight. We aren't even students anymore!"

I took the poster from her hands and rolled it up tightly, stuffing it into a canvas sack.

The plan was simple: the *Directorio Revolucionario*—José's insurgent group of which I was now a part and had, begrudgingly, conscripted Mirta—was going to force Batista out of power. Batista was getting ready to make a speech later that night at the palace, a grand, sensational gesture to show the world he was still in charge. José decided that just before the president's address, half of the group would storm the presidential palace and surround Batista's living quarters and force him to step down, while the rest of the group—Mirta and I included—would march to *Radio Reloj* and announce a successful coup.

This, José convinced us, was the only way.

He said if we didn't act now, Batista would stay in power, our families would suffer, and we would be condemned to an undemocratic, unjust Cuba for the rest of our days.

Still, I couldn't believe we had come this far.

"I am just the messenger of justice, *querida,*" José whispered to me last night in his bed, our final evening together before the attack. He reminded me of the bullet-ridden bodies of students that had recently appeared around campus—a grotesque reminder of Batista's brutality and increasing paranoia.

It was those images of lifeless students and chained classrooms that forced me to keep my resolve.

"Look, Mari, we can even write about all this if you want," Mirta bargained, deploying her final negotiation tactic. She listlessly folded the remaining cardboard in front of her, looping the long pieces of twine that hung from its edges between her fingers. "I promise I'll help you get a message to the Americans. My uncle knows someone who works at the dock where the shipment of foreign papers comes in. You can document everything—your first real piece of journalism! He'll make sure it gets on the boat. Let's just do that, no?"

Mirta knew how much my apprenticeship at *Radio Reloj* had meant to me and how desperately I wanted my own byline.

But it still wasn't enough.

"Do you want to go back to Las Tunas and end up like your mother, Mirta? Or mine? Working on a farm, popping out babies, and hoping the Americans buy one pound of *azúcar* just so you can feed your kids for the month? I don't want that life. I don't deserve it. And neither do you."

Mirta took a deep breath, running both hands through her short, dark hair. She told me countless times how she had begged her mother for months to let her go to university, vowing that things would be different for their entire family. She couldn't stomach the thought of going back, head bowed in shame, no longer a student with the promise of a future.

"*Dale,*" Mirta relented. "Pass me the bag."

"*¡Esoooooo, comadre!* That's the spirit."

I handed her the bag with the 0.30 Cristóbal carbine José had asked me to store at our boarding house. Knowing the authorities might search his room if they got wind of our plan, he had asked me to hide the duffel bag stuffed with towels to conceal the rifle inside. Batista's men wouldn't suspect it in the possession of two college women, José promised, assuring me that we would only use it in case of emergency.

Life or death.

Mirta and I waved innocently to Señora Collado as we exited the boarding house, angling awkwardly through the double doors under the weight of our supplies. We were set to meet José and the rest of the crew at the *Calle 19* apartment at 3 p.m., and from there, make our way to the radio station.

As soon as Mirta and I stepped onto the sidewalk, I could smell the salt water from the ocean drifting in the breeze.

I had butterflies.

When we arrived at the apartment, José was wearing a crisp

white shirt, leaning against the concrete stairs that led to the building's basement. More than a dozen students scurried past him down the stairs, their backs bent carrying heavy boxes.

"Raúl has the rest of the materials," José said as soon as we came into view, kissing me briskly on the top of my head. "Grab the masks and canisters from him."

Despite his best efforts to appear calm, I could tell José was nervous. He paced unsteadily back and forth, his hands in his pockets, issuing short directives. He was never this uneasy.

Mirta and I headed down the stairs to the drafty cellar where Raúl, a second-year student in the architecture department, stood beside a wide wooden table awaiting instructions. I scanned the group to see how many people had actually shown up. Fourteen other students and recent graduates, most of whom I recognized from our Monday meetings, stood huddled together tossing grenades into empty canvas bags.

"Okay *muchachos,*" José said, his voice low and rumbling. "It's time. For those of us heading to the radio station, we travel in groups of four. Each car has a designated driver. Remember to stay several meters apart, and if anyone gets stopped, say you are headed east toward Vedado. Do not continue, or they will follow you to us. Wait until 4:30 p.m. and we will meet at the university after the announcement."

José estimated we had only three minutes to occupy the station before Batista's guards reached us. He had prepared a speech to read over the radio, announcing the end of the old regime.

"This is the dawn of a new generation," José bellowed as he walked toward the door. "It begins *ahora.*"

We nodded collectively, inspired and too scared to back out now.

José wrapped his arm around me and squeezed tightly, slinging the bag with the rifle I had just handed him over his shoulder.

"*¿Lista, querida?*" he whispered into my ear. "Ready to change our lives?"

I smiled nervously.

"I'll be fine," I answered softly. "But I'm worried about Mirta."

Mirta stood with her hands in her jean pockets, her body swaying back and forth.

"¡*Anímate*, Mirta!" José shouted over his shoulder as we readied to leave. "Change waits for no one!"

Mirta gave a weak smile back.

One by one, we climbed the stairs and exited the building, Mirta and I pairing up with José and Raúl near the front.

I squeezed Mirta's hand tightly, willing her to keep up.

Together, we climbed into the first car, an old cream-colored Ford. My stomach grew tighter as soon as we passed the university.

Suddenly, I had a bad feeling.

Did we bring sufficient supplies? What if the gate to the station was locked? Did anyone else know we were coming?

I tried to calm my nerves, assuring myself that we were among the smartest students in our ranks, the ones who most understood the urgency this moment required. Certainly José had considered every possibility long before tonight.

After several minutes, the radio station finally came into view, its tall, paneled walls looming in the distance.

Mirta's face was drained of color.

"Be courageous, *hermana*," I whispered. "Everything is going to be fine. You'll see."

I assured her as much as I tried to assure myself.

The first group to arrive, the four of us got out of the car and approached the building's back door. Heavy iron chains snaked through the door's metal handle. Just as José and I reached for the rusted lock, a red flare darted into the cloudless sky, bright enough to be seen in the afternoon sun.

"That's the signal!" José pointed to the fiery beam. The flare meant that the others had breached the palace walls. This was their warning: the clock had started.

We had three minutes to announce Batista's fall.

"Quick, Mari, grab the key!" José shouted.

My hand trembled in my right pocket as I fumbled for the gold, coin-shaped key the station's manager had given me earlier that week. I hadn't returned it after closing the building.

I twisted the key inside the metal bolt until I heard a click. The door swung open with a bang. José rushed past me, racing up the steps to the second floor. Raúl and I trailed just behind him, landing on the top of the staircase, the adrenaline making us short of breath. José pushed the door to the transmission room open, the "On Air" sign dangling just above its threshold. Marching to the L-shaped wooden desk in the corner, José grabbed the black wire microphone that sat securely on the edge.

Emilio's microphone.

I pressed the switch mounted on the wall, the red plastic light buzzing brightly as the airwaves crackled to life.

"Mirta, connect the headset!" I pointed to the round disks that had fallen to the floor.

Mirta stared at me, locked in a daze.

"*¡Ahora, Mirta!*" I screamed, hoping to jolt her from her stupor. I watched the hands on the mounted clock tick by.

Mirta finally bent over to pick up the cracked headset and plugged it into the speaker.

"Three . . . two . . . one . . ." I counted down as the bright light flashed. "We're live!"

José took a deep breath, bringing the microphone to his lips.

"People of Cuba! At this moment, the Dictator Fulgencio Batista has just been executed. In his own presidential palace, the people of Cuba have gone to settle accounts with him."

My blood ran cold.

Executed?

"It is we, the *Directorio Revolucionario,* who have dealt the final blow to this shameful regime," José bellowed.

I glanced at Raúl standing beneath the speaker on the wall, beads of sweat dripping down his face.

Did he know about this? Had he helped José with a completely different plan?

A plan to *kill* the president?

My heart pounded wildly inside my chest, confusion and terror ripping me apart in equal measure.

I watched in horror as José clutched the paper, his hand trembling as he read his own words.

"To each and every Cuban listening to me: you are now free. Batista has just been eliminated—"

Before José could finish, the room suddenly went dark.

Mirta shrieked.

"They've breached the building!" Raúl shouted, grabbing José's elbow. "They've cut the transmission! *¡Vámonos!*"

José looked at me, his cheeks flushed. "*¡Ven, Mari!* Let's take the back staircase. The car is waiting."

We raced down the marble steps to the first floor, bolting through the door and tumbling onto the sidewalk.

Three cars, each with a designated student in the driver's seat, waited for us in the narrow alley behind the building.

"*¡Apúrense!*" Otto shouted from behind the wheel of the first car. "They're coming!"

Sirens from several approaching vehicles rang in the distance.

Mirta, José, and I jumped into the backseat of the old sedan while Raúl joined Otto in the front.

I stared at José's profile, stunned and immobile, my body going numb. What had he just done?

What had *we* just done?

Speeding out of the alley, Otto winded through narrow streets toward the city center.

"Head to the university!" José shouted, his voice overpowered by humid air rushing through the open windows.

"*¿Ahora?*" Raúl turned to face him, incredulous.

"Yes!" José barked back. "The transmission went out too soon. Our three minutes weren't up. That means the other group is in trouble."

"Enough!" I shrieked, finally finding my voice. "You said they were only going to surround the palace. Force Batista to step down! An act of protest! Of defiance! No one was supposed to get killed!"

José stared at me blankly. The certainty of his own actions, the resolve of his own will, written all over his face.

"I love you, Mari. But it had to be done. There was no other way. I can explain later, but right now we need to meet the rest of the group at the university."

"No!" Mirta cried, tears streaming down her face. "We've done enough."

"Our job isn't done until Batista is gone!" José roared suddenly, the look in his eyes—unleashed and wild—sending a chill down my spine. "There is a reason the transmission stopped. It means the job wasn't complete! *¡Vaya, Raúl!* To the university!" he instructed again.

Raúl shook his head in exasperation as Otto pressed the gas.

I grasped Mirta's hand as her body shook with silent sobs.

José sat with his jaw clenched, his eyes flinty; hot, sticky air from the window blowing through his shiny black hair.

Together, we sped out of the tunnel, the transmission tower getting smaller in our rearview mirror. As soon as we entered the wide, winding curves of San Lázaro street, the base of the university staircase came into view.

"Move!" Raúl shouted, the vein in his neck throbbing as he suddenly reached for the dashboard.

An army vehicle appeared directly in front of us.

Otto tried to avoid the dark green Jeep, swerving wildly into oncoming traffic.

"We're blocked in!" Otto whimpered, his voice shrill and panicked.

I heard the crush of metal before I saw it.

One of the police cars struck us from behind, sending our car spinning as the hot metal of the rear collapsed from the force of the collision.

Mirta turned around in horror. "It's them, Marisol. They've found us."

I could feel her hand trembling in mine.

I peered through the scratched glass of the windshield and saw three more Jeeps approaching, all military grade.

Mirta was right once again.

We had been caught.

CHAPTER 14

Lily

Cambridge, Massachusetts
December 4, 1991

I crossed the Yard and walked into Canaday, peeling off my pastel cardigan as I placed my key in the mason jar. The silver ring hit the glass with a jangle. Chris and Hana were cuddled together on the futon, their legs intertwined, bodies sprawled against the faded blue cushion.

"Am I interrupting?" I asked, dumping my backpack beside the door.

Chris sat up and closed the leather notepad resting on his lap.

"Not at all, love," Hana cooed, swinging her legs to the front of the couch. "Want some *soju*?"

"That'd be great," I said, reaching for a paper napkin at the center of our acrylic coffee table. Hana had officially made me a convert.

"What have you two been up to?" I asked.

"Not much, just jotting down some notes from our meeting this afternoon," Hana said, pointing to Chris's journal. "Two upperclassmen started complaining about the Final Clubs' hours again, claiming they shouldn't be allowed to operate past two in the morning since they aren't officially affiliated with the university."

Chris was a member of the Falcon, one of Harvard's private, invite-only organizations that defined our campus social scene. These were Harvard's most exclusive social circles. They were a murky cross between single-sex fraternities and secret societies, unchecked by the university and funded by the incomprehensible wealth of the clubs' alumni donors. Hana was on track to be "punched," as they called it, for the Butterfly—the only women's club.

Together, Hana and Chris also volunteered for the student council to balance out their well-heeled social life.

They called it a powerful form of "community activism."

I called it résumé padding.

Just as I was mulling over whether to set aside my lofty morals on classism and ask for an invite to the Butterfly's Winter Solstice party, there was a knock at the door. I turned the handle without bothering to look through the peephole.

Vikram stood there, his normally impeccably ironed shirt disheveled and a look on his face I couldn't quite read.

"Forgot your French assignment?" I smiled.

He was silent.

"Hey man, come on in." Chris stood to greet him.

Vikram walked inside and mumbled a hello.

"Want a drink?" Hana offered. "You don't look so hot."

"Cheers, that'd be nice."

Chris gave Hana's cheek an adoring pinch before she left to grab another bottle of *soju* from the stash in our mini fridge.

"You okay?" I asked, noticing that Vikram still hadn't moved from the door.

Hana returned to pour the clear liquid into Vikram's cup, filling it to the edge before sitting down on Chris's lap. Chris nuzzled his face into her neck while Hana purred.

Shifting uncomfortably, Vikram and I stared at each other.

"Have a seat," I said, motioning toward the blue beanbag in the corner. I leaned awkwardly on the edge of the futon beside Hana, who sat stacked on top of Chris like a Russian doll.

"What's going on?" I finally asked, looking at Vikram.

"I have to leave," he blurted out, the words erupting from his lips, hot and noxious, as if he couldn't hold them in any longer. "I have to go back to England."

I sat there, confused. Was this that dry British humor he was always going on about? Had I missed the punch line?

"Do you mean for winter break?" Hana asked. "In a couple of weeks?"

"No," Vikram answered sharply. "Tomorrow."

"Huh?" I blanched. My stomach felt like it had just fallen to the floor. "Why?"

"My mother called to say my father collapsed in the grocery store. She says I must return immediately. I leave tomorrow and will be gone for the rest of the semester. The dean has already approved the medical leave."

I couldn't understand anything Vikram was saying. He was speaking slowly and deliberately—almost mechanically—and yet the words were coming too quickly.

"You spoke to the dean?" I asked, picturing him already so many steps ahead. Had he organized his leave, packed his suitcase, arranged his travel—all before I even knew?

My heart beat faster.

Was I angry? Disappointed?

"I called Dean Kelly as soon as I hung up with my mum. The fellowship is only a year, so I can't risk not completing it. If all goes well, hopefully I can come back."

Hopefully. There was that word. The blank space around it meant there was a real possibility of exactly the opposite happening.

He might never come back.

Chris stood up slowly, breaking the awkward silence that had fallen over us. "Well, the pickup team won't be the same without you, man," he said, placing his hand over his chest. "The guys will miss our favorite midfielder, but don't let Man United get too far ahead in the Champions League," he added with a wink, hoping to lighten the mood.

Vikram gave a weak smile.

"For sure, and thanks for all your hospitality, guys. I hope to see you on the other side."

"Of course, *dahling,*" Hana said in her best British accent, stepping toward the beanbag to give him a hug.

I couldn't move.

"I need to finish packing," Vikram said slowly, looking in my direction. "Lily, could you please walk me out?"

I nodded. I could feel my throat burning, tears threatening to fall.

I opened the door, holding it ajar for Vikram to follow. Once we entered the hallway, I leaned against the iron railing of the staircase.

"Lily, I . . ."

"It's okay . . ." I interrupted.

"My dad is . . ."

"Sick. Yes. Sorry for not responding better sooner," I said, gently hitting my forehead with the palm of my hand. "How are you feeling? How's your mom?"

"It's pure chaos, honestly. We should have been more prepared and we weren't. I'll figure it out tomorrow when I'm home. Listen, I—"

"No, it's okay," I cut him off once more, not sure I could withstand whatever he was about to say. "Go handle things at home, and hopefully everything will resolve quickly and you can come back."

"Yes, I would really like that."

Vikram paused.

We both stared at the floor, silence passing between us like an electric current.

"I will miss you, Lily," Vikram said, finally.

Too afraid to speak, I closed the distance between us, wrapping my arms around Vikram's neck. He smelled like clean laundry and expensive aftershave. The tears I'd tried to keep inside finally fell, dripping onto the skin peeking above his collar, the cool gold of the necklace he said his father had given him pressing against my forehead. I let my hand fall to my side, searching gently for his fingers.

Vikram reached forward until he found mine.

I threaded my fingers through his, touching softly at first.

Then, he squeezed back.

I didn't want to let go. There were still so many open questions between us. Just as I parted my lips to speak, Vikram suddenly pulled away. He bent over quickly to pick up his bag from the floor, steadying himself with his left hand on the banister. "I must get going," he said, backing away from me slowly. "I'll see you around."

Vikram turned, bounding down the steps two at a time, the metal door to the entryway echoing through the hall as it clicked into place behind him.

I stood there alone, panic rising inside my chest. Was this the end? Did Vikram always intend for it to end this way? Or was I the only one who had hoped for something more?

Through the fog of hurt and confusion, an image of my mother's most recent letter pierced my thoughts. Everything I'd felt in Vikram's arms—even for that brief moment—felt like a daydream I'd had before, something I'd recognized almost instinctively, like watching someone else through the glass.

This was what my mother had described with José. Reading her last message, where she had fallen in love with a young activist at the university, it was as though she had put into words exactly what I was feeling now. Had José also made her levitate with hope, only to bring her crashing down in despair?

I ran my fingers through the top of my hair, wild curls holding onto each finger as if looking for salvation.

All I knew, standing alone in the silence of the empty hallway, was that I couldn't have come this far, from the bottom of a mountain in a place no one had ever heard of, to let a boy with a pretty face and an English accent derail me.

My life is bigger than Vikram Desai, I told myself, repeating the words as if in a trance.

But I didn't believe that.

At least not yet.

I left the empty foyer and walked back inside our dorm room. Hana stared up at me from the seat of the futon as I slowly pressed the door closed behind me. Chris looked down nervously at his hands.

"I'm so sorry, Lilz. I know you two had a special friendship." Hana stood and crossed the room, wrapping me in her arms, my tears forming dark splotches on her light blue pajama set. "Let me grab you some tissues from the bathroom. I'll be right back. This is all going to be okay, I promise."

Hana grabbed her bathrobe from the hook behind the door and made her way down the hall.

Chris sat uncomfortably on the far edge of the futon while I remained frozen at the door.

Finally, he looked up.

"He could have done better, Lily," Chris said quietly.

"What?" I stammered.

"Vikram could have given you more assurance. Did he promise to call? Write? Anything?"

"No," I answered, staring down at the jagged hole in my white sock. "But can we really blame him?" I asked, struggling to regain my composure while fighting the inexplicable urge to defend Vikram. "His father's sick. It's not like we were anything special . . . *I* wasn't anything special."

"Stop that," Chris said suddenly, the force in his voice catching me by surprise. "Don't say that. I've watched you two spend every waking moment together since that night at the bar, and to anyone watching you *were* a couple, which means you deserved a proper goodbye."

"It's not like he ever asked me to be his girlfriend, Chris. That's the risk I took by never clarifying . . ." my voice trailed off.

"Respect isn't a risk, Lily. A man doesn't need to *ask* you to be his girlfriend, he needs to *treat* you like one. And then *you* get to decide."

Just then, Hana walked back into the room.

"Here's a fresh box, love," she said, a family-size pack of Kleenex in her palm. She reached up to hug me as my silent tears fell once again. "You'll find your person, Lily. Don't worry. You'll get what you deserve."

"As long as you *remember* what you deserve," Chris interjected, rising from the futon. "I'll let you two have a moment to yourselves. Hana, call me later."

"Of course, sweetheart." Hana blew him a kiss. "In the meantime, let's get our Humpty Dumpty back together again, shall we? One 'Sayonara Soju' coming right up!"

CHAPTER 15

Marisol

Elk River, North Carolina
January 2, 1992

Marisol turned the key to the front of the cabin, the bag of rags she carried from work heavy over her shoulder. The rusted metal hinges of the screen door announced her arrival, the flakes of chipping black paint falling off as she pressed the handle.

Stepping onto her knotted blue rug, worn from years of tiny footsteps finding their way, she placed her bags down gently on the floor.

There, she saw her daughter slumped on the couch.

She still hadn't moved.

Two weeks ago, Lily had come home for winter break. Marisol and Kem could hardly contain their excitement at having their baby girl back under their roof for two whole weeks. Their house was always livelier, abuzz with energy whenever she was within their four walls, dropping her backpack on the rough wooden floor of their cabin, the music from her CDs blasting through the speakers as she danced through the hallway in her socks. Her laughter brought Marisol back to the moment she and Kem first fell in love;

their daughter, a physical reminder of the redemption—and joy—they had both found in each other.

But this most recent visit was different.

Marisol could tell something weighed more heavily on her daughter as soon as she appeared on their small porch with her frayed duffel bag. The entire time she was home, Lily sat by the window watching the mountain snow fall, lost in a world of her own. When Marisol encouraged her to eat, she barely touched her plate. This was not the Lily that she had always known, playing crosswords with Kem and helping Marisol heat the *cafecito*. No matter the circumstance, her daughter always had the energy to be dutiful, offering to help, to anticipate, to provide.

But now, Lily was in a place she couldn't reach, withdrawn and disconnected.

This put Marisol in unchartered waters.

Not knowing the source of her daughter's angst—and not having the words to address it—sent an uneasy, silent current through the air. Theirs was not, and had never been, a relationship of direct questions and complete answers. Marisol showed tenderness through fresh food, warm bellies, and clean towels. She encouraged achievement, helping her daughter meet metrics that no one could strip from her: good grades, fluent English, clothes that Marisol herself could make good as new with the skill of her own hands. That was how she spoke to her daughter, through the language of action.

Marisol peeked beyond the frame of the kitchen door and watched as Lily lay prostrate on the couch, facing the back of its overworn frame.

Marisol knew not the source of her daughter's anguish, but she recognized the shape of its languor, this depressed passivity.

This was loss.

The loss of love.

It was a feeling Marisol knew more intimately than she cared to remember. Could this be about the British boy Lily had mentioned in her letters? Marisol hadn't thought much of it at first, but by the time he appeared in the second letter, she suspected something more than just "studying" was at stake. Was this Lily's first boyfriend?

Marisol cringed remembering the boy who had left Lily waiting on the porch on prom night. She felt physically ill every time she thought of her daughter's fallen face the moment she realized he wasn't coming. *Ese pendejo hijo de puta descarado*. He was not courageous enough to take Lily to that dance, so unsure, or unwilling, to cross the racial lines that had squeezed the life out of so many generations, snuffing out young love before it could begin. Marisol thought that so much had changed since she first arrived in Appalachia decades ago, when "whites only" signs still adorned the store windows on the tiny paved streets of what they called downtown. And yet, when that white boy left her daughter speechless and fighting back tears at the base of their narrow staircase, Marisol realized that the abiding, silent segregation that had shocked her decades ago still persisted. Even when the signs were forced to fall, the racial pressure that forced Marisol to recognize who she was in this country—and now, who her daughter would become—was stronger than ever.

Which is partly why today, even as she watched her daughter suffer silently on their couch, Marisol couldn't directly ask Lily what had happened. She couldn't bring herself to ask the questions now that she didn't have the words—or the courage—to ask back then. Of course, Marisol wanted to know the contours of her daughter's heart, to understand the parts of herself she kept hidden; it was that part of her daughter she had tried to reach with her letters. But she simply couldn't bring herself to have the conversation in person, the words too delicate, the pain too fresh.

Besides, Marisol and Lily seemed to have reached a silent truce, an unspoken promise not to mention what was in those letters directly. They didn't discuss the contents of their confessions, these small, novel peeks into each other's lives.

But Marisol was worried. She had never seen this version of her daughter, listless and apathetic.

Which is why, by the time the final day of Lily's two-week winter break approached, Marisol decided she had to do something. She leaned over the kitchen counter, the wet peel of the plantain suspended in her hand.

"*¿Querida, me puedes ayudar con los plátanos?*" Marisol hoped the call to duty would awaken some response from her daughter, even if only reflexive. Lily knew from long weekends spent with her mom as a child, how far Marisol traveled to get the thick bananas in the winter.

Marisol saw Lily stir from beneath her blanket.

"*¿Ahora*, Mami?"

"Yes. Now, *querida*."

Lily walked over to the sink where Marisol stood, dragging her feet as if weighed down by invisible anchors.

Marisol passed her the knife.

"*¿Tienes hambre, cariño?* You haven't eaten all day."

"No, not hungry. Just tired."

Marisol paused, reaching for a discarded peel. "So many exams. How is your French class going?"

Marisol felt the air shift between them.

Lily's hands hovered over the next plantain.

"There was this guy . . ." Lily trailed off quietly, unable to finish her sentence.

Were those tears in her eyes?

"The British boy?" Marisol ventured, surprising even herself. This was a clear breach of their unspoken contract, but she couldn't stand to see this child of hers—now a woman—suffering in pain.

Lily looked up at Marisol, her eyes wide and wet.

"Yes," she answered simply. "He left."

Lily looked down and began peeling the next banana, this time with renewed focus. Then, she looked up again, as if something suddenly occurred to her.

"What happened . . ."—she paused—"to the boy in your letter? The one who led that student movement?"

Marisol inhaled sharply.

Now it was Lily who had broken the rules.

Marisol spent every moment since she got off that boat pushing the flashing images of his young face away from her mind. She swore she would never speak his name again, and yet here she was: the person she loved most, asking her about the person she had once loved most.

Marisol looked up from the pan, stiffening. She stared back at her daughter, her spatula hovering over the popping oil. Marisol wanted to offer something, *anything*, to close the gap between her and her daughter, to mend the distance between their stilted conversations and sporadic letters.

But there was only so much she could bear.

Marisol's hand drifted up to the three silver coins strung together around her neck to form a medallion.

"Everything you need to know is in the letter I gave you," she said quickly, motioning to the cutlery beside the sink. "There's nothing more."

Marisol patted her daughter's hand, trying to soften the blow of her rejection.

"Ven, pásame el cuchillo."

As Marisol reached out for the knife in her daughter's hand, the dark memories that would haunt her sleep that night were already seeping into the edges of her mind.

CHAPTER 16

Marisol

Havana, Cuba
March 13, 1957

We were surrounded.

"Stop the car," José said calmly, his voice sounding like it belonged to someone else. Otto pulled over, one set of tires gliding onto the embankment beside the freeway.

José turned.

"Stay here," he ordered again, staring at me intensely.

I sat frozen.

José was communicating something, a message I couldn't decipher.

I simply nodded in return.

Finally, José broke our gaze and turned back around, reaching for the black bag on the floor of the car. As he unzipped it, towels spilled from the top.

It was the bag I had stored at our boarding house.

José pulled out the rifle and loaded its magazine.

"Stay here," he repeated, his eyes ablaze.

Then, suddenly, José opened the car door and rose from the vehicle in one smooth motion. He waived his rifle wildly in the air.

"¡Que nuestra sangre señale el camino de la libertad!" he roared, as five men in fatigues descended from the first Jeeps, their guns pointed in his direction. José let out a battle cry and charged one of the officers, his arms spread wide with the rifle in one hand, his chest exposed and vulnerable.

He fired one shot into the air.

A spray of bullets ricocheted in return.

A deadly call and response.

I watched in horror as José clenched his stomach, his eyes wide in surprise. Slowly, he looked down, a dark crimson stain spreading from the center of his white shirt.

Mirta howled.

José fell limp to the ground, his body landing with a thud.

I gasped, unable to form words.

Bile rose in my throat.

"¡Marisol, ven!" Mirta shouted, shaking me by the shoulders to jolt me from my stupor. She tugged both of my arms, pulling me from the vehicle as she strained against my dead weight. Together, we tumbled out of the back seat, my body stiff and in traction, falling on top of hers.

Just as we hit the concrete, Raúl and Otto bolted from the front seat.

They ran from our stalled car, its doors flung open, and barreled toward the center of the street.

A second military truck screeched to a halt in front of them.

Four men in faded green fatigues jumped out of the bed of the old Jeep, its roof gone, only the frame of its canopy remaining.

"¡Paren!" they shouted. "Stop!"

No sooner had Raúl and Otto started to shout back, hands in the air, than paramilitary men were on top of them, bats in hand. All I could see was a flurry of punches; bats crashing down on their frail, pubescent bodies, kicks unleashed with a violence I had never witnessed. I heard their cries, bloodcurdling screams that would later come to haunt me in my sleep.

It was then that I realized our most grave miscalculation all along: we were simply no match for these grown men, grisly and bearded, hardened by preparation and greed. Why had I ever thought that a tiny group of students—armed with fresh ideas and a few stolen grenades—would be any match for an entire army practiced in crude brutality?

Just when I thought it couldn't get any worse, the two soldiers stood over the boys, pistols aimed at their heads.

Two shots.

Mirta screamed.

One of the guards turned in our direction. In three quick strides he was upon her, bringing his baton across Mirta's head with a crack. Blood dripped from her skull, her body limp.

I shrieked in horror as the two men hoisted Mirta over their shoulders and dumped her in the open bed of their Jeep. Its engine roared to a start. One of the officers, the last to leap down from the truck, kicked José's body.

That's when he saw me.

I froze.

I watched as a sick realization spread across his face.

"*Oye*, don't rough that one up too much," the officer snickered to another man from the convoy. "We can still enjoy her before we're done. Bring her back with us."

I began slowly walking backward, my hands outstretched in front of me. A shard of glass cracked beneath my foot. I turned and broke into a run.

I took several long strides before I felt a hand grab my hair, yanking me back with a pop. My body crashed against the concrete.

"Where do you think you are going, *camarada*?" the guard breathed into my face, sitting on top of me, his legs straddling either side of my body. I could smell the cheap cigarettes and rum on his breath. He stared down, a crazed look in his eye.

"Get . . . off . . ." I shouted between breaths, my arms flailing wildly.

The weight of his frame absorbed my blows.

I felt a crack against my check, a closed fist splitting my jaw as blood squirted into the air, landing on the guard's fatigues.

"Now, now. Look what you've done," he taunted. "I suppose we have to go clean you up . . . together."

The guard grabbed me by the hair, lifting me off the ground. I kept swinging, a flurry of aimless blows landing somewhere between his face and collarbone. He grabbed me underneath my arms and flipped me over. Another man in fatigues ran toward us and, together with my captor, hoisted me bottom-up over his shoulder.

The two men carried me toward a dark green Jeep, identical to the one they had thrown Mirta in just moments earlier.

"*Vámonos,*" the soldier shouted to the driver as we approached. "This one's coming to the prison."

What did he mean "this one"? Who was the other?

They tossed me inside like discarded trash. My body landed with a thud, my hip hitting something soft beside me covered in tarp. The second guard leaped inside the bed of the truck to tie my hands and feet with a fraying rope.

Before taking his place in front with his comrades, my assailant paused and stared directly at me. His piercing eyes, dark and stormy, sent a chill down my spine.

"Don't move," he said, pulling back the corner of the tarp.

There, I saw white skin turned blue and purple, stringy hair matted with blood. Her eyes were sunken in her skull, open and lifeless.

Mirta.

"Stay still," the guard said once more. "Or *you* won't be so lucky."

The engine roared to a start.

CHAPTER 17

Lily

Cambridge, Massachusetts
February 12, 1992

After returning to campus from winter break, I found myself wandering aimlessly through the libraries, always the last to leave before closing. The campus security guard bolted the doors behind me.

Nothing was the same without Vikram.

He had sent a few letters since he left, scribbled musings on the backs of train tickets between Featherstone and London, or handwritten notes torn from our French workbook. I looked forward to these brief peeks into his life, trying to temper my excitement each time I saw a *par avion* postage stamp.

On my way back to my dorm, I made a stop to the basement mailroom. I lingered there, savoring the silence of the dusty cellar, not yet ready to go upstairs. Instead, I leaned against the wall with his most recent letter in my hand, the scuffed envelope crackling as I ripped apart the seam.

January 29, 1992

Mademoiselle Lily,

I would like to send you "une strophe" or two, but here's a brief synopsis of the reasons why I am not going to:

1. *My primary poetry expertise in French is so great that I have next to no ability in English.*
2. *I am currently still in my state of "bumbleness," stunned that I'm writing you from the U.K. instead of leaning over a stack of books to whisper to you in the library.*
3. *Anything I did write would be far too soppy.*
4. *I have tornado strengths that need to be calculated!*

I arrived home safely in Featherstone after spending the weekend with Akshay and Shivani in East London. Wedding plans are in full swing, but I had to come back to take my dad to see a new cardiac specialist. Not to be a downer, but things aren't looking so good. I called Dean Kelly last week to tell him I needed to stay home a bit longer. Unfortunately, I may not make it back before spring semester is over. But I am trying. I would like to have at least one more "Cambridge Craze" tea before you are officially a sophomore!

Speaking of which, have you sorted out your plans for the summer? Did you hear back from that internship in South Africa? I do hope it is yours; they would be lucky to have your talents.

I hope you are well, Lily. Please write if you get a moment. I would love to hear how your classes are going, if Madame Carole misses me yet, and if any of your future travels may bring you across the Pond. (I happen to know a British boy who would be thrilled to welcome you to Heathrow . . .)

Must run now. Mummy Desai needs some help with dinner. (That's a tale, I'm afraid. She knows I am hopeless in the kitchen.)

À tout à l'heure,

Vik

I folded the letter and placed it back in its envelope, staring at the miniature depiction of Big Ben on the stamp. I could feel the words jumping off the page and almost see Vikram staring back at me with the right side of his mouth raised in a mischievous smile. It was hard being reminded of the companionship I missed in his absence, but at least the mention of South Africa gave a pause in my pain.

I got the internship.

The guidance counselor at the Office of Career Services told me last Friday that the internship coordinator was opening a position at the South African embassy in D.C. and that I could coordinate with the lead researcher at the University of KwaZulu Natal. They would give me a stipend—allowing me to stay stateside in university housing at American University starting in July—and if my research went well, I could study abroad with them in Durban next semester.

Life had been a whirlwind since I got the news, finally a good break in my direction.

Everyone had a plan this summer—this time, *including* me.

Smiling, I walked upstairs and locked the door behind me.

The room was silent.

Hana was with Chris at a soccer game and I had the place all to myself.

I reached for the bright red handle of the telephone perched on the corner of the desk and curled up on the futon beneath the windowsill, its cushions deflated from overuse.

It was my turn to call Eric; we'd been leaving unanswered voicemails for each other for the past several weeks, each of us swept up in the excitement of our first semesters away from home.

I needed to hear his voice.

"Hola, Princesa," Eric answered in an exaggerated Southern drawl.

"Hello, my love. How's school?"

"School is fine. Design rehearsals, exams, internship hunting. My parents, not so much."

"Why? What happened?"

"I told them, Lily."

I sat up straight, scooting to the edge of the futon.

"You did? What did they say?"

Eric sighed heavily. I could sense a shift on the other end of the line.

"About as well as could be expected: AIDS, death, eternal hell. The usual."

Eric laughed bitterly.

I could tell he was trying to hide his disappointment.

His pain.

"You know that's bullshit, Eric," I whispered, overwhelmed by the profoundness of his parents' rejection and unsure of how to console him.

"Your mom spends so much time in church, she must know that if she believes in a God, He made you in His image. Isn't that what the Good Book says?"

Eric was quiet.

Was he crying?

"So they say, Lily. But I was tired of hiding. I couldn't do it anymore."

"I understand, *querido*. But what made you do it now?"

"I've met someone."

"Ah!" I squealed, my excitement taking over. "Who?!"

"His name is Mario. He's from Spain. A photographer. Met him in Hell's Kitchen."

"What's that?"

"A haven for the gays. The theater district here in New York."

"Wow, Eric. That's amazing. You think this is serious?"

"I think it can be." He paused. "*If* we stop hiding."

"Good for you, E. You deserve this. You deserve to be loved in the light."

"What about you?" he asked.

"What *about* me?"

"I'm talking about Vikram, the boy who left for England. Has he finally confessed his undying love for you?"

I wrapped the phone cord around my finger, the coils squeezing the flesh until it turned white.

"Not exactly . . ." I sighed.

"He sounds like a reincarnated Todd Milhaven to me."

I winced, the memory of Todd's betrayal hurting more than I wanted to admit and certainly more than I wanted to show.

"This is different, Eric. Vikram is different."

"No, Lily. *We're* different." Eric paused, the words he didn't say filling the void.

Eric had known he was gay since middle school.

I was the only other person who knew, officially, but that hadn't stopped the boys in our high school from stuffing his locker with pink tulle and a plastic tiara the night before they nominated him for "Homecoming Queen."

A sick joke.

For Eric, who privately suffered from what the townspeople referred to as "an affliction"—and for me, one of the only Black kids in our class—the pain of watching from the outside became both customary and expected. We stared through the glass as our peers' lives moved through the typical teenage milestones:

Homecoming. Prom. First kisses.

While we didn't have the fanfare and acceptance of our classmates, we had always had each other.

"Any man who doesn't love you loudly, Lily, isn't the man for you," Eric said plainly. "You too, deserve to be loved in the light."

CHAPTER 18

Marisol

Havana, Cuba
April 21, 1957

Do you know what it's like to have your body ripped apart from the inside out? To feel your soul leave your frame, rise above you, and stare back down at you, mocking you with its freedom?

That's how I felt when I looked up and saw his eyes boring into mine, vicious and vacant. He lurched and grabbed, pinning down my forearms, his nails digging into the tender skin beneath my wrists. The hairs on his chest rubbed against my breasts, the weight of his naked body oppressive and unyielding. His grunts, a constant steady rhythm; each thrust sending the smell of rum seeping from his pores into my nostrils.

Until finally . . . there was nothing.

Only the sound of his breathing filled the silence. I heard the metal clasp of his belt buckle hit the floor before I saw it. Slowly, he lifted himself onto his knees. I could feel him searching the ground in the darkness for his glasses and uniform, separating them from my torn nylon pants and ripped T-shirt.

He cleared his throat.

"*Quédate aquí,*" he ordered, standing up beside me, staring down at my naked body, contorted and misshapen.

As if I could go anywhere if I tried.

He threw a rag at my head. It landed between my eyebrows, half of the worn white cloth spilling onto the tile.

I didn't flinch.

I stared into the blank space behind my rapist's head, too numb to react. The thought of my own impotence made my face flush with shame.

The moment he first penetrated me, I could feel the resolve leaving my body, my will to survive leaking onto the hard ground beneath me. That moment would forever mark my life's "before" and "after": the fault line between who I thought I could become with intention and who I was resigned to become by circumstance.

When my captor saw that I didn't move, he shouted something I couldn't make out, sounding too close and too far at the same time.

I was losing consciousness.

Or was that sleep taking over my body? Had I been awake all this time?

The door closed behind him, its latch sinking into place. There I lay, my naked back on the ground, my feet going cold from shock.

Was this the price I would pay? The cost of consequence I hadn't calculated?

I stayed there, unmoving. Time became a concept that meant nothing. I must have spent hours on that cold, hard floor—nights that turned into days, the sun peeking through the bars of my cell without warning.

They had taken me to *El Castillo del Príncipe,* the old military fort in the middle of Havana where Batista and his men took their political opponents.

That is where I expected to die.

In some ways, I wasn't sure if I already had.

I had heard about the camp, through newspaper clippings and whispered warnings, the clandestine jails where Batista's critics disappeared.

I never thought I would live to see one, much less be chained inside.

The first month I spent there, I had only one ratty, bug-infested blanket. Through slits in the door of my cell, I watched the soldiers crouch together just beyond the barracks, shoveling heaps of rice into their mouths on bent metal spoons.

"*Ese chamaquito* won't even see us coming," I heard a familiar voice say. I could see the shadowy profile of my rapist. He was talking to a group of six other soldiers.

"Once *El Hombre* stops Castro out East, that little lawyer will have to run back to Mexico."

A chorus of laughter.

"That *Directorio Revolucionario* kid thought that stunt at the palace was enough to stop *El Indio*? I heard Batista outsmarted almost fifty of those half-wits and had escaped to the third floor, safe and sound," one of the guards scoffed, passing a newspaper to the man sitting quietly beside him.

"And Echeverría," the first one continued, "I heard he dropped like a fly when you got to him, Silva."

Silva.

That was what they called the man who raped me.

The man who killed the only love I'd ever known.

I closed my eyes, seeing images of José's body, warm and wet, his blood spilling from once-supple skin, his mouth forming a thin, rigid line.

How did a life destined for greatness, a name we were all meant to chant in victory, get cut so brutally short? His future, stolen in cold blood; his hands—now swollen and stiff—clutching a victory speech he never got to deliver.

Had José always known it would come to this?

I flinched, replaying the crazed look in his eyes before the first ring of gunfire, the rifle loaded between his palms.

Had he tried to protect me from the truth of his plan? His *real* plan? Did he hope to deliver me a Cuba safe from dictatorship, filled with freedom? The gift of a martyr?

José didn't want my life to end with his, the tragic tale of two revolutionaries snuffed out by a single bullet.

But I wasn't a revolutionary.

I had just fallen in love with one.

"*'Castro heads for victory after attack on palace,'*" Silva continued reading aloud from the newspaper. "He's trying to seize the capital, take advantage of the opening."

"He's been in *la sierra maestra* with that *gringo* journalist all week," the first guard replied. "I heard he barely had anything to do with that university kid who organized the palace attack. We found the rest of the idiots who escaped that night holed up in an apartment on Humboldt Street. We finished them."

Silva scoffed, abruptly tossing the newspaper onto the fire. Sparks flew as hot orange embers charred its edges. "They're all fools marching to their own death. Castro wants everyone to think he can run the whole country but he can't get his own ragtag 'soldiers' in line."

Another round of laughter.

CHAPTER 19

Lily

Cambridge, Massachusetts
April 29, 1992

Spring had finally come and it felt like the entire campus had shaken off the long daze of winter.

Walking back from Lamont Library, I unclasped the top button of my pastel pink cardigan, my latest find from Filene's Basement on a recent trip to Copley Square. I'd spent all morning tucked in a library cubicle filling out paperwork from the State Department so that I would have access to the South African embassy on the first day of my summer internship in D.C.

I couldn't wait.

As I approached the door to my dorm, I heard the loud, unmistakable buzz of our emergency telephone ringing from beyond the walls.

I rushed to turn the key.

Almost no one called that number.

I dumped my backpack on the futon and raced across the room, quickly reaching for the telephone.

"Hello?" I breathed heavily into the receiver, terrified of what, or who, I would find on the other end of the line.

"Thank God you picked up," Hana's voice crackled through the speaker.

"Hana? Is that you? What's going on?"

"I'm with Chris at Harkness Commons. He's freaking out. I'm not even sure what to say. You need to come see this. It's all over the news."

"What is?"

"Just come, Lily."

I had never heard Hana like this.

"I'm on my way," I replied.

I nearly ran the half mile to the law school student center, the cleanest, newest building on campus that had quickly become a favorite study haunt for the undergrads who knew about it. Through the glass windows, I could see rows of students seated inside, huddled around a large television screen mounted against the wall.

"They fucking let them off," Chris spit out when I arrived, his eyes still glued to the television. Hana sat beside him, rubbing his shoulder. Confused, I lowered myself onto an empty chair. I looked up at the screen that had captivated the room, trying to make sense of the close-up images of four men in suits shouting over the sound of a heavy gavel.

Gasps erupted from a packed courtroom.

"These officers have been found innocent, acquitted in the trial of Rodney King," a reporter's voice boomed from the speaker.

Then, familiar black-and-white images flashed across the screen.

"Twenty-six-year-old King led officers on a high-speed chase last spring, accused of evading arrest while intoxicated. He was apprehended in south Los Angeles on the corner of Normandie and Florence. Twelve officers cornered him, four beat him until he lost consciousness."

The same video that had made my stomach turn a year ago rolled on: police hurling their batons with fists raised in the air, barking orders amidst the chaos. Chris reached for Hana's hand as the second officer moved closer to the human mass flickering at the center of the screen, reduced to a lump of near lifelessness. I flinched as a fourth officer lunged forward, baton coming down with a crack.

The announcer continued.

"This video was taken by a bystander who filmed the incident on his personal camcorder at the time of the encounter."

Chris put his face between his palms. "Fucking unreal. They got away with it. All of them."

I felt sick, as if I were seeing the video for the first time. When the King arrest first made national headlines, I had been in Elk River finishing my last year in high school. I came home to find my parents glued to the evening news, their hands gripping the edge of the sofa. My mother let out a yelp when the first baton came down. Unable to look away, we all stared in horror as the man at the center of the screen lay prostrate and cowering, making a futile attempt to shield his face with his open palms. Eventually, my father got up and left the room, so incensed he could hardly speak, save to grumble something about how white cops always tried to prove they were better than the Black and Brown people they policed. My mom shook her head with tears in her eyes.

Now, a year had passed, and the innocence of those officers had been decided.

"But the jury *saw* all the evidence," I said incredulously, the angry chants from outside the courthouse erupting from the TV screen. "How could the jury just acquit them?"

"Are you serious, Lily?" Chris stared back at me, his eyes ablaze. "Is this really a surprise to you? How do things work in the backwoods of North Carolina?"

I jumped. Backwoods?

"What's the matter? Is the truth uncomfortable? Do people like you and me walk free where you come from?" he continued.

I had never heard Chris so enraged. In fact, I'm not sure I'd ever heard him say so many words. I had also never heard him identify us . . . together. Sure, all of us were "others" in some way, but Chris and I were the only ones who were Black.

And Blackness, we knew, was treated differently in this country.

But did *Chris* see that? Chris was half African, his mom a Belgian school teacher. Most of the men I'd met on campus who occupied some state of racial ambiguity didn't choose to be Black. They acknowledged it, perhaps, but they didn't embrace it. For me, at least back home, things were different: we were all Black by virtue of not being white.

It was never clear to me whether Chris felt the same.

Hana reached over to gently rub his shoulder. "I'm sure Lily understands . . ."

"Do you?" Chris interrupted.

"I do," I answered, firmly meeting his gaze. "I speak Spanish, if that's what's behind your question. *And* I am Black. I come from the same slave stock as the rest of us, my ship just landed in Cuba. I get it. We all get it. That man could have been my father, my uncle, my brother. Hell, one day he could be my son." I paused. "And he could be yours."

After a moment of silence—our eyes locked—Chris sighed, slumping in his chair. "Exactly," he breathed heavily, as though my acknowledgment was enough to release him; the reality that he wasn't alone, confirmed.

"That man also could have been me," Chris added softly, his voice barely above a whisper.

I blinked in confusion.

"I was pulled over three years ago during my senior year of high school. I was the designated driver for a car filled with my drunk teammates. Of course, I was the only Black one. A cop stopped us right as we were crossing the border into the suburbs. As soon as we passed Eight Mile, he put on his sirens and chased us down, forcing us to pull over behind an abandoned building. He made me get out and put my hands on the hood while he unzipped my pants and strip-searched me right there on the side of the road.

"My teammates just watched.

"The same guys I'd spent every hour with at practice, telling me they had 'my back,' suddenly had nothing to say. I was frozen. The officer tapped and prodded like I was on some fucking auction block. Then, he cracked the back of my knees with his baton just for good measure."

Hana's eyes filled with tears.

"Eventually, he made me take a breathalyzer test just to have a reason for stopping me," Chris continued. "Of course, I passed—but that still wasn't enough."

"He arrested you," I gasped.

"He did. Took me straight to lockup. I spent forty-eight hours in a Detroit jail. A Detroit motherfucking jail. Can you imagine the things I saw that night? The shit I had to witness? I was valedictorian, a soccer player headed to Harvard on a scholarship. I had never even *met* a police officer. And then, all because some fucking cop wanted to take the piss out of a nerdy Black kid . . ."

Hana reached for his hand as he trailed off.

"Chris, I am so sorry," I mustered.

"Me too. I didn't mean to be rude, Lily. It's just . . ." He paused. "It took my mom twelve hours to find a lawyer to take the case. She emptied her savings account just to get the guy on retainer. And of course *she* had to do it, because my dad couldn't walk into that precinct with an accent and black skin and command their respect. The police had no idea I was her son. They just assumed—"

"You were Black," I finished.

"Yes. The cop obviously couldn't produce the paperwork showing I'd failed a breathalyzer test, and when my mom demanded he give me another one with the lawyer present, they balked and sent me home. That quickly. Her anger as a white woman was worth more than my life as a Black man. I learned that night what it meant, truly, to be Black in this country—what it meant to drive while Black, to be locked up while Black, to face the justice system while Black. I could have lost everything. How many men who look like me do? I was only saved because I had a white lawyer and a white mom. And now I have my freedom. The same can't be said for Mr. King."

Chris pointed to the screen.

"He may never see or walk properly again. But those motherfuckers are all free."

I looked down at my hands, unsure of what to say next.

"We have to do something," Hana said, attempting to fill the void. "Things are going to get worse. L.A. is gonna break."

"What do you mean?" I asked.

"This is just the beginning, Lily. Watch. I know my city. The Black folks are gonna get angry, then the Koreans are gonna get scared, and the white folks are gonna want 'order.' It's gonna be a shit show."

"So then, what?" I asked. "What do we do?"

"'*We*'?" Hana turned to Chris. "Babe, we just may have a little revolutionary on our hands after all," she laughed.

I smiled and rolled my eyes.

"Grassroots activism," Hana continued. "That's what they did in the sixties and look how much has changed."

"Not much," Chris added cynically.

"Well, we have to start somewhere," Hana said, grabbing Chris's chin and turning his face toward her. Hana was especially tender with him now, making me wonder how much, if any, of that story he had shared with her before.

"I'll leave you guys to it," I said, taking my cue. "See you back at the dorm, Hana."

"I think I'll stay with Chris tonight," she answered, sliding her chair closer to his.

Suddenly, Chris rose from the table and enveloped me in a hug, his arms wrapping around my shoulders. "Thanks for the talk, Lily. Sorry I was such an asshole."

Chris never struck me as particularly emotive, and the two of us had certainly never touched. But I was moved by this moment of solidarity and something else I couldn't quite name. Chris was, I realized, perhaps the only other person in the room who knew viscerally what I had felt watching that video.

"Sounds good," I mumbled, patting the back of his shoulder briskly.

I picked up my bag and stepped into the night, a slight spring breeze in the air.

Alone, I made my way toward the river.

CHAPTER 20

Marisol

Havana, Cuba
June 30, 1957

Days turned into nights, nights into days.

I could no longer tell the weeks—or the months—apart.

I looked down at the fragments of dirt that had blown into my cell. I had begun drawing on the dusty floor with strokes of my finger, counting the stars that I could see between the uneven iron bars.

Most nights, the guards sent in two meals per day, kicking the plate into the corner of my cell or sending someone to drop it just inside the door.

Typically, it was the man who continued to rape me.

He had marked me, taken me as his own.

One morning, hours after Silva slunk out of my cell, I heard loud clanging from the chains outside the door. The bolt was being removed.

It was just after dawn.

I cleared the dust from my eyes, the cracked skin of my elbows scraping the ground as I struggled to sit up.

"Cinco minutos," I heard Silva's voice say behind a small figure cast in shadows, standing in the entryway of my cell. He slammed

the door closed, leaving me alone with the intruder. As soon as he walked away, the figure stepped forward into the light.

It was a woman.

"Muéstrame las heridas, niña," she said without affect, shuffling toward me as her long black robe dragged against the ground. "Where are your wounds?"

In the fragment of light that fell into my cell, I could see a sliver of white cloth framing her small, heart-shaped face. She had uneven wrinkles carved into the thin, papery skin around her eyes, round spectacles perched above a narrow nose. A long black robe cascaded down her back while a dime-size medallion hung from her neck, a tiny figure etched at the center. A saint of some sort.

She was a nun.

The woman must have been slightly older than my mother.

My heart ached at the thought of her.

The woman reached for my forearm, gently lifting my elbow, and saw a trail of purple bruises spreading from my shoulder. These were the faded reminders of my resistance; I had since given up trying to fight back the nights Silva crept into my cell.

The nun placed her hand under my chin and turned my head from side to side, taking in my swollen cheeks. Then, she pressed two fingers softly beneath my rib cage.

I flinched, the flesh near my breast tender and throbbing.

Tracing the dark line that had emerged below my navel, the nun gently placed her hand on my stomach.

"Casi cuatro meses," she whispered, staring at me intently.

I stared back, confused.

"You have roughly five months left."

She pulled a small black bag from beneath her habit. On the front was a white medical cross.

Was she also a nurse?

"Drink the water they give you. Leave no food on your plate. And walk, if you can, around this cell."

She took out a small bandage and wrapped it around a bright red sore on my wrist, the open flesh turning white at the edges from infection.

"Stay alive," she whispered. "The baby will help."

Then, as quickly as she entered . . . she left.

That night, I could feel the guards' plans for me shift.

They started sending in extra bread and tin cups of rainwater, careful to make each one cleaner than the last. I nibbled at the corners of day-old bread, my stomach protruding from beneath my rib cage.

I existed like that for several more weeks, until one night, I heard them shouting at the base of the camp, just outside my cell.

"A decision had to be made!" one of the officers barked. *"Es tu progenie*. Your child!"

"¡Pero ya tengo mujer!" the familiar voice spat back. "I cannot bring home a baby that doesn't belong to my wife."

Silva.

He and another officer were arguing . . . about me.

"How much longer do we need to keep her here?" he pleaded, sounding shrill and unnerved.

"As long as it takes!" the first man answered. "Give her extra rations. Keep her fed. The nun *knows* about the baby, you idiot. We can't get rid of it now!"

"I cannot—" Silva interrupted in protest.

"No!" the man shouted. "You cannot kill your own flesh and blood. It is against the will of God!"

His final rebuke seemed to temper the scuffle.

"But—" Silva interrupted again, weakly this time.

"You only have to keep the baby," the officer relented with a sigh. "We don't need the girl."

CHAPTER 21

Vikram

Featherstone, England
May 24, 1992

Vikram rolled over in his king-size bed, rubbing the sleep from his eyes. He could see the sun peeking through the crème-colored Venetian blinds, the vase of fresh flowers his mother had placed on his nightstand smelling of lilac.

He couldn't believe he was still here.

Months had passed since the call that interrupted his studies and upended his life. He'd spent every moment since shuttling his father to a revolving door of specialists and squeezing his mother's hand, helping her make sense of the difficult diagnoses spilling between mouthfuls of medical jargon. His father's days were numbered, that much was clear. But on Friday, the principal cardiologist at St. Thomas's Hospital declared his father had reached a status that was tenable; he could continue his routine medications knowing the challenges that lay ahead.

"*Beta,* are you awake yet?" his mother's soft voice echoed at his bedroom door.

"Yes, Mum. Getting up now," Vikram answered groggily.

"Mind if I come in?" she asked, already taking a seat on top of his disheveled covers.

"How are you doing, son? This has been a lot, I know." She reached for his hand, the sun spots on her papery skin darker and more vivid than Vikram remembered.

Vikram was surprised by his mother's question, not because he doubted how much she cared, but rather because the realm of the emotional was not a Desai specialty. His father, Samir, acerbic in wit and even shorter on words, did not offer much by way of banter. And Aditi, his mother, surrounded in a house filled with stoic men, had silenced her need for emotional intimacy long ago.

"I'm fine, Mum. How are you holding up?"

"Getting old is no fun," she sighed. "It is the unwelcome surprise you expect. You know your time will come, but the swiftness of its arrival is as brutal as it is stunning." Aditi leaned closer, the smell of her familiar perfume reminding Vikram of the days he'd spent sitting on her lap, nestled against her bosom.

"I always figured I would be the one to go first, but you know your father," she nudged him playfully. "He can't stand to come in second place."

There it was, Vikram thought smiling, that cheekiness he'd inherited from his mother, demure as she seemed to everyone else.

Suddenly, she leaned in closer, caressing the side of Vikram's face.

"It's time for you to go back, *Beta,*" his mother announced flatly.

"Where?" Vikram asked, propping himself up against the dark maple headboard.

"To Cambridge." Aditi adjusted the yellow silk of her sari.

"But Mum, there is still so much to take care of. You've got Dad, plus the wedding—"

"All those things will still be here," she interrupted. "The wedding is not for another ten months. You must go back before things get bad again for your father. Plus, if anything happens, your brother is in London."

Vikram decided it would be a kindness to let this lie exist between them. He knew, as did his mother, that they couldn't count on Akshay. Akshay was consumed in his own world, one he had built with Samir's approval and in his image. Both were doctors who had long left the ailing bedsides of patients to pursue the more lucrative horizons of medical cosmetology and the pharmacies that supplied them. All of this meant Akshay was free from any real filial duty, just so long as he maintained the accolades that sustained his father's satisfaction. He was the son for which their father had prayed: the doctor, the eldest, the soon-to-be husband.

"Akshay and Shivani are coming over for brunch. Please come down and say your goodbyes. And speak to your father, he wants to connect with you before you depart. There is a flight available next week."

"You already found a flight?"

"I did. I called your father's office to book it. I will tell him that the dean requested your return and it was me who decided you must go back now."

"You spoke to Dean Kelly?"

"Yes, but your father does not need to know that." She stood up quickly. "Come down for brunch and we can have a chat before you go."

Vikram marveled at his mother. Ever since he was little, he could remember her wielding her soft, quiet power to navigate his father's more tempestuous moods. It was an art. Vikram listened to the door close softly behind her, her slippers padding down the winding staircase to the first floor, past the foyer and into the kitchen.

Vikram rubbed his eyes.

Cambridge? Next week? That meant he would finally see Lily again. He felt butterflies in his stomach just at the thought of it.

They had exchanged a few letters since he'd left; Vikram trying to keep his messages light, not wanting to burden Lily with the heavier thoughts he'd had since their last encounter.

Vikram reached for the bronze handle of his nightstand, opening its single narrow drawer. The glass vase rattled on top.

He pulled out Lily's last letter.

May 18, 1992

Monsieur Vikram,

I see why Madame Carole thinks you are such a talented writer.;) It was so good to hear from you again.

Things have been going well, but I must admit, I do miss our chats. It feels lonely in Lamont Library without you. (Although, I think Marcelo the security guard and I have at last become friends. Now when he kicks me out, he does it with a smile . . .)

Update: I got the internship at the South African embassy! I'll head to D.C. for a few weeks this summer, which will be a nice break from campus and sure as hell beats going back to Elk River. Plus, with everything that's been happening since the Rodney King trial, it feels like there's still real work left to do here stateside. Maybe I can see how things are playing out in D.C.

Speaking of which, Hana and I have been volunteering nonstop with the Institute of Politics. We're planning a campus rally against police brutality later this month. Since the verdict came down, things have been on fire.

Literally.

Surely you've seen coverage in the U.K., but L.A. completely imploded, and now protests have spread to every major city. The Black Students Association here on campus has been leading the charge for campus police reform. Chris has been trying to recruit the athletes to help us, but it's disheartening how many of them refuse to join.

It's all been so exhausting.

I still don't understand how many people just don't get it. They think this is a black-and-white issue, about Black and white people. In reality, it is anything but. This is about power and the abuse of power. People act like you can't choose sides, but you can—and I'd argue you should—when there is a moral question at stake, not a political one.

Anyway, I can't wait until you're back here and can solve all these problems with me. In fact, I'm tearing up a bit now just thinking about how long you've been gone. On to other things, shall we?

You are truly one in a million, Vikram Desai.

I can't wait to see all the ways in which you change this world . . .

For all of us.

xx Lily

Vikram was at a loss. Each time he read her letter, he felt more confused. Worse, he worried Lily's faith in him might be misplaced. He wasn't sure that he could solve any of the problems she mentioned; he wasn't even sure he understood them. Wasn't Lily Cuban? Why did she always lump herself into the Black student causes? Not that there was anything wrong with that *per se*, but why take on additional stress when she didn't necessarily have to?

Vikram's parents had always taught him to avoid the people and situations that carried negative associations. It was uncomfortable to admit, sure, but the African and Caribbean immigrants they passed driving through Brixton usually fit the bill: crime, chaos, discord. There was always mention of a shooting or looting in their neighborhoods on the six o'clock news. As immigrants themselves, Vikram's family knew they couldn't risk that association; they didn't have the luxury of failure. They had to survive.

Vikram folded the letter, gently sliding it back into its envelope, two American postage flags stamped in the corner. He peeled back his bedcover and stepped onto the plush carpet below, reaching for his black cotton pants lying on the floor. He threw on a T-shirt and headed down the wide staircase, spiraling from the second-floor landing.

When he entered the kitchen, Vikram could smell every good memory of his childhood. His mother had her back to the door, slowly stirring a pot as it simmered quietly on the stove.

"Good morning again, my darling," she chirped, her gold bangles clanging as she reached for the ginger. "I still can't get over how thin you look! They were starving you over there, eh? Don't you worry. I have *dal gosht* and your favorite *biryani* already in the oven. Go say good morning to your father."

Before Vikram could make his way to the living room, Samir rounded the corner, his left hand gripping a cane as it struggled beneath his weight.

"*Bah!* What are you doing up, *Pati*?" His mother rushed to grab his father by the elbow, his body doubled over in his effort to stand. "I told you I would bring your food."

"Stop making a fuss, Aditi," his father grumbled. "I can make it to the kitchen just fine. Akshay should be here soon."

Vikram reddened. Of course, Vikram had not warranted this level of effort; it was his brother.

"You look well this morning, Pa," Vikram said, unsure how to greet him. A hug felt too intimate, a handshake too formal. Since he had been home, Vikram and his father had settled on a cool peace, keeping their conversations short.

"Hello, son," the elder Desai said stiffly, giving Vikram a stilted pat on the shoulder.

Vikram turned back toward the stove to offer to help his mother, when suddenly they heard voices coming from the foyer.

"Alooooooo!" Akshay boomed, his smile wide, a light gray jacket thrown over his shoulder, hanging by the hook of his finger like a Bollywood actor. "Bring it in, you American boy!" Akshay sprinted to where Vikram was standing and put him into a headlock like when they were kids. Shivani appeared behind him, her oversize sunglasses still perched atop her perfect nose, despite having been inside the house long enough to remove them. Giggling, she approached the two brothers, reaching out playfully to separate them.

Vikram, heaving and short of breath, wrenched himself free from beneath his brother's arm. "Good to see you, too, Akshay."

Akshay smiled.

Samir shuffled toward them, stopping to give Akshay a hug. "Good to see you my boy, and of course, your beautiful bride." Akshay and Shivani simultaneously wrapped their father in an embrace, a synchronized act of intimacy that caught Vikram by surprise. Staring at the three of them, it felt as though he were standing outside a theater, watching a movie play through the glass window. They all looked so natural, the ease between them palpable and without cost. Vikram felt displaced, an outsider under his own roof.

"Come, let's get you some food," Aditi interjected, watching her youngest from the corner of her eye.

"Sounds great, Mum," Akshay said cheerily. "We're starving after the journey." The drive from London was two and a half hours. Akshay had ridden in the back of a black SUV driven by the same chauffeur that their father had hired for the past thirty years.

"Is Carrington waiting outside?" Vikram asked, wondering about the old Trinidadian man who had been a staple of the Desai household since he could remember.

"He is. He'll take us back after lunch. Unless you need him to take you to the airport? Mummy says you've already got a flight?"

Vikram was surprised to hear that his mother had already told them about his departure; she had only announced it to him this morning.

"Yes, I fly back next week," Vikram answered, taking a seat at the kitchen table beside his older brother. Akshay sat at the head; their father, coughing into his kerchief, took the seat directly opposite them.

Akshay nudged the side of Vikram's torso with his elbow. "What's the rush, baby brother? Is there someone special you're running back to? What's the story with the American birds, anyway?"

Shivani let out a yelp. "Akshay! Stop that! Not in front of your parents!"

"What?" he shot back, feigning mock innocence, sure that his question had rattled its intended target. Their parents shifted uncomfortably in their seats, acting like they weren't paying attention.

"Ah yes," Vikram sighed. "What would an Applied Mathematics post-doctoral fellow possibly be doing in Cambridge besides dating Americans? That, of course, is the sole purpose for uprooting my life seven thousand miles away and paying God-knows-how-much money to finish an entire fellowship in a year. A bird."

"Don't be snarky, little brother. You know you're there for a dual purpose. You're almost twenty-five! You're getting old. Mummy can't make you a decent matchmaking profile if you don't get on with it."

"Let him have his moment, Akshay," Shivani said calmly, placing her hand on his knee. "The girls will be lining up for Vikram when he comes home. Plus, whatever happened to the young lady you were seeing before you left? Radhika? Are you two still in touch?"

Aditi suddenly cleared her throat. "Well actually, I invited Radhika's family over for the Diwali festival. Her mother came by the pharmacy when I was doing a site visit and I thought perhaps it might be nice to get our families together when you're back later this fall."

The color drained from Vikram's face.

"Mum," he started, "let's not get ahead of ourselves . . ."

"Don't be silly, Vikram," his father suddenly interjected, surprising everyone that he was even listening. "It's time to be responsible. Your brother is right: it will look odd if you return next year without progress. Any man knows you can't just focus on your studies and not your home. Your legacy is all you have."

With that, the air felt like it left the kitchen.

Vikram mentally kicked himself. He shouldn't have been surprised by Samir's interjection, only that it had taken so long. Vikram knew he'd never live up to his father's expectations professionally, but goddamnit, he *had* tried. He was still trying, if he were honest with himself, much to his own embarrassment. It felt like the only way he could salvage some sliver of respect from his old man, before it was too late, would be to at least bring him a bride whose family's name he would be proud to print on an invitation.

Like Shivani.

His parents had nearly fallen over themselves when Akshay first told them about his plans to formally court her: the Gujarati girl from his freshman seminar whose parents belonged to the temple just beyond the university campus. Unsurprisingly, her extended family members belonged to Akshay's temple back in Featherstone, and of course, after dozens of excited calls between aunties on both sides, they discovered they were distant relatives. Vikram's mom had become so overwhelmed at the prospect of a marriage that she had withdrawn Akshay's perfectly curated biodata from the matchmaking agencies she had hired just four months prior.

Within days, pressure began mounting for Akshay to propose, and once he finally did, Vikram's mother wept like Krishna himself had come to deliver the gift of eternal life. Even Samir had moisture in his eyes that threatened to form a full tear.

Vikram wasn't sure he could offer them that same hope.

"*Beta*, I do think you should spend some time with Radhika when you return. It is important that you lay down some roots. I will set up other meetings for you in the meantime, so that at least you can get started."

Meetings.

Vikram hated the sound of it, so cold and sterile. But his brother was right; he wasn't getting any younger. At least with Radhika, there was some element of choice; they had dated briefly in college so he knew her well enough.

"You will need to come back soon," his father continued, interrupting Vikram's thoughts. "You need to find a wife, but a wife will not be impressed by a bachelor with no financial future. An applied maths degree without a job isn't exactly a point of pride. That's why the business will be waiting for you, ready for you to take the reins."

Vikram cleared his throat. "As I have told you before, the business is not for me. I—"

"What are they teaching you in these schools?" his father scoffed, punctuating his anger with a feeble attempt to slam his fist against the table. "Do you know what I would have done to have a business handed to me—wrapped with a ribbon—when I came here from India? Do you know how many men would die for such an opportunity? A gift that you can see only as a curse? Spoiled!"

Aditi took her napkin from her lap and stood up.

"*Beta*, I think your father is saying that it will be time to come home soon," she said, passing the hari chutney across the table to her husband. "Stay in Cambridge and complete the rest of your fellowship, but with all the unrest we've seen on the news—after that man ran from the cops and got himself beaten—I'm not quite sure why you would want to stay there much longer. Either way, we will expect to see you later this fall."

Akshay and Shivani exchanged conspiratorial glances.

Vikram noted how they never seemed to help him when they knew their support was needed most—when it could turn the dial, or at least reduce the emotional temperature of the room. Vikram looked down at his naan, the shreds of cilantro sitting on top.

He was too weary to fight this battle now.

CHAPTER 22

Marisol

Havana, Cuba
November 19, 1957

The contractions came in a rush, all at once.

I woke up to feel the ground beneath me soaked with water.

Water from inside my body.

I screamed.

Writhing alone on the prison floor, I heard heavy boots kick open the door.

"*¡Llévala!*" Silva barked, the father of the child now breaking its way out of my womb. Two of the younger soldiers scurried closely behind.

I felt pairs of rough hands turning me on my side as they squeezed my swollen stomach through the narrow frame of my cell, rushing me outside into the cool night air.

My ankles were still bound when they dumped me in the bed of the truck—the same one that had brought me here almost nine months ago.

Where were they taking me now?

I cradled my stomach as the truck made hard turns over the

broken asphalt just outside the city. As we drove farther into the darkness, farther away from the prison, I could hear the ocean roaring somewhere in the distance.

Or was that me?

My body felt like it was being ripped apart.

"*¡Apúrate!*" Silva screamed, slamming the brakes.

Two men rushed to the open canopy where I lay, dragging me from the vehicle. We had arrived at a small, makeshift hospital nestled near the water, hidden somewhere amongst the trees.

Silva emerged from the driver's seat and stood in front of me, glaring at my slumped, convulsing body.

"There is only one man here who concerns you: the doctor. He will deliver this baby. Talk to no one else. My men will be stationed outside. And don't try anything stupid," he seethed, reaching for my neck, his face inches away. "You are only alive because that seed growing inside of you is mine. And rest assured, I will make sure that child never knows its whore of a mother existed."

My blood ran cold.

I gave birth that night in a tiny hospital outside of Havana.

It was a boy.

The baby struggled to take his first breath once he came out of me, writhing as his face turned blue, the umbilical cord wrapped tightly around his neck.

My body went limp with relief when I heard his first screams.

He was beautiful.

Light auburn curls, still wet with my blood, wrapped around the nape of his neck. His eyes were small and swollen, barely open from the months living inside me. He had perfectly pink lips, round and full, and a wide nose like my father.

I searched his face for signs of his own father, the monster who had ruined my life.

"*Dale la leche*," the dark-haired doctor who had just pulled him from me ordered brusquely. "The baby is premature and malnourished. He may not make it through the night."

Who was this man who had defiled his medical license to be on the Batista payroll, nursing bodies maimed in the darkness? How much had they given him to treat their wounds and bandage their battle scars, paid for in silence?

I pulled the baby closer to my bosom, willing his tiny mouth to suckle my swollen breasts. He wouldn't latch, his weightless body flopping against my arm.

"Feed him when he cries. The nurse will be on duty. I'll be back in the morning." The doctor slid back the thin white curtain as he swiftly exited the room.

Shortly after, I heard the sound of metal.

A door closing.

He must have locked us inside.

Finally alone, I marveled at the tiny creature before me.

I was in awe.

Stroking the silky tendrils of curls that framed his swollen face, I had never felt anything like the wave of emotion, the primal urge to protect him, that swept over me. It was visceral, feral. I needed this baby. And he needed me.

That is, if he survived.

The baby's chest caved inward, his tiny ribs spreading as he struggled for air.

A gurgling noise erupted from his throat, his mouth forming a tight circle as he writhed in pain.

A grimace, but there was no sound.

I screamed, my eyes wild with panic.

The curtain around my bed swung back open.

A nurse ran toward me, a long black robe dragging behind her on the floor.

It was the nun, the same one who had examined me five months ago.

I recognized her immediately.

"Déjame ver el bebé," she hurried, rushing to check his pulse. She leaned forward as she pressed two fingers firmly in the center of his chest, her thin necklace dangling in front of the baby's face. Then, she flipped him over, his body lifeless like a handsewn doll. She tapped the flesh below his neck as she raised his head, still covered in slick white film.

The baby sputtered, secreting a putrid yellow liquid with an odor that seemed too strong to come from such a fragile frame.

"No tenemos mucho tiempo," the nun whispered forcefully, her words spilling out all at once. "They'll be back shortly."

"Hurry, take these clothes," she continued. "They are the best I could find and they shouldn't draw any attention. Slip these over your head."

She was reaching for my arms, arms that had just taken back my listless baby boy.

"Clothes?" I whispered, my voice weak from exhaustion. "For what?"

"The journey. You need to leave now."

What was she talking about? My head was spinning, a dusty haze of confusion settling over me.

"¿De qué habla?" I asked, motioning to the bloody towels beside me, still wet with the baby's placenta. "We can't go anywhere."

"Not the baby."

The nun stared at me intensely, trying to assess whether I was able to process her words.

"If you stay, you and this baby are as good as dead. I have seen this before, and I cannot in good faith watch it happen again."

What was she saying? My eyes filled with tears, marveling at the cruelty of this woman's suggestion.

"They will kill you, *niña*," she pressed on. "As soon as they see your baby, they will take him and make you disappear. And you heard the doctor, there is very little chance that this child makes it through the night. He looks premature. His best chance is with me."

Rage rose like bile in my throat, the words bubbling up hot and venomous.

"I am not leaving my child," I said with as much strength as I could muster, my knuckles turning white as I gripped the edge of the birthing cot.

"If you take him from this hospital, this child will die." The nun stared at me, her face cold and inscrutable. "The baby is struggling to breathe. He is emaciated. And so are you. If you want to survive, you must leave now. The guards are asleep outside and the doctor has left for the night, but they will all be back in the morning."

She reached for a key tucked in the folds of her habit and began removing the locks tethering me to the metal bed frame.

"I will tell them that in the haste of caring for the sickly infant, I left your chains unlocked and the door open. You escaped."

I stared back at her in disbelief, my mind trying to make sense of her warnings, her swift movements.

"What about my son?"

My son.

The word for this child—for who he was to me—sliced through my heart like a knife.

The nun sat on the edge of the bed, the threadbare cushion sinking under her weight. She sighed. Her eyes softened as she took my hand in hers.

"Had it not been for this angel, the soldiers would have executed you long ago. This baby saved your life."

My hands trembled, shaking my son's birdlike frame, his

sharp ribs protruding through his translucent skin as he fought for air.

"You both will not make it out of here alive," the nun pressed again, her urgency returning.

Somewhere deep in my spirit, I knew she was right.

This beautiful baby of mine and I could not exist in this world together.

Not at the same time, not in the same place.

These monsters would never allow it.

I was a liability to this son of mine, to his life and to his freedom.

I couldn't watch him die.

Tears streamed down my face as the weight of my decision hit me, my breath coming in heaves. My heart felt like it would stop inside my chest.

How would *I* survive this?

Just as I pulled the baby to my bosom, the unmistakably familiar sound of clinking metal rippled through the hallway.

Someone was unbolting the front door.

Quickly, the nun grabbed my shoulder. "Put the child in the cot. Slip on the clothes I left in the bag. There are enough *pesos* for bus fare in the pocket of the trousers. Walk through the infirmary at the end of the hall. You will see a back door. I have left it open. And take this . . ."

She reached around her neck and unclasped the silver medallion that rested on the center of her chest. Etched in the foreground were three gold coins engraved with an image of a man's hands clasped with the tiny palms of children.

"Esto te va a proteger," she whispered, placing the heavy necklace in my palm. "Saint Nicholas, the patron saint of children. *Que vayas con Dios."*

With that, she stood abruptly and whisked the curtain closed, disappearing into the hallway.

Through the sheer panels of linen, I could see her animated conversation with a guard who had entered through the main doors. Snippets of conversation floated through the empty corridor.

"Malnourished . . ."

"Needs sleep . . ."

"Baby not well . . ."

"In the morning . . ."

I stared at the rifle dangling from the guard's belt.

She was trying to stop him.

He had returned to confirm that I had fulfilled my duty, that I was no longer needed.

That I could die.

I inhaled, breathing in the smell of my newborn baby.

I reached for the small pair of scissors on the tin tray of bloody medical supplies the doctor had used during the delivery. I brought the silver blades close to the baby's scalp and clipped a lock of his hair. As I placed the scissors softly back on the tray beside me, I noticed a jagged line just below his ear.

A birthmark.

"Siempre seré tu mama," I whispered into his wet curls, still matted with my blood. Then, I wrapped his swaddle tighter, lowering him onto the makeshift bassinet at the foot of my cot: a small, hollow basin of wood with two rough, folded blankets. I gently placed his tiny body in the center, his face toward the sky.

I leaned over the edge, lightly kissing his forehead as my tears fell into his face.

He didn't stir.

How could this baby survive in a world that had so brutally bore him?

"One day I will come back for you," I whispered, my heart shattering into a thousand pieces.

I stepped away from the cot and pulled the bloody, mangled nightgown above my shoulders, my body wincing from the pain. I limped to the corner of the room and stared at the light gray trousers and short matching tunic the nun had placed in the bag. One by one, I slipped my legs inside the rough material before pushing my arms through the sleeves. I caught my reflection in the broken mirror above the washbasin.

The cracked glass split my reflection in two.

Is this who I was now? A shattered, broken imitation of a mother? A woman who abandoned her only child?

I kneeled down beside the baby, nestled like a bird among the pool of ripped cloth. I smelled him one last time, memorizing his scent, every note of fresh life, of a future without me.

Then, he opened his eyes.

Green, piercing and calm—his tiny eyes stared directly into my own.

"Please forgive me," I whispered, tears blurring my vision. I reached down to touch his cheek. He burrowed his swollen face into my hand and closed his eyes once again.

Peeling myself away, I walked to the edge of the room and grabbed the small canvas sack that held the doctor's medical supplies. I emptied it and stuffed two rolls of gauze and the pair of scissors inside, wiping them clean of my own blood.

Quietly, I crept toward the door, slightly ajar, and I pulled back the white curtain, its rusted rings screeching softly as I slid them across the rod. I peeked through the glass.

I could hear the nun still arguing with the guard, but their voices sounded farther away. Somehow, she had lured him to the other side of the corridor where they were beyond my line of sight and away from the back door.

I crept into the hallway. Crouching along the baseboards, I caught a glimpse of the blood soaking my inner thighs, a dark spot spreading across the faded trousers. I looked back toward where the baby lay in his cot, wondering one last time if I could make the escape with him.

"Ayúdame a caminar por la Palabra," I heard the nun's voice drift

down the hallway. *May I walk by faith and not by sight.* She was praying with the guard, stalling him before he pressed his way into my room.

This was my only chance.

I threw the canvas sack over my shoulder and dragged my swollen feet against the dirty tile.

Just as I placed my hand on the brass knob to open the door, the shrill sound of my son's cry pierced the stillness of the night.

I froze.

But there was no turning back.

That was the last time I heard his voice—and the last time I knew that he was alive.

CHAPTER 23

Vikram

Boston, Massachusetts
June 1, 1992

Vikram sat on the plane, his fingers running idly along the edges of the paper nestled inside his pocket. He had taken Lily's most recent letter with him for the journey.

Between the septic smell of hospital visits, thoughts of Lily were all that kept him going since he had been back in the U.K.: her mischievous smile when she knew she wanted to test a rule worth breaking, the quizzical way she looked up at him from the corner of her eye when she was unsure.

But now he was the one who was unsure. Vikram swirled the ice cubes in the empty Styrofoam cup in front of him, a reel of memories from the past few months scrolling through his mind.

His family's insistence on seeing Radhika, the ease of his brother's relationship with Shivani, and the seamless way the pair folded into his family haunted him. The whole point of marriage was survival of the system, right? The preservation of legacy and culture, protecting the peace of the unit. But what if—just what *if*—there was another way?

Vikram couldn't bring himself to say anything to Lily when

they'd parted in the hallway of her dorm six months ago. His mind was pulled in a million directions that day: would his father live until the plane touched down? Had he put toothpaste in his carry-on? Could he ever truly make Lily an honest woman? Would his parents let him? And if he couldn't, was he simply stringing her along? Even if he could get past all of that, how did she feel about him?

He wanted to tell Lily what had been on his heart for weeks, but it was a feeling so fragile, he couldn't fully describe it to himself. This isn't how he had felt with Radhika. With her, there was always contentment, but no butterflies. The excitement came from their sameness, the welcome surprise of encountering someone in a place that felt a million miles from home, but discovering something so familiar that it anchors you. She was petite and slender, with thick, shiny black hair that cascaded down the middle of her back. She was what Vikram had been told he should be looking for—what he had intended to be looking for—all along. So when they connected at the Indian Student Society their final year at university, it felt like they had been destined for the altar at first "hello." Everything in their relationship was fast-tracked. It happened so fast, in fact, that Vikram needed to put on the brakes, using this post-doctoral fellowship as an excuse to get out of the country and bide his time. He just needed time to think.

And then Lily happened.

The speaker blared overhead, an announcement from the stewardess crackling through the plastic paneled ceiling: *"Ladies and gentlemen, we have now begun our descent into Logan International Airport. Please place your belongings under the seat in front of you . . ."*

Vikram grabbed the cap of the pen he had stolen from the airport lobby, quickly flipping over the back of his boarding pass and laying it on the tray table. He looked back and saw the attendant collecting rubbish from the group of unruly passengers beside the loo at the back of the plane and reckoned he had about five minutes before she reached his seat in 11F.

Now then!

Where to begin? I've made it onto this tiny tin in the sky, hoping to scribble out a strophe or two before Olga gives me her most naughty stewardess glare . . .

I'm not sure what else to say besides . . .

I miss you.

I wish I could be more poetic.

But Lily, I miss you. And I have missed you.

Sure, the tea and long walks were grand, but the marrow of who you are—the way you listen with your whole body, the way your eyes get big in anticipation of what I'm going to say next—it's like you believe or see only the very best in me. Or rather, like you've always known who I could become. You force me to become better with new perspectives, new insight—things I've never even considered.

I guess what I'm trying to say is . . .

What *was* he trying to say? And why couldn't he say all of this before? Why did it take him until the last moments of his flight back to Boston, after months of being away, to finally build up the courage to put his true feelings to paper?

Turbulence jolted the plane.

He could feel Olga approaching the final five rows, before she came to business class.

I want more. And I think we could be more.

I hope I haven't lost my courage to tell you this before this plane lands, this letter reaches you, or Olga scolds me—whichever comes first.

Think about it.

Yours,

Vikram

Staring down at the smudged ink of his boarding pass, Vikram didn't know what his heart felt, exactly, but he knew that the woman he hoped would one day read his letter likely wasn't the one his parents hoped for, or expected.

But maybe, just once, their displeasure was a risk worth taking.

Vikram quickly folded the letter, running over the creases with his fingernail before stuffing it into his pocket, just in time to fold his tray before Olga reached his aisle.

Olga.

Was that even her name? She looked like an Olga.

The plane began its wobbly descent, bodies jostling, cups spilling, passengers stifling gasps as they tried to mask their nervousness. Finally, Vikram felt the wheels of the plane unfold beneath his feet, the massive machine skidding haltingly against the tarmac.

A round of applause peppered with a few cheers.

Who were these people who applauded on airplanes, anyway? He had always wanted to know.

Vikram gathered his messenger bag, sliding his notebook along the inside pocket. Checking to make sure he didn't leave anything behind, he shuffled out of his window seat and into the aisle, grabbing his suitcase from the overhead bin.

Vikram could feel his body begin to relax. He was going home, after all. Whatever "home" meant these days.

Blending into the crush of passengers exiting the baggage claim area, he made his way through the glass doors that deposited him into the lobby—a sea of anxious, non-ticketed bystanders and teary-eyed loved ones. Vikram always thought airports were either the saddest or the happiest places in the world: people embarking on a future of promise and reconnection, or facing an ending, terminal and uncertain.

As he rounded the corner of the metal barriers approaching

the main exit, Vikram searched for the signs pointing him in the direction of the taxi stand.

Suddenly, he stopped.

Through the blur of travelers feverishly crisscrossing in front of him, he couldn't believe his eyes.

There, just in front of the main doors, Lily stood.

She looked him directly in the eye, as if she had been waiting for him to notice her. Adjusting the cloth belt cinching the waist of her bright floral dress, Lily smiled sheepishly, her fingers fidgeting with a small, yellow cardboard sign that read simply, "Welcome home, Vik."

Vikram stood frozen in disbelief. He had sent Lily his general flight details in their last exchange, scribbling excited musings about seeing her on the back of his flight confirmation. He had even asked if she had time to see him later that week, but never in a million years expected she would read the arrival time on the ticket, much less show up.

And yet, here she was.

A rush of excitement surged through Vikram's body, the buzz of elation so powerful it overtook his senses. Is this what they meant by absence making the heart grow fonder? Fond was an understatement; this was an avalanche.

Vikram's head began to spin. He needed to be close to her.

Immediately.

Vikram broke into a jog, dodging overstuffed suitcases and harried passengers until he reached her.

Lily beamed, her face breaking into that natural, wholesome smile Vikram had spent the past few months fantasizing about, just before more lurid thoughts of her filled his mind.

When Vikram reached her, Lily jumped, standing on the tips of her toes and throwing both arms around his neck. He dropped his suitcase to the floor. Vikram grabbed Lily around the small of her back, bringing the full weight of her body into his.

There, in the middle of Logan International Airport, he kissed her.

Those felt like the most gentle, tender seconds of Vikram's young life. His lips met hers, soft and full, eager and searching. He gathered the sides of Lily's face into the palms of his hands, sliding his fingers into the curls that ran along the nape of her neck. Together they stood, intertwined, inside a world of only their making.

Finally, Vikram peeled away gently, hoping for a better look at her. Was he awake? Or was he still dreaming in his childhood bedroom?

Vikram took a deep breath and stared into the warm ink of Lily's eyes. When he exhaled, he felt the pain and uncertainty of the past few months leave his body, his anguish disappearing somewhere into the ether. Instead, he breathed in all the hope that this moment promised.

That is, of course, if she felt the same way.

Lily looped her fingers through his, their clasped hands dangling at their sides.

"Let's go, *Monsieur* Desai," she said. "We have a lot to catch up on."

Vikram took a deep breath, wrapping her in his arms.

"Lucky for us," he answered with a smile, "we have all the time in the world."

PART TWO

FIVE YEARS LATER

CHAPTER 24

Lily

London, England
January 4, 1997

I adjusted my dress, tugging at the beaded embroidery along the bodice, the lace petals sliding as I twisted the seam. The bouquet in my hand was an explosion of color, bright yellow daffodils mixed with rich red roses and pastel petals. My fingers trembled. I tried to remember what the wedding planner had told me just the night before: keep the tip of the tulips beneath my belly button when I began the walk down the aisle to accentuate the bodice of the gown. I grew nervous just thinking about all those eyes on me.

Right then, the music started to play.

The violinist plucked his first string and a thin bead of sweat formed at my hairline. I had decided to wear my hair straight, opting for something dramatic to mark the occasion. My curls had been my signature since I was a girl, but now I was entering a new phase in my life as a woman. I wanted to announce that to the world, prove it in every sartorial detail, as I stepped in front of so many faces I hadn't seen since college.

As soon as the harpist joined the quartet, the instrumental notes of Alison Krauss slipped beneath the cracks of the great double doors. That was my cue. I took a deep breath and placed my cream-colored heel onto the rich red carpet, the light from the rotunda pouring down my silhouette.

The doors swung open and the sea of faces took my breath away. There had to be two hundred people seated in the pews, filling my line of sight. I smiled nervously, trying to keep an even, steady pace as I clutched the wildflowers tied with a yellow ribbon between my hands. I turned my head demurely to each side, hoping to make eye contact with the guests I recognized, slowly making my way toward the altar.

That's when I saw him.

Those eyes, dark and intense, still managed to take my breath away. He was just as beautiful as the day I'd met him. His skin had taken on a few fine lines, marks of time and wisdom, complementing the few strands of gray that peppered his jet-black hair. He looked distinguished. His skin was moist and rich, the color of copper, shining as the light from the candles that adorned the aisle bounced off his cheekbones.

My heart pounded, my palms grew sweaty.

I swallowed.

As I neared the end of the aisle, I passed where he stood in his pew.

Vikram stared at me.

What was he doing here?

I climbed the final two small steps to the raised podium and took my place beside the pastor, who opened the ornate Bible on his lectern and cleared his throat.

"We now welcome you to the wedding of Miss Hana Kang and Christopher Bekki."

The wedding was held at One Great George Street, one of the most exclusive venues in London, its staggering Edwardian architecture breathtaking to even the harshest London skeptics.

I angled my body, standing elbow-to-elbow between the four other bridesmaids in coffee-colored gowns, trying to control my breathing. I stared vacantly, barely registering the lifetime of promises being made beside me.

It had been almost five years since I'd last seen Vikram.

Every fantasy I'd had about how this moment would go, what it would feel like to finally see him again, fell short of the suffocating wave of emotion taking over me. Nothing could have prepared me for the way my heart would break, all over again, with Vikram standing just feet away.

When did Hana invite him? Why hadn't she told me?

I stared down at the bouquet in my hand, too afraid to look up for fear that I'd catch his eye.

Beside me, Hana stood at the center of the altar, yellow candles casting their light on her face as she gripped the cream-colored pages of parchment containing her hand-written vows. She wore a fitted silk gown that hugged the curves of her petite frame while small clusters of baby's breath laced through a single French braid forming a halo around her head.

"Chris, you were everything I didn't know I needed," Hana declared in her deep, sultry voice as she leaned into the microphone.

Chris wiped away a tear gathering at the corner of his eye.

"Who knew all those years of dining hall coffee and too-sour Scorpion Bowls at the Kong would have amounted to this?"

The crowd broke into laughter. Absently following the cues of the audience, I laughed along.

Hana was delirious with joy, basking in the pride this moment had clearly brought to Mr. and Mrs. Kang and their entire church congregation. Her family from South Korea spilled out of the pews, nodding adoringly and whispering their approval. Hana looked radiant. And behind the veil, I had never known a more centered version of my closest friend.

Chris and Hana had become inseparable since our freshman

year and seemed to only grow more into—and in tune with—each other as the years went on. Chris was still playing soccer, his Major League dreams finally taking off two years after he graduated. He played a few seasons abroad in Greece and even played in the African Cup of Nations representing Côte d'Ivoire, his father's national team. He and Hana had stayed steady the entire time, conversations over faulty international connections and disparate time zones proved not to be too much for their long-distance romance. Chris eventually convinced her to move overseas when he began coaching in London, and together, they settled into a beautiful apartment in Notting Hill paid for by the ever-elusive Mr. Kang. Now, here they were, standing at the altar to which they had invisibly and always been headed.

After a final reading of First Corinthians by the Kang family pastor, I waited for the recessional to begin before darting for the service entrance at the back of the venue.

I couldn't risk seeing Vikram as the guests spilled out of their pews.

I bounded up the dark, carpeted stairwell, the artificial candles flickering on either side of the corridor. Frenzied and out of breath, I barreled toward the bridal suite where I had gotten dressed just before the ceremony, collapsing on the green velvet couch by the window, my jeans still draped across the back.

Finally alone, I burst into sobs.

I felt a dull, throbbing ache just being in Vikram's orbit. Not only was I forced to remember the excruciating pain of losing him—the nights I'd spent crying in the dark wondering if I ever crossed his mind—but my worst fear had also come true: I had never been able to replace him.

I had gone on countless dates since I graduated from school, searching for love in the dark corners of crowded dive bars and the fluorescent lights of near-empty press briefings. This was my second year at the Network Public Radio outpost in New York. Since moving, I had met guys out in public or on blind dates both as a penniless intern and now, as a fledgling reporter. I felt like a tragic heroine sitting nervously across the table of blind dates, having raced there after deadlines and press conferences. I tried my best to make room for romance, and among the unreturned phone calls and unanswered voicemails, I did manage to hold on to a few longer trysts along the way.

There was Jake, the Jewish boy from Ojai who liked me, but not enough to weather the hour-long drive to see me in The Valley; Marc, a half-Chinese half Jamaican from Yale whose accent I loved, but whose questions about the South made my head spin (*Did I have running water? Was Bill Clinton my favorite president?*). Then there was Jordan, an Indian boy who had moved to New York from Durban, South Africa. He was delightful, punctual for our dates, and was finishing his residency in psychiatry. Our conversations were incredible, but as much as I enjoyed our time together, every time we fell into bed . . . I thought of *him*.

Hana stormed into the bridal suite, casting her carefully crafted bouquet onto the carpet.

"What. The. Fuck," I said, heaving, before she could say a word.

"I didn't think he'd actually *come*, Lily! And I knew you would say no if I told you," she answered, primed and ready for my anger.

"Then why did you do it?!" I nearly shouted, bursting again into tears.

"Number one, because today is my wedding day, and by the laws of marital society it is legally impossible for you to be mad at me with two hundred guests waiting for me downstairs. And two, Chris only told me this week that he bumped into Vikram at an alumni soccer game three months ago. He said he'd mentioned the wedding, how nice it was to see him again, and that if he wanted, Vikram was welcome to come. Apparently, Vikram expressed some doubt, saying he wasn't sure if that would be a good idea, presumably because you would be here. But Chris, like a *guy*, waved it off and apparently told him it was no big deal, and of course, didn't tell me about *any* of this until three days ago."

"But what did Vikram *say*, Hana?" I pressed, my frustration rising.

"That's just the thing, Vikram never said one way or another whether he was coming. And since I found out so late, I just didn't say anything to you. I didn't think he'd actually show up!"

"Well, he's here, Hana," I huffed.

"Look, Lily. This isn't ideal, but . . ."

"But?"

"I never really forgot."

"Forgot what?"

"How hurt you were when things ended. How you spent the rest of college aimlessly retracing your steps, searching for closure that he never gave you. Or that you didn't give him. Maybe now is your chance."

"But Hana, we haven't spoken in five years! The last time I saw him was one of the worst days of my life."

The admission startled me.

My heart sank when I thought about the months leading up to our last interaction, filled with more hurt than I cared to remember, more anger than I could forget.

CHAPTER 25

Hana reached for my hand as I unraveled before her.

The once-straight hair tucked behind my ear curled slowly as the tears dripped down my face.

I had spent so many nights trying to forget everything that happened in that tiny tea shop, the backdrop to the final crescendo of our own private saga.

Vikram and I had started dating officially after he returned from the U.K., falling back into our rhythm of luxurious tea breaks and long walks along the river. We snuck between the towers of meticulously stacked books in Lamont Library and shared kisses that tasted like promise and passion. And yet, tucked away in those library corners, I could sense some quiet, invisible current pulling us apart, even when we were together.

Between our moments of bliss, Vikram often talked about his brother's upcoming wedding. He would recount his mother's unbridled excitement at having a traditional "Indian bride" for his brother, describing in detail how she traveled to India to bring back yards of fabric that she showed off to her friends. She organized entire viewing parties every week just to dream of different ways to use the hand-sewn fabric during the week-long wedding festivities. Vikram talked about the pride his father felt watching his older brother embark on a life of ambition and accomplishment, of accolades that would make any immigrant parent beam with self-satisfaction.

One night, I overheard Vikram during a particularly long, loud call with his parents. He was trying to calm his mother down, speaking in what he thought were hushed tones, taking a few steps away so the words spilling through the other end of the receiver wouldn't reach me. I never knew the specifics of that particular conversation, he never wanted to say, but I suspected somewhere in the chaos . . . was me.

Vikram turned his back to me that night, pulling the covers to his neck as he faced the rusted ladder of my bed frame. His father's gold necklace dangled from his neck. Vikram and I had never explored our bodies fully, never taken that final leap into intimacy, and that night, I sensed we never would. I knew Vikram well enough to know the thoughts that remained unspoken, the hesitation that pulled him to the edge of my bed, farther away from me.

And from us.

His parents' acceptance haunted him. I could tell from the silence between his words that my skin and coiled curls were not their idea of the American Dream; my hips, wide and curvy like my mother's, did not spell the body type of "elite progress."

Vikram's family would not approve of me.

Like the parents of the boys who rejected me in high school, who stole my hopes of giggling teenage mischief and secret kisses at drive-in movie theaters, they would wonder what their son saw in me. What future could there be, they would ask, between this girl with the skin the color of bronze who dreamed in Spanish and hailed from a mountain so small it wasn't worthy of a dot on a map?

I was not their dream, and it was hard to believe that I was his.

Worse, while Vikram grew more into his culture, he left me alone in mine.

The hours I didn't spend in the library with Vikram, I'd spent with Chris and Hana canvassing in Roxbury and Dorchester, trying to implement sensitivity training for the Boston Police Department. Since the Rodney King verdict, a rash of anti-police protests had spread across California, KKK rallies reignited down South, and the New England elite spent their time in ivory towers pontificating about the aftermath of it all.

But with every poster I made, each rally I attended, the less Vikram understood. And the less, perhaps, he *wanted* to understand. There was still this inextricable piece of me that I couldn't quiet—that I didn't *want* to quiet—and that Vikram didn't seem aware of, or able to feel.

Not viscerally, at least.

Every time the door chimed when we walked into a restaurant and the hostess refused to look at me, or when I was left waiting in the cold to get into a party at the Oracle Final Club—its confederate flag still hanging in the foyer—Vikram didn't understand or even see it. Vikram wasn't curious about, or conscious of, that part of my life.

I had always assumed in some sense that we were the same, both outsiders looking in. Him, an immigrant; me, the daughter of the mountains America forgot. But Vikram never seemed to suffer the jolting sting of rejection, the voltaic current of exclusion, or the silent condescension that painfully, unwittingly, forced me into my own awareness.

And yet, we persisted.

Despite the layers of culture that he didn't understand, at his core Vikram *did* know my heart. He had instantly recognized my seeking spirit, searching for a home, just like him. Vikram, I knew, truly saw the other parts of me. When I admitted some fear nestled deep in my subconscious about failure or achievement, he understood that instinctively. His experiences were wholly different, borne of a world both rich and foreign, but his ability to understand the ties that bound us—our hopes and dreams and fears for the future—*was* almost visceral.

Vikram, for all that he did and did not see, was unlike anyone I had ever met.

But walking into that tea shop five years ago, none of that, of course, was what I decided to say.

Or, perhaps, not what I felt I *could* say.

I entered the tiny café, the chime ringing above the frosted glass door.

Vikram was already seated at our favorite table, smile wide, hair falling onto his forehead as he stood to greet me. He kissed me lightly on my lips before I took my seat, sliding my backpack off my arm and onto the bench.

"Hello, love," he beamed, lowering onto his chair.

"Sorry I'm late," I said, sipping the jasmine tea and sparkling water he had already placed in front of me. "Hana needed my help picking out her dress for the big Final Club Formal tonight. You know, a *total* crisis." I winked, playfully rolling my eyes at Hana's sudden infatuation with all things "elite." She had complained of a stomachache just hours before, but shook it off with two spoonfuls of pink Pepto Bismol as she rushed me to the nearest boutique.

"Ah right." Vikram nodded. "Those are the undergrad fancy-schmancy clubs you all have, yes? The ones where young teenage boys try to strut their stuff and make their female classmates wait outside in the frigid Cambridge temperatures in skimpy dresses just to be denied entry so they can prove they are, in fact, the most exclusive ticket in town?"

"Those very ones . . ." I smiled.

"Well what would you do if you didn't have a secure older gentleman saving the evening with Cambridge's finest two-dollar tea?"

"I suppose I'd be freezing my *tetas* off in a skimpy dress on Mass Ave. . . ." I laughed.

Vikram smiled, squeezing lemons into my water and staring absently at the chipped mosaic of the tiled table between us.

Something felt off.

"What's wrong?" I asked. "You seem down."

"How so?"

"You just seem . . . sad. Melancholy, maybe?"

"Do I? Readjusting, I suppose. It's still a bit weird being back after so long."

It had been nearly three months since Vikram had returned from his parents' house in Featherstone. I had completed my internship in D.C., Vikram had resumed the final semester of his fellowship, and together, we had fallen into the rhythm of our new romance. And yet still, Vikram often felt millions of miles away.

The purpose of his last visit to England, of course, was to care for his father, but we also knew—somewhere deep and unacknowledged—that this was a trial run, a precursor to what was to come. Vikram was scheduled to return to England in two months' time, the final capstone project of his fellowship concluding in a few short weeks.

His parents wanted him home.

"I suppose I'm just thinking about the end of the semester," Vikram started again, swallowing hard this time. "Thinking about what happens . . . next."

There it was.

I held the ceramic mug between my palms, the warm steam from the jasmine leaves wafting into my nostrils. Vikram and I had never actually talked about his departure before. I knew he was meant to leave, he always was. He knew it, too, but seemed to take great care to never mention it directly. Why was that? I wondered. I had assumed for both of us there was a sort of *carpe diem* to it all, wanting to be present in the moment, while also not being too juvenile or unnecessarily dramatic at the thought of leaving a college experience that was, by its very nature, designed to be temporary.

Plus, I had already felt the pain of him leaving me before.

"How are you feeling about all of it?" I ventured. "Are you ready?"

Vikram sighed.

"In a word? No. I mean, it was to be expected. But I guess I didn't expect to like it here as much as I did. If I'm honest, I kind of thought you Americans would all be gauche and filled with loads of crap, pardon my crassness."

I gasped in mock surprise. "You? Judge us? Never!"

Vikram smiled, looking down at his cup. "Perhaps you're not *all* so bad. Maybe interesting, even. Especially the genus of women from the American South. My word. Layered, those!"

I playfully tapped his arm.

"I kid, I kid," he conceded. "Well, not really," he added with a wink.

I watched him slide the gold mandala pendant of his necklace back and forth along its chain.

"You're nervous," I said. "Why?"

His eyebrows furrowed in apprehension.

"I guess I'm just thinking of everything I've built here over the past year, of everything it meant to me—*means* to me," he corrected. "And, of course, you. Us. Whether there is an 'us.'"

I looked at him, silently.

How could I answer that honestly? What truth could I share? That I wanted him to pick me, but knew he wouldn't? That I wanted to avoid asking a question whose answer I couldn't handle? That asking him to choose between his family and his girlfriend was an impossible choice I could never forgive myself for forcing upon him? And that sensing any hint of hesitation would confirm my worst fears of rejection and desirability—fears that I had tried, unsuccessfully, to leave in Elk River?

I looked down.

"*Can* there even be an 'us'?" I whispered.

"What do you mean?" Vikram asked, a pained look spreading across his face.

"Your life is there," I explained. "You've always said that. And you've designed it that way. The pharmacy . . . your dad . . . and even if you do manage to do the movie thing . . ."

"Film production," he interrupted softly. It was the only real dream Vikram still allowed himself to have. Secretly, he wanted to produce films, trading in the royalties from his father's pharmacy for camera equipment that he'd dreamt of since he was a boy.

"Exactly," I continued. "Proving yourself in that world is going to be hard enough as it is, not to mention proving yourself in *your* world. To your parents. And all of that doesn't happen here."

"But it could. Couldn't it?" he asked, with equal parts hope and hesitation. "Would you *want* it to happen here?"

I looked away, unsure of what to say next.

The bell above the door chimed as a student entered, already slightly inebriated from the weekend's festivities, stumbling toward the counter.

"It doesn't feel fair, Vikram, to answer that for you *or* for me. I mean, my life is here too, at least for the next three years. I have to finish my program, apply for jobs. Grad school, maybe. And I can't be the reason why you sit around and wait. It's dishonest. It would rob you of your own opportunity to dream, of seeing everything you've worked for finally in motion."

"But what if you are part of that dream, Lily?" he pleaded.

Were those tears in his eyes?

"Vikram," I sighed, waving my hand in the direction of the window. "This isn't real. None of it is. This is a small snapshot in time.

Only a moment. Nothing we have done here, learned here, known here is a proven concept yet. Including us. We cannot possibly make a decision that would upend the complete trajectory of our lives, simply because we got on well for a couple of semesters."

Vikram stiffened.

"Is that all this was to you? Us just 'getting on well'?"

The small vein above his eyebrow throbbed. I could see the hurt in his eyes.

"Of course not . . ." I added quickly, reaching for his hand.

Vikram jerked his hand away, placing it out of my reach beneath the table.

"Vik, don't be like that. You know what I mean. It's just that we can't do this to each other. We have our whole lives ahead of us. We can't make decisions now that will fuck up the rest of our plans."

"Fuck it up?" Vikram shook his head, incredulous, his eyes wide with shock. "Now I'm a fuck-up? Something that's going to get in the way of your laser-like focus? Your climb to the top? What is with you, Lily? Why is your ambition so soulless? What the hell are you running from, anyway? Nothing is ever good enough for you, is it? Nothing and no one. You build this little wall around yourself to protect you from anyone reaching you, to keep them from seeing anything they might not like. Or that you don't want them to see. It's like your whole fucking life is about eliminating liability. Canceling out risk. Are you ever going to be happy? To be settled—from the inside, out?"

I sat there, stunned, feeling like I'd just been slapped.

"I think it's safe to say that our night has come to an end." I gathered my backpack, avoiding his eyes so he couldn't see the tears forming in mine. "Perhaps, so has this relationship. I'm going to excuse myself so that I can get 'settled from the inside out.' I hope you can do the same."

I stood abruptly, my chair siding against the linoleum floor with a screech.

"See you around," I said, tossing the words over my shoulder as I marched off, trying to save the pieces of my heart Vikram hadn't shattered.

That was the last time I saw Vikram Desai.

CHAPTER 26

Five years since the glass door to that tea shop swung closed, Hana reached for my hand.

"I know you were hurt, Lily," she said, her voice softening as she sat in a pool of white bridal silk. "Trust me, it was hard to watch your on-again off-again odyssey. But as your friend, I can admit that I have never seen you like you were with him. You were carefree, light, unencumbered. Vikram may not have changed, but what if the circumstances have? Maybe now is the right time to finally answer those questions for both of you."

I moved closer to the edge of the four-poster king bed and rested my head on her shoulder. So much time had passed since Hana and I talked every day like this, huddled by the noisy radiator of our old dorm.

"You're not getting soft on me before the party, are you?" she whispered into my hair, her arm wrapped tightly around my shoulder.

I laughed.

"I just . . . I don't know what to say, Hana. It's been so long."

"Try," she answered simply, stroking the back of my hair. "Tell him what you felt back then and ask how he feels now. But be quiet enough to hear his answer, Lily. Regardless of what happens, you do deserve closure. It is the very least he can do."

—

My heart pounded as I went downstairs to find my table, pausing by the bar for a glass of champagne.

"Cheers, mate," I heard a familiar voice say. A manicured hand peeked from beneath a tailored sleeve with an engraved Indian flag on the cuff link, pulling two glasses from the large silver platter.

Vikram turned to face me.

He extended one of the golden flutes as if he had been waiting for me all along.

"Now then," Vikram smiled, "fancy seeing you here."

I tried to keep calm, slowly reaching for the glass as the cool condensation dripped down the stem onto my fingertips. I had practiced this moment again and again in my head, but nothing, it seemed, could have prepared me for the vision standing in front of me, the same boy, now a man.

I sipped the champagne, hoping to steady my heartbeat.

"Didn't scare you off yet, did I?" Vikram stared at me intensely, the corner of his mouth rising in a slight smirk.

"Not yet," I answered, leading the way down the corridor that connected the bar to the main dining area. The wedding planners were herding the guests to the Great Hall in preparation for dinner.

"Have a chance to talk to Hana? To confirm that I'm not a wedding crasher?"

"I did, indeed," I answered, my eyes narrowing, peering at him from the side. "Although I still can't say I'm not surprised."

"Of course you are. Remember, I had three months to think about this moment. You had three seconds."

"Did you?"

"Did I what?"

"Think about this moment for three months?"

"Much longer than that, I'm afraid," he sighed. "But I wasn't sure I could do it—*would* do it—until three hours ago, when I finally gathered enough courage to leave my flat. And I assure you, I am still just as nervous as you are right now."

I turned to face him. That was the honesty that had initially drawn me to Vikram, his heart open and vulnerable, spilling its contents between us.

It had always been his hallmark.

Our hallmark.

Until it wasn't.

"I have played this moment over a thousand times in my head," Vikram continued, the words tumbling over themselves. "Every time it is different, and yet none of the times were like this. Now that the moment is finally here, I'm at a loss for words. There is so much I want to say and I don't know where to start."

"Just start with whatev—"

"I'm sorry," Vikram blurted out. "I want to start there: I am sorry. I shouldn't have spoken to you like that at the tea shop. I was sad and scared of going back to England. I was defensive."

Vikram put his hand on the back of my seat, pulling it out from beneath the table where my name was inscribed on a small placard in gold cursive.

I lowered myself onto the chair as Vikram gently gathered my hand in his, taking the seat beside me.

"I was shocked when Chris invited me at the alumni footie match. I had no idea he'd even moved to London," Vikram smiled. "Seeing him was a reminder of a much brighter chapter, before board meetings and pulled hamstrings. But it was also a reminder of you."

I swallowed.

"Lily, you have haunted me since our last conversation. Relentlessly. Every head of curly hair that passes me, each sharp belly-laugh from a passerby . . . you are everywhere, in everything."

He reached up and pulled the bottom of one of my now straightened strands.

I wanted to tell him about all the months I'd spent replaying that same conversation, a punishing loop of our last moments together. I wanted to tell him about all the wasted months I'd spent trying to replace him, searching for a shattered composite of all the things I'd missed about him.

"Then why?" I asked instead. "Why didn't you pick up the phone?" I could feel my tears beginning to pool. "If Hana and Chris hadn't gotten married, if Chris hadn't seen you at the soccer match, if he hadn't *invited* you—would you have ever said any of this?"

The first tear fell onto the light silk of my dress.

"We've lost so much time, Vikram."

"I'd like to think I would have spoken up, eventually. But Lily, I've been trapped. I came back to take the job at my father's headquarters here in London. Since then, frankly, I've given up. No more movies, no more chasing the Hollywood dream. But it also means that things have finally gotten still. Not good, just . . . still. And I've needed that. After the chaos of my father's health—of losing you"—he looked down and paused—"all I do is try to push that magical year abroad as far as I can from my mind. I couldn't think about you and still survive."

"I hardly believe you've just been sitting a world away pining . . ."

"Of course I haven't avoided the arrangement circuit, *beti*," he winked, mimicking his mother's warm accent.

We both laughed, a small break in the tension.

Vikram tugged at his jacket sleeve, color rising in his cheeks.

"I pined, yes, *and* tried to forget. I tried to forget you on every poorly brokered date my mother arranged, tried to forget your smile, your touch; tried to find a distraction from my own frustration with the very life I've spent so much time trying to escape. But who could forget you, Lily?"

My eyes filled with tears.

Vikram reached for my hand.

I looked down at my fingers, interlocked between his, gazing at our now-protruding veins and unfinished lifelines.

This was the moment I didn't think fate would ever afford us.

"I am a mathematician, Lily," Vikram continued. "I solve problems. I eliminate variables. And with you, there were so *many* variables. I knew I wanted you, I knew it with a singular focus. But that year was supposed to be the year of my studies, my most accomplished yet, the final feather in my cap of achievements to let my parents know that I was finally successful. And then you came along."

I bit my bottom lip, hoping to stem the flow of tears.

"You are brilliant and beautiful, Lily. Honest without shame. Or self-consciousness? I don't know what it is, but I want more of it. I have spent every day trying to capture a high that I knew wouldn't come from anywhere else—in any other universe—besides with you."

"Then why didn't you fight for us, Vikram?"

"Because you didn't *let* me, Lily. You said no."

I looked down at my lap.

He was right.

"I wasn't sure where any of it was headed—with you, with us, with my career after college. I was desperate for us to continue, Vikram. I was. But I was desperate for you to *convince* me that we could. I was scared, too, perhaps more than you. I wasn't sure you really wanted this . . ." I motioned to myself, taking in my dark hair and towering frame. "I wasn't sure you wanted *me*."

I watched as Vikram fought back emotion.

"But you're right, I wasn't courageous," I admitted, staring back at him. "I should have given it a chance—given *us* a chance."

Vikram sat in silence. He wiped his glass, running his finger along the rim.

"That means a lot, Lily. And the truth is, maybe just the possibility of hearing those words is why I came tonight. That tiny ember of possibility—of a fate I couldn't fight for back then—is what I have always, somewhere, kept alive. It's what finally pushed me to put on this ridiculous penguin suit three short hours ago." He smiled, tugging at his impeccably fitting black tuxedo jacket.

"Because you, Lily Walker, are worth it."

A single tear made its way down my face, likely carrying the carefully applied rouge on my cheek along with it.

Vikram squeezed my hand and brought it to his chest.

"In fairness," I smiled, "I didn't think we would get to this part of the conversation so soon." I reached for my glass, raising it mid-air. "But then again, I wouldn't have it any other way."

We both laughed, our foreheads nearly touching as we marveled at the absurdity, and near impossibility, of this moment so many years later.

But inside, I felt cleansed. I felt the unmistakable relief of having found something lost.

Just as Vikram opened his mouth to speak, the DJ started blasting Soul For Real's "Candy Rain." The rest of the bridesmaids and groomsmen began to trickle in from the cocktail room, and soon, there was a full party approaching our table.

Our time alone was up.

I looked at Vikram as if to apologize for the chaos, but Vikram seemed unbothered. He looked down at our clasped hands, as if my hand in his was answer enough.

Then suddenly, on cue to the beat, Vikram stood up and pulled me along with him. He twirled me around and drew me closer, placing one hand on the small of my back.

"There's plenty of time to talk about what happened," he whispered, "but for now, let's imagine what could have been."

I inhaled sharply, the scent of his cologne making me lightheaded with lust and memory. My breasts pressed against his chest and I could feel the solid weight of his body against mine, thicker, firmer, than I remembered.

"Now, where were we?" he whispered again, this time close enough for me to feel his breath on mine.

I looked up at him.

Even after all these years marked by the subtle changes of time, he was still familiar to me.

He stared down and smiled.

And then, he kissed me.

Pure.

Fucking.

Electricity.

I could feel his heart beating through his starched white shirt, my hand reaching up to grab the nape of his neck. His lips, full and smooth, were better than I had fantasized all those nights while alone, searching for comfort in men who I wished had been him.

Vikram and I stayed like that—bodies throbbing and hands searching—for what felt like eternity.

We had waited long enough.

Time had frozen and we deserved it.

When we finally pulled apart, I caught Hana and Chris staring. They exchanged a glance, some unspoken judgment passing between them. Through the dance floor packed with well-wishers, I caught Chris's eye. He reluctantly smiled, whatever tacit criticism quickly evaporating.

"Let's get out of here, shall we?" Vikram whispered in my ear. He pulled me away, holding my hand as we made our way to the elevator bank.

No sooner had the elevator door closed than Vikram pressed me against the glass, one hand grabbing the side of my face as he kissed me firmly, his other hand propped against the elevator wall.

"Yours . . . or mine?" he breathed heavily into my ear.

"Yours," I panted.

Vikram led me to his suite. Room 1101. He held the door open with his palm as we stumbled across the threshold, lips locked, leaving the past and all its uncertainty behind.

Vikram slid his hand beneath the strap of my dress, guiding me gently to the center of the room, the door behind us clicking into place.

The light from the hallway disappeared with it.

"Listen," he whispered, "before anything happens, I'm not sure how you feel, but there is one thing I want you to know."

"What is it?"

"That it was you, Lily. It has always *been* you." Vikram wrapped his arm around my waist and pulled me into him. "I wanted you then, and I want you now."

Tears pricked the corners of my eyes.

I took the small magnetic room key from his hand and gently placed it on the nightstand beside the queen-size bed.

"Now then," I said, leaning into him as I unhooked the clasp of my dress, "let me at least answer your question."

"Which question?" Vikram asked.

"Of how *I* feel."

I kissed him slowly.

Intentionally.

Then, I reached for the wall behind his shoulder and turned off the lights.

That night, our bodies said the words we couldn't find so many years ago.

I want you, Lily.

I missed you, Vikram.

Choose me.

Why did you let me go?

I'm here now.

Is this enough?

CHAPTER 27

Marisol

Elk River, North Carolina
January 4, 1997

Marisol faced the mountains outside, slowly stirring the pot of warm rice in front of her, the steam steadily rising in the cold. Her body stilled as she waited for her husband to turn the door handle. She could see his back through the small window of their cabin, watched as he sat on the small wicker stool and removed his dark blue shirt, the material thick from the flammable protective coat he was forced to wear when he worked on the boiler of the train.

Kem always joked that he fell in love with Marisol's *arroz con pollo* before he fell in love with her, teasing that she must have added some Cuban *Santería* to charm him at first bite. Marisol always laughed when he said this, the fine lines beside her mouth forming small half-moons.

But she knew the truth: she had captured his heart long before then.

Marisol continued to stir, remembering the unlikely journey that had led them to each other.

Kem kissed Marisol's forehead lightly when he entered the

house, reaching for the ceramic plate on the edge of the counter. He gave her a gentle squeeze as she ladled a spoonful of white rice onto his plate.

As he took his seat at the wooden table that had carried them through so much life, each scratch a fading memory, Marisol marveled at how much Kem looked like their daughter, a physical reminder of the unlikely redemption they had found in each other.

What would he think, she wondered, if he also knew there was a boy, somewhere in the world, who possibly looked just like her?

Havana, Cuba
November 20, 1957

I slept all the way to Camagüey.

Limp and ragged, I took the same dilapidated bus that had once carried me to university—full of promise and full of hope—back the way I had come.

As the bus doors swung open, I descended the short set of stairs, flecks of dried blood falling off my pants with each step.

The familiar sounds of vendors haggling just outside the station welcomed me home, the smell of warm *pan* wafting from their carts as I stood on the platform.

Everything looked the same as I had left it: before school, before the protests.

Before my son.

I hung my head, wrapping my head in the excess cloth from my tunic to avoid the crowd as I made my way out of the station.

No one could recognize me.

I needed to disappear.

Walking a half kilometer through the tall green cane leaves, I arrived at the square shack that had once harbored my childhood dreams.

My home.

I stood in front, staring up at the thatched palm fronds of our roof, remembering the way the water seeped through the corners during a heavy rain.

Just as I lifted my hand to knock, the door swung open. My mother stood there, eyes wide, her mouth open in shock. She took one look at me and pulled me into the house, hurriedly slamming the door behind me.

"Marisol . . ." she said, incredulous, barely able to finish my name.

I fell to my knees and wept, the rough red mat she still kept on the dirt floor scraping my knees. Sobs erupted from my swollen lips as my shoulders shook from the force of my cries.

"They said that you . . ." my mother struggled to speak, still unclear what to make of my condition, an apparition materializing on her threshold. She broke into tears, a wail of agony, dropping to the floor beside me.

Suddenly, my father rounded the corner, the back door swinging in his wake.

"*Ay Dios santo, creador de la tierra . . .*" My father shook his head in disbelief.

My brother entered behind him, a gasp erupting from his lips.

"Mari?" Mateo rushed to me, joining me beside my mother and wrapping me in his arms. "What are you doing here? Batista's men came here after the attack on *Radio Reloj*," he said breathlessly, trying to make sense of the confusion. "They said you died, along with some girl named Mirta. They said that you were traitors . . ." his voice trailed off, unsure of whether to continue.

A sick confirmation settled like a rock in the pit of my stomach. The nurse was right.

They had never planned to let me live.

Those cowards.

They had already killed me for everyone who mattered.

"If they already came here, we don't have much time," I managed. "They'll be back. They have something that belongs to me."

My father looked down at the fresh blood that was now pooling beneath me on the floor. My mother stared at me in horror, a knowing look crossing her face.

"They'll kill me," I reiterated. "And they'll kill you if you help me."

The words hung in the air between us; the truth of them, deadly.

"Mateo, get the papers," my father ordered. "You know where they are."

Papi kept all of our documents—birth certificates and the few treasures we owned—tucked beneath the frayed strings of the mattress he shared with our mother. I still remembered the stained brown folder filled with yellowing pages.

Mateo returned with my old *carné de identidad* and a death certificate.

My death certificate.

My father pressed the pages into my palm.

"Leave the death certificate with us. Only take the *carné*," he ordered. "You'll need it to board."

My hands trembled.

"Board where?"

"There's a boat leaving tonight. A shipping vessel. Several of the croppers I work with are traveling back to the United States with the American workers who came here for the rainy season. Go with them. Say you are there to sell sugar. Just show them your *carné*."

I turned over the small paper document in my hand. There was a paper clip in the top right corner where I had left it. On the back was a photo of me, Mirta, and José shortly after we'd met at the student government meeting, a photo I'd sent back to my mother.

I stared at our faces, captured in a moment that felt like a lifetime ago.

"It leaves tonight?" I asked, looking up at my father.

"Yes," he answered sternly, looking at me with equal parts sadness and disdain. This was what he had warned against, what he told me would happen if I went to school and became tainted by the ills of the city.

I would lose my way, he'd cautioned.

But I had done so much more than that.

My mother covered her mouth, trying to prevent her sobs from escaping and the neighbors from hearing. Her only daughter, presumed dead, only to return and be ripped away once more.

She reached for my face, both hands grasping my cheeks.

I collapsed into her arms.

Together, we wept.

My father stood by idly, awkwardly watching our embrace as my brother silently disappeared to the kitchen. Moments later, Mateo came back with a piece of torn paper and black pen.

"Marisol, mira," Mateo began as he started writing down a telephone number. "Tío Camilo has a home in Havana. If you need to get word to us, call there first. He'll know how to find me."

My eyes grew wide. Mateo had grown so much in the eight months since I'd been held, more than a year since I'd left for university. Why had he kept up with my father's cousin? How did he have contacts in Havana? Was he planning to leave, too?

I held the paper in one hand. With the other, I reached out for my younger brother, now a man. He hugged me; we both knew this time could be the last.

My father leaned against the doorframe.

"You must hide in the tobacco shed until nightfall. It's not safe for anyone to see you before you make it to the boat. The neighbors will tell."

I nodded, tears falling to the floor.

Everything he was saying was true. Nowhere—and no one—was safe.

But what about me? Where would I go?

I stared down at my mother's fraying rug, unable to look my parents in the eye.

I had wagered everything.

And lost.

CHAPTER 28

Lily

London, England
January 5, 1997

I opened my eyes, my head spinning.

I took in the room around me: light seeping through the edges of the gray cellular blinds, the overhead fan buzzing, last night's gown draped over the edge of the dark green velvet loveseat of the hotel room.

And then there he was beside me: the figment of a dream I wasn't brave enough to have.

I shifted my weight, nestling my nose in the crook of his neck.

Vikram, sound asleep, held his arm around me, mouth agape, breathing heavily.

Was this the future our own cowardice had stolen? Did I just miss the signs? Was I too deep into my own insecurities—my own memories of rejection—to let him love me the way I'd craved?

"Vik," I whispered, gently rubbing his shoulder. "Wake up. Please." I lay on my side, facing his profile.

Vikram stirred. The light through the window fell across his cheek. He turned to face me, finally opening his eyes.

"Yes, my love?" he answered.

My love.

Was *I* his love? Did he mean that for me? Or did he not know where he was, the fog of sleep not yet cleared from his mind?

Vikram stared back at me, somehow knowing everything I was thinking.

My Vikram.

He still knew me.

"Was it worth the wait?" he asked.

"Which part?"

"All of it, I suppose," he answered sheepishly, motioning to the crumpled sheets wrapped around our bodies.

"This. Me. Last night. Us?"

I slid my leg across his lap, propping myself on top of him.

I pressed against him, firmly, until I could feel him come alive beneath me.

"Only if we make it count," I answered, holding his face between my palms.

This was our time, I thought to myself, our chance to rewind the clock, to cleanse the mistakes and heal the misunderstandings that pockmarked the timeline that should have been ours to begin with.

This time would be different.

Vikram stared back at me, seeing the invisible marquee of feelings scrolling across my heart.

He squeezed my hips, holding my entire body between his hands.

"I'm still yours, Lily. I never left."

The following morning, I boarded the plane to JFK, leaving my heart at Heathrow.

Vikram and I had a tearful goodbye, our fingers parting one final time as I passed through security.

But while crestfallen at the prospect of returning to a life without him, hope was still mine.

Vikram and I were back.

We had promised to write, to call—to continue.

I returned to the tiny apartment I shared with Eric in Hell's Kitchen, straining against the handle of my navy roller bag as I dragged it up the stairs one by one, pausing on each step to catch my breath. I could smell Eric's cooking wafting from our third story walk-up, the red exposed brick framing our faded welcome mat.

Eric had stayed in New York with the money his grandmother had given him after graduation, hoping to start his own small business in textile design. For the past year, he'd let me live in his spare bedroom for a pittance, a cozy two-bedroom apartment that Eric's grandmother still insisted on calling a "*pied-à-terre*."

Together, we were each other's home away from home, a reminder of the life we had left behind, and the life we still wanted.

"Was the wedding fabulous?" Eric asked as soon as I entered the apartment, dumping my bag and throwing my body against the brown, L-shaped sofa that was too big for our living room.

"Of course. It was *Hana's* wedding," I smiled. "Would we expect anything less?"

Eric laughed.

He had met Hana during a couple of visits to Cambridge and once during my internship in D.C. They had hit it off as I knew they would, Eric even nursing her back to health during one of her particularly bad stomachaches. He made her his grandmother's "Carolina Cure"—a concoction of rum, honey, and ginger that he swore fixed everything—and together they watched Lifetime movies on my creaking twin bed.

Eric passed me a slice of well-done ribeye, handing me a bottle of A1 sauce before I had to ask.

He sat down across the couch, sliding another bowl in front of me. His famous mac 'n' cheese.

"Was *he* there?" Eric looked at me pointedly.

How had Eric guessed?

"He was," I admitted. "But I had no idea they'd invited him."

"Did you two talk?" He tilted his head, peering at me over the same horn-rimmed glasses he'd worn since high school.

"We did a bit more than talk . . ." I buried my face in my hands, looking back at him through the crack between my fingers.

Eric gasped. "No! You didn't!"

He threw the fuzzy blue pillow he was holding in his lap at my head.

I gave him a guilty smile as we doubled over in laughter.

"Miss Walker!" Eric teased, covering his mouth in mock surprise. "Why *now*? After all this time?"

It was a question I had asked myself the entire plane ride home.

Why was this time different?

Or was it?

I reached for the warm bowl of cheesy pasta perched on our acrylic coffee table, topped with small pieces of bacon, just like we used to eat back home.

"I'm not sure," I answered honestly. "I guess we've both grown up."

"Grown up and not apart?" Eric asked skeptically. "Remember the nights you called asking me for advice because you were hopelessly in love, but he never made a move? And then when you finally *did* date, how he wouldn't touch you? Never actually 'sealing the deal'—or even telling his parents about you?"

I rolled my eyes.

"Lily, who knows if he's changed, but *we* sure as hell have. Look at you! You're not just some girl from Appalachia anymore. Nor are you the misfit nerd who those high school assholes rejected because they had never met anyone 'different.' You're a fucking NPR reporter now! And all those sniveling idiots who rejected you because you grew up on the other side of the tracks or had tight curls that their dusty Revlon crimpers couldn't imitate—are eating their words. All I'm saying is, you have a big life now, Lily. It all paid off. So don't run back into the arms of someone who knew you when you *felt* small, just so you can remind them that you did, in fact, become big."

I looked down at my half-eaten elbow pasta.

"Vikram isn't Todd," I protested softly. "He's different. And I think this is finally our chance, Eric."

"I hope so, darling. For your sake and mine." Eric picked up his empty bowl and carried it to the kitchen sink. "Mario and I can't patch you up as well a second time around," he whispered over his shoulder, disappearing into his bedroom and closing the door.

"I'll be fine!" I yelled from the couch.

Eric and Mario were still going strong, commuting even as the older graphic designer's work took him frequently back to Spain. Eric loved him, I knew, and Mario felt the same—loving Eric wholly, publicly, and without reservation. In fact, I had never seen Eric hold anyone's hand before Mario. Now, whenever Mario was home, they proudly strode together down Eighth Avenue.

I rolled my suitcase into my room and dropped down onto the thick down comforter I'd found on the discount rack at Century 21.

Was Eric right? That maybe Vikram hadn't changed?

Frankly, even if he hadn't—did it matter? Wasn't the old Vikram what I wanted: the old flame, the old lust, the old comfort?

And truthfully, it wasn't just about him.

I cleared my plate from the table and walked to the sink, leaning against the edges of the silver washbasin. The cracked concrete of the neighboring building stared back at me through the window as memories of green ivy and smoky coffee shops whirred through my mind, images of another time and place. I saw a vision of my younger self filled with possibility and an entire runway of options still ahead.

As much as I craved returning to Vikram, I mostly craved returning to the Lily he knew then, wide-eyed and full of hope.

CHAPTER 29

Marisol

Elk River, North Carolina
November 20, 1957

The boat that carried me through uncharted waters was one of several to leave Cuba.

That night, it left at eight o'clock, promptly as promised.

I was the only woman inside, wrapped in my mother's old rags and a hat, disguised to look like an older laborer from the city.

I stared forward as the boat's engine roared to a start.

My mind was blank.

My heart was empty.

Watching the restless waves crash against the bow, I contemplated my uncertain fate: my lover was killed, my son left a crater in my soul that could never be filled, and I knew that I would spend the rest of my days atoning for the decision to survive.

As the vessel lurched forward, I sat in silence, flashes of the past few days—the horrors of the past year—keeping me awake.

Finally, after what could have been minutes, perhaps hours, I noticed one of the workers crossing the slippery deck toward me. His gray boots squeaked against the lacquered wood as he approached the ledge where I sat.

He must have seen the look in my eye, despondent and barely alive.

"¿Señorita, está bien?" he asked timidly, keeping the distance between us.

I remained silent, looking down at the cracked skin of my palms.

The stranger lowered himself gently onto the seat beside me, and in broken Spanish, asked where I was headed.

I hardly looked up in response, not wanting to invite any intrusion, any discord, into my already impossible journey. By then, I had come to recognize the cruel eyes of broken men with brutal intentions. And yet, when I turned to face this stranger, something about the softness in his eyes told me he was no threat.

The man explained that he had been docked in Camagüey for six months, working on the railroads as a *fogonero*, or stoker, for Batista. The money, he tried to explain, was better than it was back home where people who looked like him were paid less.

The man looked like my father. He had brown skin the color of wood after a plentiful rain, deep brown eyes, so dark they looked like a starless night sky. His arms were long and sinewy, his muscles ropelike.

Sensing my need for silence, the man sat down quietly beside me. He simply looked at me, timidly, seemingly unsure whether I was okay.

More hours passed, until the boat finally docked in Miami, our bodies jolting against the hull as several men tethered it to shore.

Nearly all the passengers stood to gather their belongings.

I remained frozen.

"Ma'am," the stranger finally ventured, "isn't this where you want to get off?" He spoke in English this time, a lilt that sounded different from the round intonations I'd heard from foreigners on the radio.

I looked at him, unsure of what to say.

Of where to go.

"Miss, you can't just travel alone." He looked around, almost nervously. "It's not safe. This boat is docking next in Virginia, and that's a long ride."

I didn't understand most of what he said.

But it didn't matter.

I had no destination.

"*Mira,*" he swallowed, this time trying again in Spanish. "I'm headed back to North Carolina, a train ride away from Virginia. It's in the mountains. There's a lady in my town who runs a boarding house for single women. My mother stayed there shortly after she had me." He looked at his hands, a look of unmistakable shame briefly furrowing his brows as he wrung his navy worker's cap between them. "Maybe she can help you?"

I looked up at him, tears filling my eyes.

I hadn't entirely understood, but I nodded.

Did I bear the fresh, unmistakable stench of tragedy? Had he sensed my vulnerability? Or did he just take pity on a single woman traveling alone on a worker's boat?

To this day, I don't know what made him ask to accompany me, or what made me follow that stranger onto the next dock and take a train into the middle of a mountain I'd never heard of.

After all, I was no one's responsibility.

But when I stepped off that boat in Virgina—breasts still aching from birth and trousers covered with the stench of dried blood—the man, much to my shock, never left my side.

He helped me gather my belongings, no more than a frayed sack with loose rags, my *carné* and photo tucked inside.

Then he paused, turning to face me.

"Miss, I don't know who you are or what you're running from. But starting over is hard," he said softly. "I've done it. And if you'll let me, I'd like to help you."

He extended his hand.

"My name is Kem."

CHAPTER 30

Lily

New York City, New York
January 19, 1997

In the weeks since I'd returned from London, I was the happiest I'd ever been.

Between "I love you" and "goodnight," Vikram and I arranged to speak almost every day. Scratching off numbers on the back of the long-distance calling cards, I walked to the 49th Street bodega ready to wager my last dime for a few minutes of hearing his voice.

Vikram was back in London and had resumed life as usual, the life that in many ways he had grown to resent. He worked at the headquarters of his father's pharmacy and said our nightly phone calls were his breath of fresh air, breaking the monotony of his day and breathing life back into his future.

That future was all I could think about, dreaming of how to close the gap of our long-distance romance. Would he move here? Could I find work in London? What would happen to my half of Eric's apartment here in New York?

The mere thought of Vikram—and the potential that busted at the seams of our burgeoning relationship—powered my days. I would think about him as I pulled on my jeans, sitting snuggly on my waist after all the fish and chips I'd enjoyed in London. I would think about him on the walk to work, imagining us alongside the happy couples who parted with short kisses and sweet giggles as they descended onto the train. Then, I would rush home to call him as soon as I left work, scrambling out of the spartan midtown office NPR shared with its local affiliate station.

Francie, my boss, seemed to notice my distraction.

Shortly after I'd landed from London, Francie had called to tell me she was assigning me to the civil trial of O.J. Simpson. Simpson was a beefed-up ex–football player who had just beaten criminal charges of killing his wife and her friend. The "trial of the century," they'd called it. He was all anyone could talk about my senior year of college.

I had actually been finishing my post-grad internship with the Urban League in Los Angeles when Simpson's first trial ended. Instead of continuing to South Africa, I had decided to follow the turmoil continuing to spread though L.A. and was staying with Hana's older cousin, who let me rent a room in her basement for a few hundred dollars.

The day Simpson was acquitted, a little more than a year after his arrest, the relief and rage that rippled through the city fell along racial lines. I was so tormented by the images I'd seen—the once-whispered racial slurs now spoken aloud and written on protest signs—that one night, unable to sleep, I wrote a short op-ed about the parallels between that trial and the aftermath of the Rodney King verdict I'd witnessed as a college freshman. Black folks were still looking for justice, I'd explained, many of whom had watched white men get away with crimes of every type: gruesome and violent, corporate and traceless. So why couldn't a Black man benefit from the same broken system, they argued?

That's how Francie found me.

Two days after I convinced the small paper in Glendale to run my piece, the *L.A. Times* asked if they could run it, too. To no one's greater surprise than my own, the article spread like wildfire.

The rest, as they say, was history.

Francie called from NPR and asked if I'd had any "formal" news experience. She didn't balk when I told her the truth: I didn't. I could never have afforded to live and work for free in a big city newsroom, I explained. But while I may not have had *news* experience, I did have experience.

I also told her that no one who had ever taken a bet on me had ever lost.

Francie was stunned, clearly unsure if I was an arrogant dipshit or a genius.

But I guess it worked.

She offered me the job the following week and I'd been in New York ever since. The only problem? Francie had me stuck writing puff pieces and transcribing useless interviews, removed from the history-making moments and cultural commentary that had attracted her to my work in the first place.

Which is why the chance to follow Simpson's civil trial, a full circle moment, was a big deal.

"Have a seat," Francie instructed, pointing to the white, bean-shaped couch she kept impeccably clean in the corner of her office. "Since you've been back from your little European vacay"—she paused—"you seem . . . different."

"How so?" I asked, embarrassed by the implications of her question. Was she calling me lazy?

"I can't put my finger on it," she said, appearing to struggle for words, or perhaps trying to choose them wisely to avoid a call from human resources. "You just seem, I don't know, *slower*. And if you plan to board the plane when that trial wraps in two weeks, then I need you to get your act together."

My act together?

"I'm just *keeping it real,*" she added quickly, in her best effort to "connect" with me, her only Black employee.

"You seem sluggish. So if you're not up for the assignment—"

"I am," I assured her, not wanting to hear the rest of her sentence—or threat.

"I'm fine," I repeated. "It's probably just the jet lag from a few weeks ago."

"If you say so, Lily. But this is it. This is the chance you asked for. And remember: I'm the only one who took the bet."

I placed my hand over my chest in a gesture of thanks. "I am eternally grateful, Francie."

Francie always did this. In every interaction, no matter how big or small, I was forced to perform my gratitude to her for "choosing" me. I constantly needed to prove my appreciation for a post in which I had, in fact, excelled. None of my colleagues, I noticed, were required to perform this public prostration. They were paid more than me despite fewer years with the company and were assumed to have earned their positions. Mine was considered a "gift."

I walked out of Francie's office and sat back down at my cubicle, staring at the clock until it was time to leave. All I wanted to do was call Vikram.

Would he understand?

As soon as I got home, I went to my bedroom and reached for the phone perched on my nightstand, its thick white cord coiled in a knot. I picked up the calling card lying just beside it and waited for the long buzz of the international dial tone that had become the soundtrack of my life.

Vikram didn't answer.

We usually talked at the same time every night shortly after my walk home from work, but this week he had already missed two of our calls.

Feet swollen and body tired, and now with more time on my hands than expected, I reached for my robe hanging on the back of the door and decided to take a hot bath. On my way to the bathroom, I grabbed my notepad nestled beside a large pile of mail with an envelope addressed to me in my mother's handwriting.

My mother still wrote to me occasionally and we had grown closer in the days since graduation. While our letters had become less frequent, I called her more instead, knowing somewhere deep down that I craved the guidance and grounding of her motherhood in real-time. Perhaps now she was more open to it. My mother had sighed with relief as soon as I crossed the stage with my diploma in hand, assuring herself that now I was okay, having made it through what she believed to be the riskiest period of my life. I'd crossed the threshold, in her estimation, into a world where neither she nor my father had been granted access.

Still, there was something about those letters that had helped us take the quiet risk of knowing each other.

I turned on the faucet, holding the envelope in one hand and lowering myself into the bathtub with the other. Resting my neck against the cold edge of the ceramic basin, I reached for my notepad, careful to protect it from the droplets of water sliding down my elbow. I steadied my paper on the ledge beneath the windowsill.

Mami,

Work has been crushing.

My boss doesn't believe in me as much as she used to. I keep trying to convince her that I'm not an "unlucky gamble" or a "risky chance." Why do I have to keep justifying that I belong? She makes me prove my value time and again, each day a new slate, while everyone beside me plugs away in progress: more work, better opportunities, higher pay. It doesn't help that all day I spend documenting injustice—from the police force to crooked politicians—inequality that's obvious.

And yet my boss can't see that her own silent double standard is the exact same thing we're seeing in the streets.

The same things, I imagine, that you saw back home.

Before home was here.

Why don't you ever talk about it, Mami? About what happened in Cuba? What would happen if you spoke the words? If you told me why I could sometimes hear you cry at night, hoping Dad and I wouldn't witness your silent sobs?

Do you miss it?

A place where the people looked like you?

Where justice—or injustice—was served in your language?

You said in one of your letters that you wanted to become a journalist.

You never told me if you did.

Is this life—my life—what you thought it would be? What being a journalist would look like?

For me, it's harder and more gratifying than I'd imagined. Somewhere between the endless transcriptions and dizzying public documents, there are answers. Answers to what goes wrong, answers to what we're getting right—and answers to how we can be better.

Live better.

Speaking of which, I've even found some answers for myself.

Remember the boy we talked about in the kitchen that day over winter break? The one from French class?

I've found him again.

And this time, I think it's right.

He's The One, Mami.

Maybe one day you can meet him?

And Mom . . .

I love you.

x

Lily

CHAPTER 31

Marisol

Elk River, North Carolina
January 3, 1959

When our train finally left us in North Carolina, we walked off the platform into the darkness of night, exhausted and weary from the overnight journey.

Kem made sure I was settled into the boarding house, a series of stacked bunks for women who worked the tobacco fields in the summer, not unlike the *Bombonera* home for girls.

For the first few days, I survived off the charity of the local church, rifling through boxes of previously worn gloves and layered jackets. Together with one warm meal provided by the house mistress each evening, I endured a winter more bleak than anything I had imagined.

Several days after our arrival, Kem returned to the boarding house and offered to escort me across the crumbling train tracks into the city to find work, waiting outside while I timidly turned the doorknobs of tiny brick businesses and privately owned homes.

But for every store that boasted a "for hire" sign, there was another sign that dangled just beneath it: *No negroes allowed.*

I learned quickly after having those doors slammed in my face, that here, apparently, *I* was the negro. Back home, *"negro"* referred to Black people with skin the color of mahogany who worked the sugarcane fields with my father. I, on the other hand, was *una mulata;* my coarse curls and skin the color of copper, the product of generations of mixing between Spanish conquistadors, African slaves, and the indigenous people decimated by the bloody history between them.

But this new label—and the rejection that came with it—would become one of many to teach me who America was, and who *I* was in her unwelcome embrace.

Domestic work was the best I could hope for.

I looked down at the rags between my hands, pausing before shining the rest of Mrs. Mitchell's candelabra, now used to its hidden chips and small pieces of missing crystal. She was the first person to hire me after that first cruel winter, back when I was still new to this country and new to its lessons.

I wiped the fragile ornaments that dangled from the ceiling while Mrs. Mitchell sat beside me at the kitchen table, heaping spoonfuls of sugar into weak coffee that looked like dirty water. Preparing to go to her bedroom, she closed the newspaper in front of her, sliding it gently to the edge of the table.

As I bent down from the ladder, I caught a glimpse of the front page.

The set of piercing brown eyes staring back at me took my breath away.

It was him.

"May I . . . this?" I asked in my broken but growing English, pointing to the black-and-white pages. *"¿El periódico?"*

"The periodical?" Mrs. Mitchell repeated. "The newspaper?"

I nodded eagerly.

"Of course, honey," she replied, peering down at the photo to see what had captured my attention. "Take it with you."

There in black and white, Fidel Castro waved to crowds of people gathered outside the presidential palace.

The palace we had once thought would be ours.

"Is that where you are from, Marisol? *Kewwww-buh?*" Mrs. Mitchell asked, distorting the name of the land that had given me life, turning it into something unrecognizable.

Perhaps now, it was.

I nodded briskly and tucked the paper under my arm, gathering my bucket and stained smock. It was four o'clock. I thanked Mrs. Mitchell and quickly began walking the mile back to my boarding house, wrapped in the thick layers of cloth she had given me after my second week working for her. Sweat dripped from the fraying black band I used to tie back my thick curls, now falling past my shoulders.

When I arrived, Kem was waiting for me.

"*Buenos días,*" he greeted, his smile wide.

Kem sat in the bright red swing that hung from the porch, his brown coat buttoned tightly around his neck.

I smiled back, a small butterfly in my stomach.

More than a year had passed since he first ushered me to these shores, safeguarding my passage into this town—into my new life.

Why had he stayed for so long?

Each day after finishing his shift at the railroad, he brought some tiny, unexpected token—a fresh muffin, a pulled daisy—and sat with me.

He said he wanted to make sure that I was okay.

That I was whole.

I showed Kem the paper in my hand, waving it in the air like I'd seen the newspaper boys do before tossing it into the yard.

"*Sí,*" he said, "I saw. You want me to read it?"

I nodded.

Kem extended his hand, reaching for the rolled-up pages. He slid toward the edge of the swing to make room for me. I sat down beside him.

"Cuba: First Step to a New Era," he read aloud from the headline, spreading the paper open between us. "Batista's done, Mari," Kem said softly. "Looks like he fled. He went to the Dominican Republic. Castro beat him."

I shook my head, staring at the cracked wood beneath the peeling soles of my boots.

Kem continued to read from the paper: "The whole youth of Cuba was behind Fidel. Thousands of boys and girls gave their lives, thousands suffered abominable torture at the hands of the police and army, and thousands spent varying terms in prison."

Black-and-white photos splashed across the page showing throngs of Cubans standing behind Castro, draped beneath billowing flags and holding painted signs between calloused hands that read, *"Patria o Muerte."*

Patriotism or death.

Is that what the Revolution had cost me?

Kem placed the paper between us. "It's over, Mari."

I nodded silently.

But it wasn't over for me.

I thought back to the island, the smell of salt water, the sound of laughter during those early days on the university steps.

Everything I had loved, I had left behind.

My friends, my family . . . my child.

I would never go back.

I leaned against the rusted swing, still covered in snow. My feet dangled from its bench.

Who was I then? Back when I had the energy—and illusion—to wage a battle for my own freedom? When I thought that I could finish university and get a job? When I wanted my mother to keep the money from her own coffee and sugar, and for men who looked like my father to have a chance at their own dreams? Why did I dare dream of a country with democratic elections that didn't rely on censorship to protect its frail image? Where I could live without fear of being whisked away in the quiet of the night if I upset the men in charge?

Every presidential hopeful had promised us those things.

Castro, chief among them.

But that's where I was wrong.

To think that men—each of whom thought they knew better than the next—could fight for power, steal it, and then use it fairly, was a fantasy.

Power is meant to be shared.

But only women know that.

And yet foolishly, we believed men.

We *followed* them.

Even the ones with good intentions.

And now, it's too late.

There was nothing left for me.

I had a child who likely didn't survive and who wouldn't remember me if he did. My best friend was gone, no grave to mark her short life, and the man who loved me—who promised me a fate far from the one surrounding me—would never hold me again.

I had no memory untarnished by the sick pain inflicted on me by broken men with unchecked power.

I swung my legs against the bench as I looked out onto the mountains in front of me, the sky blue and infinite.

Gusanos, they call us; the ones who fled.

Maybe we are.

Worms who burrowed into the earth for shelter, waiting for the storm to pass.

CHAPTER 32

Lily

New York City, New York
February 3, 1997

I sat on the cold lid of the toilet seat, tears streaming down my face.

The plastic stick, yellow with my own urine, trembled in my hand.

Two blue lines.

One for my present, one for my future.

What the fuck had I done?

This was the proverbial fork in the road, the fork that could puncture everything I had worked for.

Or maybe . . .

I stopped myself.

I didn't even want to let myself imagine. I couldn't give myself enough hope to finish the thought.

But if I did . . .

I stared at the pregnancy test.

Could this be the fresh start Vikram and I needed? The final push toward the future we both wanted, the one we'd dreamt about for hours on our long-distance phone calls, fantasizing about shared last names and a white picket fence?

I had to tell him.

Tonight.

We were already scheduled to talk at five o'clock, knowing this was the last time I'd be able to call before my flight to L.A. Tomorrow the Simpson trial was likely to render its verdict, and I was leaving from JFK first thing in the morning. I was expected to hit the ground running; Francie said the city was on edge and I should be ready for fireworks if Simpson didn't have to pay a dime in this final trial related to the double homicide.

I packed one of the two blazers I owned, tucking its black polyester seams inside my trusted navy blue suitcase.

But as much as I tried to focus on the trial—on the hundreds of pages of documents I needed to study on the flight—all I could think about was Vikram.

Would he be as stunned as me? Sure, I'd had sex before; I knew how babies were made. But I hadn't considered the possibility that night. I hadn't planned on any of it: not the sex, not falling in love—hell, I hadn't even expected to see him at the wedding.

But I needed him now.

I needed him to tell me what to do.

Two nights of carrying this secret alone was already too many, and each time I took a new test the results came back the same.

Without even realizing it, it was actually Eric who first tipped me off that I might be pregnant.

"No offense, Lily," he'd said, peeling an orange as he looked up from his *Will & Grace* rerun. "But do you think you should slow down on the barbecue chips?"

I laughed, tossing my empty bag of Lays at his head. It was the second bag I'd eaten that day.

"No, but seriously," he continued. "I heard you making some weird noises in the bathroom. Are you vomiting? That 'heroin-chic' look is so last decade. There really is no need to look like Kate Moss when you can look like Lily Walker."

"Thank you . . . I think?" I answered, rolling my eyes playfully.

"Seriously, go get some nausea medication if you're not feeling well. Rite Aid is still open."

He was right. The truth was, I had been feeling sluggish for the past two weeks, like I was waking up on a cruise ship as soon as my eyes opened.

"Just saying," Eric persisted, "I haven't heard that much vomit since Big Mama had Don Jr. She couldn't get out of bed for weeks and threw up all over the bathroom sink like clockwork before taking me to school. But Lord knows *you* haven't seen this side of a man's anatomy since . . ."

Suddenly, Eric stopped laughing. He looked at me, eyes wide.

"Wait, do you think . . ."

"Cut it out, E." I waved my hand dismissively, trying to mask my nervousness as I rifled through my wallet to see how much cash I had for the pharmacy. "It was one night. The probability of that is less than you getting pregnant with Mario."

Eric threw his head back in laughter.

No one besides Eric knew about my rendezvous in London. Not even Hana. We hadn't spoken since she'd been on her honeymoon in Bali.

"I'm gonna go see if there's some Pepto at the drug store. Need anything?"

"Just replace my chips!" Eric yelled as I closed the door.

I stood in the hallway.

My blood ran cold.

Deep down, something in my spirit knew Eric was right.

Turns out, he was.

One freezing walk to Rite Aid and three boxes of home pregnancy tests later: I was having a baby.

And so was Vikram.

My head spun.

I felt sick. This time, for different reasons.

What would Vikram say?

Things had felt off in our last two calls. Every time I tried to pin him down regarding some minor detail about our future—*When could he possibly visit? Did I need to start saving for a plane ticket? Did his company have a branch stateside?*—he avoided my questions, mumbling something about needing more time and inevitably scurrying off to some work "emergency."

What was he going to say now?

Would he be mad? Think this was my fault? That I had just ruined his future . . . and mine?

Or was there some sliver of possibility that he would believe this to be our cosmic confirmation? A sign from the universe that we were, in fact, meant to be together? That our love was so powerful it had created a life of its own?

I sat by the phone, watching the minutes tick by on the clock, staring at my packed suitcase and biting what was left of my nails.

I tried calling again.

Finally, Vikram picked up.

"Hello?" I began, as casually as I could.

"Now then . . ." he said, the sleep in his voice making it a low, gravely whisper. "Everything all right?"

"Yeah, you know, just putting one foot in front of the other. Getting ready for L.A."

A pause.

There never used to be pauses between us before.

"What are you doing?" I pressed through the silence.

"Nothing, just coming back from my parents' house," he answered, sounding less sure with every word. "We had dinner with Akshay and his wife."

"Oh that's nice," I said, unsure of why I felt there was something bigger behind his admission, some truth tugging at the corners of his words, waiting to be revealed.

"How are they?" I ventured, playing Marco Polo to find the truth he wasn't saying.

"They're fine, Lily. Business as usual. They just said . . ."

"Said what, Vikram?" I was getting exasperated. This cat-and-mouse game was trying my patience, tweaking my anxiety.

Vikram sighed.

"That they found someone, Lily."

"Found who?" I asked.

Silence.

I could only hear the buzz of the landline between us.

My body seemed to know his words meant something that would change us—something that would shift our course—before my mind could interpret the message.

"They found someone for me to marry."

I don't know exactly what happened in that moment, but my mind went blank, my body lost feeling. The color outside my window suddenly dimmed, the pall of Manhattan more gray than it was five minutes before. I was confused. I didn't understand.

"What do you mean?" I mustered.

"My parents set up an arranged marriage. Assisted, rather. My family has decided that I will marry Radhika in the fall. They settled the details some time ago, and now that I've found my footing in the company, they say it's time that I take the final step. For all of us."

The "final" step? "Some time" ago? Wasn't he just with me in London?

"When did this happen?" I stammered, my head spinning.

"Shortly after Hana and Chris's wedding."

"Then why the *fuck* didn't you say something, Vikram?" I asked, my pain deeper than my rage. I could barely speak. I was too busy trying to understand the bomb he had just dropped on my life.

On our lives.

"It wasn't confirmed then, Lily. They had mentioned *hopes* of a marriage, talks of meeting with her family formally, but there were no details. I thought it was mostly bluster. And then when I saw you, I just . . ."

"You just *what,* Vikram? Made me your concubine for the night? Forgot you were set to be married?"

"Stop it!" he shouted, for the first time showing any emotion. "You were nothing of the sort! I loved you, Lily. I—"

"You *loved* me? You couldn't have loved me. You don't love someone and marry someone else. You don't tell someone you love them for the first time, and in the same breath, say it will be the last. Loving means staying, Vikram. To love me means you'll stay with me. Is that what I hear you saying?"

Another long pause.

Tears soaked the light gray sweatshirt sitting snugly across my swollen breasts.

"I can't, Lily. You know that. I just . . ." He paused. "I just can't. I've been watching my father die slowly for the better part of a decade, and he must see me settled—see his legacy secured—before he leaves this earth. I owe him that much."

"Did you ever tell them about me? Your parents?"

Vikram sighed. "Lily, I . . ."

His silence was answer enough.

"So I was your secret?"

"It's not that, Lily, we just don't talk about dating until it's—"

"Serious. Until you've found someone who is *worthy* of being taken seriously."

"Don't be like that, Lily. This isn't ideal for anyone, least of all for me. But sacrifice is necessary. This is the hard choice," he added, "but it is the right one."

"And I, therefore, am the wrong one," I concluded, the sound of my own voice reverberating off the walls of my empty bedroom.

"So this is it?" I added, feeling the weight of all he'd just said, the inevitability of what came next, closing in on me.

"Listen, I still want to stay in touch . . ." Vikram whispered, sounding defeated.

"*Stay in touch*? Like I'm some colleague you met at a networking event? Vikram, this is beneath you. More importantly, it is a disservice to your own word—to everything you told me. Everything you promised. But it's also a disservice to me. Don't you think I deserve just a fraction of the care I've shown you, reflected back to me? A modicum of decency? Of empathy? Consideration? Say what you will, but I have always been honest with you. I have never lied to you and I have never obfuscated the truth."

"Lily, I meant every word—" Vikram protested.

"Enough," I shouted, raising my voice for the first time. "Remember this moment, Vikram. Because this is the last time you will ever speak to me."

I hung up the phone and collapsed on the bed.

CHAPTER 33

Marisol

Elk River, North Carolina
March 13, 1973

Siéntate, cariño," I instructed my husband stiffly, relying on the language of my youth to give me the courage to say the words I still needed to find.

Kem hung his axe on the wall just beside the porch screen door, leaning its red handle against the cabin. He had been working a double shift for the past two weeks, chopping lumber to earn extra money.

My hands trembled as I laced my fingers inside his calloused palm, leading him to the scuffed wooden chair, only one of two that made up our tiny kitchen dining set.

Kem studied me, unsure of what I was about to say, and yet still trying to assure me without words.

I stared into his eyes, two dark pools of deep brown; pools that had become my safe harbor.

I grabbed both of his hands, placing my elbows on the round edges of the table.

"I'm pregnant," I blurted out, eager to relieve myself of the words I'd kept bottled inside.

Kem looked at me, eyes wide and bewildered.

"How do you feel?" he asked, scanning my face for any signs that told him what *I* thought he should say.

I swallowed hard, unsure of how to answer.

We had taken our vows inside a tiny church at the town's edge three years after we stepped off that boat. Since then, Kem knew that I did not want children.

I didn't deserve them.

What type of woman was I, anyway? A mother who abandoned her child for a chance at her own survival? Why should I deserve a second chance?

It had been nearly sixteen years since I last heard the howls of my infant son pierce the night sky.

In all that time, Kem and I had never spoken about the specific horrors that drove me here, the ones that landed me in his path. But somewhere deep down I suspected he knew; awakened by the stifled cries that jolted me from my sleep, the sharp gasps that found me when his touch was unannounced. For years, we existed with open questions between us, an intuitive dance between the said and unspoken. Kem never pried, sensing, I suppose, that any sudden movement would send me further away from him. Instead, he accepted what I could give, and together we made a life of our own.

I wrung my hands together, the skin around my nailbeds peeled from the harsh chemicals I used to clean.

I had let the dream of a healthy child—of a whole family—die long ago.

Now, here I was at thirty-four, staring down at my penance.

"I can't do this," I whispered.

"Yes, you can, Mari." Kem took my hand in his, just as he had years ago on that porch outside of the boarding house when he first asked me to marry him.

"*We* can do it," he paused. "If you want to."

I stared down at my swollen breasts, my sore ankles.

The body has a way of reminding us of what the mind has forgotten.

Was I strong enough to withstand another loss, should it find me again?

I closed my eyes and reached up to stroke Kem's cheek. Then, I placed his hand gently on my stomach.

I watched his eyes light up as he felt the flutter of life growing inside me.

While I held his hand in mine, hovering over the small unseen miracle we had created, all I could hear were the cries of a lost boy miles away, calling out for a mother he would never know.

CHAPTER 34

Lily

Los Angeles, California
February 4, 1997

"Miss Walker?" a voice called over my shoulder as I descended the escalator. I turned to see an older Black man with a sign bearing my name standing in front of baggage claim.

"Yes?" I answered.

"I'm Virgil, your driver. Ms. Francie Martinez sent me?"

Francie had ordered a driver? She must really want this story—and quickly. That wasn't a good sign.

"Yes, of course. This is all I have," I replied, motioning to the small navy suitcase beside me.

Virgil reached for the handle and led me out of the air-conditioned terminal and into the arid heat. I always forgot that Los Angeles was a desert until the sun reminded me. I reached for the sunglasses inside my purse.

I climbed gingerly into the back seat of the car, a dark gray Mercedes with light leather seats, and could feel Virgil peering at me from the rearview mirror. We sat silently for the first few miles, easing onto the I-105.

"You from around these parts?" he finally asked, the blueish hue of his cataracts visible from the mirror.

"No, not at all," I answered with a smile. "I'm from the mountains. North Carolina."

Virgil's face lit up.

"You don't say!" he said with a deep drawl. "I have people in those parts!" His smile reached the corners of his eyes, revealing a wide set of yellowed teeth. "My daddy's people are from the Blue Ridge Mountains. Came there from Jamaica. Railroad workers. Got a whole bevvy of kin down that way."

"There aren't many of us out here in the wild," I said with a laugh. "My grandfather was from Jamaica, too. He immigrated to Cuba as a boy and had my mom there. But my dad's family is all from North Carolina. They worked on the railroads, and before that, the coal mines."

"Well would you look at that," Virgil said wistfully, adjusting the rearview mirror to get a better look at me. "And don't you ever forget."

"Forget what, sir?"

"The sacrifice it took them to get here, and the sacrifice it took to stay."

I was quiet.

Who was this sage behind the wheel?

"We are the fruit of survivors," Virgil continued. "The proof of redemption. The story of your kin is the only story that's yours in this whole chaotic world—and it's the only one you'll have to give to your children."

My children.

I nodded, tears filling my eyes as my hand wandered idly to my stomach.

I rested my head on the window, palm trees and mansions peppering the winding canyons, reflecting off the glass.

This was all I had, I repeated to myself, this tiny being growing inside of me. This tiny human carried the hopes and the dreams of every single person who had come before. But as grand as that thought was, the intoxicating implications of legacy and duty, the timing couldn't have been worse. I would much rather have waited, at least until I could afford one of those mansions staring back at me from the highway.

But what control did I really have? This was apparently my time, the cosmic order of things.

I just didn't want to do it alone.

Would I have to go back to Elk River, a single unwed mother? Another Black girl people dismissed as poor, indigent? Irresponsible?

I thought of Mami.

Is this how she felt when she was pregnant with me? Was I the culmination of her grandiose dreams—or did she simply get trapped, stuck in a town and in a marriage where she had to survive?

Now, I would be her full circle of failure: two generations later, her grandchild, growing up in the same cabin at the bottom of the mountain she'd spent so many years dreaming of escaping.

I hoped one day she would forgive me.

But as afraid as I was of her disappointment, I knew one thing for sure: this child was mine, and I was hers.

And I wasn't going anywhere.

CHAPTER 35

I pulled up to the courthouse just as the local news trucks were arriving. Virgil parked the car on the side of the courthouse as I made my way up the back entrance. I still remembered the reporters' door from when I had dubbed myself a "freelancer" during the last trial, gaining access to the galley with a bootleg reporter's badge. Back then, no one had actually commissioned the op-ed that was still swirling in my head, the one that would ultimately kickstart my career.

As I made my way up the winding marble staircase at the center of the courthouse, I felt a jab in my stomach. The pain—quick and sudden—took my breath away. I bent over, clutching the iron railing. Could the baby be moving already? I estimated I was more than a month along based on my last period. I had an appointment scheduled when I returned to New York at a clinic in Midtown. I needed to see the blood results—hear a professional say the words—before I could tell anyone else.

So far, Eric was the only one who knew. He consoled me over tear-soaked pillows and bowls of ramen noodles, vowing that together we could figure out the "how" of it all.

"Life isn't a plan, Lily. It's a promise. A promise for more: more surprises, more experience, more beauty. All we have to do is keep going and take care of each other along the way. Which for us, makes tomorrow no different than yesterday, right?"

I cried into his shoulder, relieved and overwhelmed.

What had I ever done to deserve him?

Back at the courthouse, I leaned against the railing as harried court reporters rushed past me. I slowly unfurled my body, waiting for the sharpest pain to pass. Dull waves of nausea hit me in their wake.

Finally, I stood up.

After a few more steps I was back in the courtroom—this time, a civil courtroom—brighter and airier than the gray criminal courthouse that held Simpson's last trial. I took my seat in the galley, squeezing uncomfortably between the other reporters.

My peers.

I pulled my notepad from my purse, uncapping my pen and writing the date in the top right corner of the page. I slid to the end of the pew, making room for two more reporters with *L.A. Times* lanyards hanging around their necks.

How long had it taken them to get there? To earn a coveted spot at one of the best papers in the country? I had long dreamed of moving back to L.A. and sending in my résumé.

Was that dream dead now?

Less than thirty thousand dollars a year was barely enough to pay the bills in a place like Manhattan. Big leaps, big dreams, and cross-country moves weren't exactly for new moms. Certainly not single ones.

Jolted from my thoughts, I heard the courtroom doors swing open with a bang.

In walked O.J. Simpson, broad, tanned, and imposing as ever. His time out of jail had done him well; he was slimmer, but still had the bulk of pumped iron in his shoulders. He walked with a swagger and unassailable confidence that told you he wasn't planning to pay a dime to this family, or any family for that matter.

"Order in the court!" the judge said with a bang of his gavel, hushing the whispers that had trickled in since his arrival.

Simpson settled comfortably in his seat, ready for a show.

"If it doesn't fit, you must acquit," the lead defense attorney reminded the jury in his closing argument, harkening back to the famous line from Simpson's criminal trial. He clearly relished this intimate audience, each juror leaning forward with rapt attention. "And if he didn't do the time, he shouldn't pay a dime," the attorney concluded with grand theatrics, smiling smugly as he took his seat beside the ex-footballer.

I thought I'd be sick from the shitty puns alone.

But legal nursery rhymes aside, was he right?

The defense for Simpson's civil innocence hinged on race, specifically on racial bias. His lawyers argued that he was ensnared in the ugly web of prejudiced policing, made worse by the highly publicized media circus surrounding his criminal case.

The truth was, race was almost always at play with these types of cases, cases that unveiled the darkest side of the human psyche, a psyche motivated by survival and scarcity. And when survival was at stake, race was the easiest and sharpest tool of warfare in a country so damaged and worn down by its abuse. Was O.J. proof of a dirty system, finally righting itself? Even if he was the guilty recipient of unmerited mercy? Was he redemption for L.A.'s Black population, so many of whom were able to recount an experience of being wrongfully pulled over by a cop or given a false speeding ticket just for *Driving While Black*?

After several hours of heated exchanges between the attorneys, I closed my notebook, sure that I had enough to write my first piece pending the final verdict. The jury was set to reconvene at the end of the day, giving me enough time to type my notes from the hotel room.

When I walked out of the courthouse, Virgil was already waiting for me, parked in the same place he had dropped me off earlier that morning. Together, we bounded down Beverly Boulevard toward the Roosevelt, a small boutique hotel built in the 1920s.

I could barely afford coffee there when I was last in L.A. as an intern. The hotel's décor harkened back to flapper girls and *The Great Gatsby*, the height of Hollywood glamour during the Roaring Twenties. I knew right away it was where I had wanted to stay with the slim *per diem* Francie allotted me.

Virgil approached the golden archway that framed the hotel's main entrance, shifting the car into park. After pulling my suitcase from the trunk, he walked behind the long tail of the car to open my passenger door. As the door swung open, I reached for his hand, placing one freshly polished kitten heel onto the concrete.

As soon as my foot touched the ground, I felt a searing pain, shooting from my abdomen to my pelvis.

I winced, taking in a sharp breath.

Seeing me falter, Virgil clutched my hand and steadied me as I tried to bring my second foot to the ground.

I gasped, this time the pain shooting from my stomach to my chest.

I doubled over, trying to catch my breath.

That's when I saw it.

A stream of dark crimson blood, thick and gelatinous, running down my leg.

PART THREE

TWO YEARS LATER

CHAPTER 36

Hana

London, England
July 14, 1999

July 14, 1999

My dearest Lily,

This is the part of the future no one plans for.

Certainly not at twenty-six.

This is the "ever after" that gets lost in the fine print.

As I stare out my window, wrapping the soft wool fringes of my blanket around my shoulders, I marvel at the tiny miracles of this life; the invisible ones, the ones we pass by on our way to work in the rush of accomplishment and achievement, losing sight of tiny blessings in the oblivion of our haste.

Now, in the stillness, I watch the butterflies land on the cobblestone path just outside our Victorian home, one of the brightest on Lancaster Street, and marvel at the small miracle—the divine intention—of each and every fluttering creature.

I will never forget your face when you first came to visit, the look of awe when you saw the bright blue paint on the outside, the even brighter tapestries I'd hung just across the threshold. "This was meant to be yours," you told me, standing among the exposed brick of our unfinished foyer.

"It's so you, Hana."

You were right, Lily.

This was meant for me.

This is the home where I dreamt of warm fires, belly laughs, and the pitter patter of children's footsteps—footsteps that I now know will never come.

Because this is the last home I will ever know.

I am dying, Lily.

I will not "bury the lede," or whatever it is you journalists say.

But the truth is, I wasn't sure how to tell you, or even if I should.

I couldn't bear the thought of you looking at me with those big brown eyes, afraid to let me see your tears. I couldn't bear to hear your words of affirmation, well-intentioned phrases meant to give me hope for another day.

Because I do have hope, Lily—just not in the way that you think, not in the way that we were taught to hope.

I have hope that in the end, it will all be okay.

I have hope that we will find peace, and that the legacy of the life I have lived will settle like dust, a subtle sheen of protection over the ones I love most.

When I thought about how to tell you this—this one unbearable truth—a clear memory popped into my mind: I remembered you walking back into our dorm room one fall from the mailroom, clutching an envelope with your name on it. You wore a faint smile on your face, one that suggested you weren't happy, per se, but felt something deeper.

I asked who the letter was from, and why you seemed so, I didn't know. . . calm? Settled?

That's when you told me about the letters that you and your mom had been writing since the day she dropped you off, the very first day we met.

I asked why you and your mother wrote such long missives from miles apart, instead of simply picking up the phone. You stared at me blankly, as if I had asked the most obvious question in the world: "Because she can't," you answered. "These are all the words she cannot say."

Now I understand, Lily.

I, too, cannot bring myself to say these words.

I need to tell you goodbye, but not with the plague of sadness that comes with foreboding death.

So, please pardon my lack of originality, but I figured I would borrow a page from your mother—with all the words I cannot say.

I have asked Chris to give you this letter when I am gone, which means if you are reading this, it is now your turn to say goodbye.

Let me go in peace, Lily, and know that I was loved and that I left this earth whole.

You were part of that wholeness.

As I am sure Chris will have told you by now, the stomachaches on our way to spring formal, the "cramps" that came before the fatigue, the inexplicable weight loss after the wedding . . . they were all signs.

Signs that I missed, signs that I caught too late.

Please do not be mad at him for not telling you; I swore him to secrecy.

A dying wish, as it were.

Who can argue with a bedridden wife?

But here we are, my sweet Lily.

I leave you this letter in hope of accomplishing only two things:

1. To let you know how completely and totally you are loved.

2. To ask a favor.

First, Miss Walker, you are the best friend I have ever known.

You are courageous, honest without fear or favor. Or self-consciousness? I don't know what it is, but I have spent every day since meeting you trying to become more like you in this way. You are a beacon of purpose, seeing and saying truths that sometimes the world is not ready to acknowledge.

Please do not change.

You are far from the girl with scuffed sneakers who stood in the entryway of C-22. I have watched you evolve into the intention-driven woman that you are. Recognize the deep distance you have traveled, Lily—in your career, in your purpose, in your personhood. You are more powerful than you realize.

And be excited that, for you, there is still more time.

Finally, I ask a favor: take care of my mother and Chris. You will all need to lean on each other now.

Engage with one another, Lily.

Life is rarely what we hope, but it can still be what we make it.

Chris is a saint. During these dark past few months, he has come straight home after work, scooping up my tiny, birdlike frame in his arms. He holds me tightly against his chest like a newborn baby, whisking me away from my perch by the fire, which now always blazes, no matter the season. And yet despite my frailty, my once full body wasting away before his eyes, he has never once looked at me differently. He still treats me as his equal, his confidante.

He sees me as strong.

But I need you to help him stay strong, too, Lily. He needs a sense of purpose, a sense of industry to get through the days ahead. Otherwise, the grief will swallow him whole, and he does not deserve that after fighting for so long.

Honestly, when we first moved here, I wasn't sure if Chris could get over the great loss of not staying on a professional team, but to his credit—always practical and ever logical—he never lost his momentum. He must have felt somewhere, deep down, that the stadium lights were meant to be shared. And that's exactly what he does. Coaching the women's professional team has been great for him. "Coach C!" I always hear the girls shouting after a win. He has earned their trust and won their admiration, and he needs to continue performing the daily task of living in his purpose, acting on his passion.

He needs to move forward.

And that goes for you, too, Lily.

Remember when you came to visit after the wedding and stayed in the carriage house behind our home? That week, we ran the whole of London like two hens in our prime, bouncing from bar to bar, taking shots of tequila and singing karaoke at the top of our lungs. It was like 1991 all over again, reliving our campus glory days, minus the cold and minus the Kong. We'd stumble home to find Chris waiting up to hear our tales of mischief on the town, smiling at our shenanigans, having already prepared two glasses of cold water and a bottle of Advil for the cramps that he knew would inevitably come (now, we know why).

Remember me like that, Lily.

Remember us like that.

High off youth and high off hope.

I need you both to carry that memory—that snapshot in time coated in the vibrancy of our youth—into a future that is uncertain, but no less bright.

There is still magic to be found.

You must be free enough to find it. Find it—and follow it—wherever it may take you.

I've learned that loving someone, Lily—truly loving them—is about trusting their will, free and undeterred. It is trusting them to make a choice that, in some small way, won't leave you behind. A choice that won't erase you, since they can't carry you into a future that isn't wide enough, expansive enough, to hold the both of you.

So be brave, my sweet friend.

Be brave enough to pick up the pen and find another kindred spirit who sees you; relax into it and rejoice in it, whenever and wherever you may be lucky enough to find it.

Find home.

I will be waiting for you, on the other side, without regret or resentment.

Because I love you in freedom.

And that is the only way, my darling sister, that I can love you forever.

Yours always,

Hana

CHAPTER 37

Marisol

Elk River, North Carolina
July 30, 1999

The Mitchells' landline rang.

Marisol looked at the black phone mounted to the wall of the kitchen.

"Good afternoon, Mitchell residence," she answered, leaning against the splintered handle of the mop.

The voice on the other end was garbled, coming through in snippets.

"Lily?" Marisol asked, holding her breath, the coiled cable now in her palm. "Is that you?"

"Mami . . ."

Lily was sobbing.

"*¿Qué te pasa, querida?* Where are you?" A string of questions—hot and urgent—flooded from Marisol's lips. Her heart pounded in her chest.

"She's dead, Mami," her daughter wailed.

"*¿Quién, Liliana?*" Marisol shouted in panic, relying on her mother tongue to spit the words out as fast as she could. "*¿Quién está muerta?*"

"Hana, Mami. *Hana se murió.*"

Silence took over the line. Only Marisol's heavy breathing and Lily's cries broke the stillness.

"Ay, *querida* . . ."

Marisol didn't know what to say, but sighed a breath of relief.

Her daughter was okay.

Her daughter was alive.

"What do you mean 'died'? When? From what?"

"Cancer, Mami. Chris just called me. She wouldn't let him tell me . . ."

Marisol could hear the suffering in her daughter's voice. She sounded unmoored, stranded in a sea of confusion.

"Come home," Marisol interrupted. "Come home now."

"*Dale,*" Lily sobbed. "*Pero Mami* . . ."

"What is it, *querida*?"

"She's gone. . . . *forever,*" she gulped, as though the fresh reality had just hit her for the first time.

Lily's labored cries revealed a depth of pain the likes of which Marisol had not heard in nearly half a century, back when those same cries erupted from her own lips.

Marisol knew then exactly what was in store for her daughter.

CHAPTER 38

Lily arrived at their cabin door a shell of the daughter Marisol remembered. She had lost weight, her hips narrow, her high cheekbones protruding.

Worse, her eyes.

Marisol saw that the light in her eyes wasn't there. That light—Lily's twinkling sparkle—had always been Marisol's North Star, the one that let Marisol know her daughter was okay, that no matter what had changed, Lily was still the same little girl inside.

But now she wasn't.

Marisol had sent a bright, curious child to Cambridge and later New York, watching her develop into a discerning, curious woman. But now, after so many years apart, years spent trying to both protect her and let her fly, the world had sent Marisol's daughter back in worse condition than it had found her.

She held open the door as Lily crossed the threshold in silence, offering Marisol a limp arm by way of a hug. Kem slipped in behind her, placing Lily's navy suitcase at the foot of the staircase, the fringes of their beige carpet fraying from time and use. Marisol placed one hand tentatively on Lily's shoulder as her daughter stood in silence on the welcome mat. Lily looked down at Marisol, her big brown eyes filled to the brim with tears waiting to fall.

Marisol pulled her daughter in for a deeper hug, no words passing between them.

Lily bent her head, her tears finally falling into the curls piled high on Marisol's head. She let out a sob. Marisol stroked her daughter's hair, straight and coarse from the hours she must have spent ironing out its kinks, ironing out its history.

Marisol wept quietly with her daughter.

She wanted to protect her.

That was all she had ever wanted.

Marisol guided Lily to the couch where they had spent so many years in silence, watching old reruns of cable shows with families that looked like theirs: *The Cosby Show, Living Single, Hangin' with Mr. Cooper,* but whose playful relationships reflected a lightness their own had never achieved.

Marisol listened as Kem climbed the stairs with Lily's suitcase, placing it on the floor of her bedroom. She then heard his footsteps cross the hall to their own bedroom, just before the crackling sound of his record player came alive. The sweet melody of Marvin Gaye wafted down to the living room, heartbreaking lyrics of picket signs and mothers' tears disguised by the sultriness of the singer's voice. This was Kem's silent signal to Marisol that she was alone with their daughter, wordlessly granting them permission to share a moment without him. He would drown out their words with his music, descending into his own world to grant them privacy in theirs. His gentle gesture, one of the many reasons Marisol appreciated him, the same man who had seen her on that boat so many years ago, somehow understanding her before even knowing her.

Downstairs, Marisol rocked their weeping daughter in her arms.

How could she have prevented the fracture—so internal, so deep—that had shattered this daughter of hers?

"She was my best friend," Lily moaned, rocking back and forth in Marisol's arms. "She *knew* me. She helped me when I was stumbling across campus with no direction. She made space for me. She included me. I'll never have anyone to understand me like that again."

"I know, *querida* . . ." Marisol offered quietly.

"No, Mami," Lily said suddenly, pulling away and looking her mother directly in the eye. "You can't *possibly* know."

Her sudden coldness caught Marisol by surprise.

"After the baby, I can't handle any more loss," Lily said, staring down at her lap.

"What baby?" Marisol asked. "Hana was pregnant?"

"No," she paused. "I was."

Now it was Marisol who pulled away, placing both hands on her daughter's shoulders so she could see the entirety of her face.

"You were pregnant, *querida*? *¿Cuándo?*"

Lily looked back down, her tears now a silent stream. She fumbled with her hands, pressing her cuticles with the edges of her nails.

Marisol reached up and stroked Lily's cheek, placing the loose strand that had fallen into her face behind her ear.

"*Hace dos años,*" Lily answered finally, barely above a whisper. "After Hana's wedding. But I lost it."

"How, *querida?*"

"I don't know," Lily began sobbing again, the anguish of the unknowing returning to her in waves. "It happened when I went to cover that Simpson trial. The doctor said it could have been stress, the travel, the altitude, the plane. Hell, I don't know. But when I went to the clinic, the baby was gone. It had bled out."

Marisol hugged her daughter with a fierceness that took even her by surprise.

"*Pero tú no tienes la culpa . . .*" she murmured in her ear.

"Of course it's my fault," Lily answered sharply, the flash of anger returning to her eyes. "I should have never taken that assignment . . . gotten on that plane . . . gotten back together with *him*."

"With who?" Marisol asked, still trying to piece together the bits of information coming at her all at once.

"The boy from school. The one from French class," Lily swallowed. "Vikram."

She started to cry again.

"Ay, *querida*," Marisol said, pulling her daughter closer to her chest. Marisol remembered the letter, the one where Lily had said she'd found love again.

But she'd never said his name.

"*Pero* it's still not your fault, Liliana . . ." Marisol assured her, tightening her squeeze to punctuate her promise.

"I am the only one to blame, Mami. I was so ashamed I had gotten myself into that situation, that I had believed his promises. I couldn't even tell Hana . . ."

Lily began to cry again at the fresh reminder of her loss.

"I understand," Marisol whispered.

"But you *can't* understand!" Lily sat up suddenly, indignant, untangling herself from her mother's arms. "You can't possibly know what it is to lose a best friend . . . to lose a *child*."

Marisol swallowed, looking directly into her daughter's eyes.

This was the moment she had dreaded, the one she knew she couldn't avoid, the moment to which all other moments—and letters with snippets of untold memories—had led.

"Lay down, *cariño*," Marisol said finally, pulling the pillow from behind her back and placing it in her lap, an invitation for her daughter to lie down.

Lily looked at her mother, suspicious at first, and then softened. Her shoulders slumped, too tired to carry her anger, too tired to decide whether to trust. Marisol slid closer to her daughter, closing the space between them. Gently, she pulled her daughter toward her, guiding her head to her lap. Lily lay down, curling her knees to her chest.

Marisol wiped her daughter's eyes with her fingers, just like she used to when Lily was a child.

Marisol took a deep breath.

"Lily . . ."

Lily looked up, hearing a shift in her mother's voice.

"There's something I need to tell you."

CHAPTER 39

Lily

Elk River, North Carolina
July 30, 1999

I couldn't make sense of any of the words my mother was saying.

A protest? A rape? A slain lover? A *baby*?

My head was spinning, my mind splitting into a million directions.

"They held you captive?" I stuttered, the only thing I could think to say. The reality of what she was describing, brutal and beyond belief.

"Yes," my mother said simply, staring at me, unblinking.

"But how did you escape?"

"On foot. After the nun helped me, I made it to the main road and back to the bus stop. I was in Camagüey by nightfall."

She sounded like she was recounting a story that didn't involve her, one that had happened to someone else.

"And your family?" I asked, too stunned to cry.

"They put me on a boat. With dozens of others. We knew Batista's men would find me—find *them*—if I stayed. I was a loose end, a threat to their mission. They would have slaughtered us all. There could be no witness to their depravity, it flew in the face of every tenet they said their government stood for."

I looked down. My mother's hand was trembling, the only sign that the words she was saying hurt her to recall.

"And Papi? Does he know?"

"He knows there's . . . something. We've never talked about why, but he knew I didn't want children when he met me."

She reached out for me quickly, as if in apology, ashamed at the truth that had just escaped her lips.

"But you were the best thing that ever happened to me, Lily—to *us*," she rushed to add. "I was simply scarred and scared. I knew I couldn't survive the loss of another baby if anything were to happen."

"But does Dad know about the rape? The child?"

"I've never spoken about either . . ." she whispered, spreading the cloth of her apron across her lap, wiping away at invisible wrinkles.

My heart broke. How long had she carried this alone?

I thought back to the past two years.

Loss seemed to be around every corner.

And all this time, I had carried it alone.

Just like my mother.

"Mami . . ." I ventured, rubbing her shoulder.

She looked up at me, as if she had been waiting a lifetime for me to speak, waiting for me to say anything at all.

"*Estamos bien, tú y yo*. We're going to be all right." I put my arm around her. "We're going to make it."

At that, my mother collapsed into my arms, weeping with a childlike intensity, audible sobs escaping her lips, her shoulders shuddering.

I had never seen her cry before.

I held her like that, my arms wrapped around her small frame, for what felt like forever.

So much of what she'd said in the last hour made no sense to me. And yet, pieced together with the snippets of the past she *had* shared in the letters, it *all* started to make sense. Who she was—and who she had always been—was always right there in front of me.

I just hadn't seen it.

Or had I?

Despite the rush of questions and confusion, there was one truth I saw clear as day, a thread I'd begun unspooling since she first began speaking.

"Mami," I whispered into her hair, her wild curls pressing into my face. "We can cry now." I squeezed her once more, wanting to let her know that I was with her, that I wasn't going anywhere.

At least, not yet.

"But in the morning, we have work to do . . ."

She looked up, confused.

"We have to find him," I said. "My brother."

CHAPTER 40

The next few days I felt like I was drowning underwater, sleepwalking awake.

Everything my mother had told me swirled in my head, haunting my dreams, taunting me when I was awake.

How the hell had she survived all that? Why hadn't she told me? Had I misunderstood her this entire time? Would I have treated her differently had I known she was . . . a *victim*? Of rape? Of captivity?

And then there was Hana.

My entire reality had flipped on its axis in a single week.

I took a two-week leave of absence from work to attend Hana's funeral and help Chris sort through her things. Turns out, Francie was particularly understanding: her father had died from a terminal bone cancer five years prior, a secret no one knew until she signed my leave of absence paperwork. "Take the time," she said. "You can't get it back."

It didn't hurt that my O.J. Simpson piece had put our little New York bureau back on the map. I had gotten the only radio interview with Ron Goldman's family, the family suing Simpson, which was a feather in Francie's cap when it got picked up by *The Washington Post* and the *L.A. Times*.

Now, she lured me with bigger stories and better assignments.

But these days, all I could think about was him.

What did he look like, this brother of mine? Was he alive? If so, did he have my mother's curls? Her small stature? Or were the signs of the man who had given him life—and stolen so much of hers—written all over his face?

I was consumed by the mystery of this brother, this other piece of my mother possibly left behind. I decided to take an additional week of bereavement leave to organize my visa and accommodations, navigating the labyrinth of travel rules left by the half-century embargo and absent diplomacy.

I needed to go to Cuba.

I needed to find him.

But first, I needed to say goodbye to Hana.

I sat still on the plane, hearing my suitcase rattle above me in the overhead bin as the wheels folded into the hull of the aircraft. The cabin pressure swelled as we descended.

I was headed back to Heathrow.

The doors of the plane opened and I bled into the crowd of harried passengers cascading down the hallway as we made the familiar journey to baggage claim. As soon as I exited the glass doors I saw Chris at the arrivals hall.

"What are you doing here?" I asked in surprise.

"I figured you needed a ride since your best gal pal couldn't give you a five-star chauffeur experience."

I laughed sadly. "Well you're not wrong, but somehow I think this is more about Mrs. Kang swarming your home with 'prayer warriors' than it is a token of your magnanimous generosity . . ."

"Let's just say I needed some fresh air while Mama Kang spends some quality time with the Holy Ghost," Chris confirmed.

"You know we're going straight to hell, right?" I asked rhetorically, peering at Chris from the corner of my eye.

We both smiled sadly, looking down at the floor.

Chris grabbed the small navy suitcase from my hand. "This is it?"

"Yeah. I actually have a lot of work to do while I'm here. There's basically just one sweatsuit inside for me to write in."

"You've got work? During a funeral?"

"Well, yeah, sort of. I have to make travel arrangements."

"For what?"

"Cuba."

Chris stopped, turning to face me.

"Really? Why? Have you ever been?"

"No, I haven't. It's complicated. Getting there is a logistical nightmare, and then there's my mom. Something's come up. And I guess after Hana . . ." I trailed off, looking down at the same scuffed Keds I'd refused to get rid of. "I just realized none of this is guaranteed, you know? I need some answers."

"To what?"

"Questions. Ones that aren't suitable for the vestibule of the arrivals terminal, and that require a drink and some Korean pancakes to answer."

"Duly noted," Chris said, placing my bag in the trunk of his car. "Then let's get you back to the carriage house. I'm sure one of Mama Kang's prayer warriors snuck a bottle of *soju* in her suitcase that you can borrow."

Chris and I made our way back to Lancaster Street, the street looking exactly as it did when I'd first visited—back when I had a best friend, back when Hana had her health, and back when we all had a future.

Together.

As soon as I entered, a swarm of women in their late-middle age paused and stared, taking me in.

"*Aigoo!* This is Lily." Mrs. Kang emerged from the back of the foyer, introducing me to her family. "This is Hana's best friend, you remember her from the wedding?" An approving cluck erupted from the group, three of the older women coming to take my jacket, one reaching for my purse. Mrs. Kang looked down at her hands. She stood still for a moment, needing to take her time, as if trying to muster the courage for what came next.

"Come, *ttal*. Have something to eat. You've had a long journey. There's *jeon* and *tteok* already on the table."

Ttal.

Daughter.

My shoulders flinched. How it must have pained her to call me that, knowing that hers—the real one she wanted to be here in this moment—wouldn't return.

I felt like an imposter.

Mrs. Kang led me to the kitchen table, an array of rice cakes, beef soup, and boiled pork covering every inch of the tablecloth. One night while we were drunk talking about our parents, Hana told me that at Korean funerals some of the food was meant to protect guests from ghosts, others to connect them to the gods.

I hoped wherever she was now, she was feeling connected.

"Have a seat," Mrs. Kang said. "I know you have traveled far, and for that, I thank you."

"*Unni*, it is my honor to be here. I am only sorry I didn't know sooner," I said. I was still hurt that Hana had not told me she was sick, and I hoped my bitterness at being kept in the dark—however irrational and ill-timed—didn't leak out.

"None of us knew, Lily," Mrs. Kang sighed, seeming to sense my hurt. "I also cannot for the life of me figure out why Hana wanted to keep this a secret, to battle alone." Mrs. Kang stared out of the small window above the sink, into the manicured backyard.

"I have been trying to figure that out, too," I sighed, warming my hands on the mug of steaming tea Mrs. Kang placed before me. "But I am sure she had a good reason. So many people carry their secrets close: fear of burden, fear of rejection. It's noble, I guess, but its lonely."

Mrs. Kang suddenly grabbed my face with both of her hands and stared directly into my eyes. Her own were wet with tears.

"You were a good friend to Hana, Lily. And she lived a full life. She loved, and was loved. What more can I ask as a mother? But there is one thing I need to ask of you: I cannot bring myself to go through her belongings. And I don't think Chris can do it alone. Can you help with her room, there's photos and—"

"Of course, Mrs. Kang. Please," I interrupted. "That is why I'm here. No need to explain."

Mrs. Kang smiled as her shoulders dropped with relief. She wiped her eyes. Then, she stood abruptly, walking back over to the sink. She stared out of the small kitchen window, her back to me.

"Thank you, *ttal*." She wiped her eyes. "I must go now to help the *ajummas* with the arrangements."

She wiped her plate briskly, walking out of the kitchen with her head bowed, hoping to hide her falling tears.

I stared at the food in front of me. I had no appetite. How hard this day must be for everyone in this house. I marveled at the unnatural order of losing a child and the resilience of human nature to survive.

An experience, I was learning painfully, was more common than I'd realized.

I placed my mug in the sink and made my way toward Hana's room. The door was closed, save for a sliver of light escaping through the crack beneath it.

I knocked.

"Come in . . ." I heard a baritone voice answer, a shuffling of papers in the background.

Chris.

His eyes were red. He was sitting on the bed, piles of documents surrounding him.

"The business of death," he said sharply, not looking up. "No one tells you that the time you're meant to spend grieving is the time that most requires your faculties, the time where you have to pay the most attention to details. One bill, one letter, one deed changes the course of everything. It is all so final, so terminal."

I walked over to the settee at the foot of the bed and picked up the pile of papers closest to me. There were stubs of tickets to flights all over Europe, some in the Caribbean, all dated within the past year.

"How long did you know, Chris?" I asked softly.

"Eight months," he said, picking up a stack of receipts. "We knew for eight months."

"But why—"

"Because she refused, Lily. She didn't want anyone to know." Chris looked up at me, the vein in his forehead pulsating.

"I could have helped you guys . . ."

"How, Lily? She wanted dignity. She wanted strength. She wanted you to be the same with her as you've always been. She wanted to live. She didn't want to gently die. She wanted her death to be a moment, not a process."

I listened silently. I couldn't argue with him.

Or with her.

I knew that this was her logic. It always had been. I remembered sitting on the carpet of our dorm one night, Hana thumbing through an article in *Glamour* magazine about aging parents and the decision to put them in nursing homes. That was the night she had told me about Korean funerals.

"Would you ever do that?" Hana asked, tapping on the glossy pages as I scribbled in my French book.

"Do what?"

"Put your parents in an old folks' home?"

"No, not really," I answered honestly. "It's not really a cultural thing. It's considered an honor to love someone in old age, to care for them at the end of their lives, the way they cared for us at the beginning of ours."

"Yeah." She nodded. "Same for us. Koreans don't really do that, at least not back home, anyway. We just rely on family, mostly. But the truth is, I don't ever want to go out like that. I'd rather get hit by a bus than have everyone stare at me with those sad, pitying eyes." She shuddered.

"*Jesus*, Hana," I said with a dark laugh. "Can you not tempt fate with a Greyhound bus?"

Hana laughed.

"But you know what I mean, Lily," she continued. "I want to die on my feet."

And there it was.

Hana didn't get the death for which she'd hoped, an end that she didn't have to see coming. So she took control where she could, refusing to be looked at with sadness, with pity.

"Are you okay, Chris?" I asked.

"I'll never be okay," he admitted. "And I'll never be the same. Whoever I was before doesn't exist anymore. Hell, I don't even *remember* life before Hana."

I didn't know what to say.

He was right.

I felt the same way.

"All I can do is keep going," Chris continued. "That was the only thing she ever asked of me. She knew me well enough to know I'd just want to stop without her. She was my motivation for everything: for money, for soccer, for living here. She was my purpose. *This* was all I wanted," he said, motioning to the house around him.

"You're right," I said.

Chris looked at me.

"About all of it. It's shitty. It's miserable. And we're at the very beginning of the tunnel of grief, the darkest part, where there's not even a hint of light at the end. But I've learned in the past month that people survive the shittiest part of life, and somewhere, somehow, in a way that can only be explained by the magic of humanity, they survive."

Chris wiped the corner of his eye.

"My mom," I said, taking a seat at the far end of the footstool, "has a son."

Chris looked up at me.

"I didn't know until last week when I went home to tell my mom about Hana. Apparently she was raped, back in the fifties, right when the Revolution was taking off in Cuba. They held her captive. They raped her repeatedly. And she had a son."

"My God, Lily . . ."

"The point is, I know her story can't stop there. It shouldn't. She doesn't deserve that. She survived a shitty situation—the shittiest imaginable—and I refuse to let that be her end. That's why I'm going back to find him—if he's still alive."

"Is he?" Chris asked.

"I have no idea. But that's not the point. The point is the pursuit of the answer. The point is what Hana said: to keep going. And you, Chris—just like my mom, just like me—have to keep going."

Chris looked down at his hands, filled with the blank pages of unanswered questions and incomplete documents. I hoped my words brought him some sliver of comfort.

At least enough comfort to press forward.

Chris and I spent the next two nights preparing with Hana's family, her father even flying in from Seoul with his new girlfriend in tow. Hana, I realized, wouldn't have been mad. Her parents had gotten separated shortly after her wedding. Their marriage, an orchestrated performance more for their community than for themselves, had finally run its course. "On brand," Hana would have quipped seeing the younger woman on her father's arm decked out in European luxury regalia. "Let people be who they are," I could almost hear her saying.

Even Eric flew into Heathrow with his partner, Mario, with plans to visit Mario's family in Spain after the service.

"Your family is my family," he whispered into my ear when he came to the wake, dropping his supple leather duffel bag by the door.

Within seconds, his arms were around me. My tears fell uncontrollably as I buried my face in his chest, the first time since visiting my mother that I had truly allowed myself to fall apart.

The weight of Hana's loss had finally hit me.

That Sunday, we had a service fit for a queen: an array of Korean barbecue, a gospel choir with diverse faces and powerful voices, a harpist to play Hana's favorite songs. The church where we held it, where she and Chris occasionally attended on Sundays, was packed: people from her graduate program at the architecture school, a few folks from college, and the young women from Chris's soccer team. At one point toward the end of the service, I saw a flash of dark hair peppered with gray, a man with a fitted gray jacket making his way toward the exit. Something about his movement struck me as familiar.

Could it be . . . ?

I shook my head. No time for ghosts. I assured myself Vikram wouldn't have dared come to something so personal, so final.

But then again . . . it didn't matter.

I had work to do.

I had successfully applied for my Cuban visa and was headed back to New York to repack my bags. I was flying to Cuba at the end of the month.

After hugs and tears with a solemn Mrs. Kang, who at once looked sad and relieved at having given her daughter the homegoing she deserved, Chris offered to drive me back to the airport.

"Listen," he said, as we pulled up to the departures terminal, the glass bottles of *kimchi* Mrs. Kang insisted I bring back rattling in my suitcase. "I need a distraction. I can't do this shit by myself. I can't go back to business as usual. I won't survive it."

"I know, Chris. You just have to put one foot—"

"Can I come?" he interrupted.

"Come where?"

"To Cuba. To help you find your brother."

"Huh?" I asked, turning to the right-side driver's seat, stunned and unsure whether he was serious.

"I can't just coach the regular season like a regular guy," he continued. "I'm a fucking thirty-year-old widower. I need a reset, a distraction while I figure this all out. And hell, maybe you could use a friend just in case, I don't know, Castro sics his comrades on you for asking the wrong question . . ." He laughed, trying to lighten the mood, to cloak the absurdity of his request.

I buried my face between my hands.

What the hell was happening?

I knew Hana wouldn't want him just sitting alone, staring at that fireplace he kept burning in her honor. Is this what it meant to be my brother's keeper? To do for her, as a sister would?

"Sure," I said matter-of-factly, trying not to give myself too much time to think about it. "I leave on the fourteenth. The airport is José Martí. I'll put you down as a 'stringer'—like a research assistant—for the visa. I promised my boss I would turn two stories while I'm there, as a sort of penance for my absence. I'll tell her you're an expense-less part of the crew."

Chris smiled for the first time since I'd arrived.

"Sounds good. Tears and mojitos."

I shook my head and stepped out of the car.

Chris walked to the trunk and pulled my suitcase out by its handle, placing it gently on the asphalt between us.

"See you in Havana." He waved awkwardly, before getting back into the driver's seat.

I raised my hand to say goodbye and watched as he pulled away, wondering what I had just agreed to.

CHAPTER 41

Marisol

Elk River, North Carolina
August 10, 1999

Marisol knelt in the dusty closet she shared with her husband, packed with every piece of clothing she'd ever owned.

She pushed her hanging dresses aside, mere rags by now, but she didn't have the heart to let them go. In the darkest corner, under piles of old sweaters she'd bought for pennies at Goodwill, was the shoebox, tattered and worn.

She hadn't opened it in forty-one years.

Knowing what was inside was torture enough, the only portal between her current life and the one that now felt like a faded memory of someone else's. Having to ignore the tattered shoe box was a daily punishment she wagered upon herself, its contents taunting her every morning as she picked out her clothes.

It was torture, she figured, that she deserved.

She had never wanted to open that box again.

But this time, she had to.

Marisol's knees cracked as she reached for the cardboard crate, gently lifting its lid. Inside were the sharpest shards of her past. A single square of yellowed paper, torn from the pages of her student journal, lay on top of a ripped folder bearing only a scribbled number and half of an address written in black ink:

+ 53 7 832 7314 // Vedado // *Calles C y 13*

Beneath it was her *carné de identidad*, her identification card, the nineteen-year-old face staring back at her. It was one she could barely recognize. On the back was a paperclip securing a smaller, square Polaroid in place. There Marisol was, wearing a white tunic, her smile wide, hair loose around her face. Her cheeks were full and round. A young man was standing close beside her, his arm draped across her shoulder.

José.

Marisol took a deep breath, tears filling her eyes as she stared at the only photo she had of the time before: before trauma, before redemption. Before her forced rebirth.

Marisol wept. She could still feel her baby boy being taken from her arms. She could still feel her father's trembling hands passing her the ID, disappointment and fear staring back at her in equal measure.

Marisol picked up the faded paper and held it in her palm, her other hand reaching for the doorknob to balance her weight as she slowly raised her body. The muscles in her back clenched as she stood erect. She walked out of the room and down the hallway, staring straight at the black phone mounted on the wall in the kitchen. She could not lose her nerve. She needed to do this while Kem was at work, and she needed to do this for Lily.

To protect her.

Of course, there had been no talking Lily down since she made this decision. Marisol tried to tell her that it was unsafe, that Cuba was not the same as it was in her youth. The regime had only strengthened, its power solidified, only this time under a different name. The government's grip over its people had frozen in time while the country decayed, and the reality of what men were willing to do with that power knew no bounds.

Marisol bore the scars to prove it.

But in the end, Marisol wondered, how could she have avoided telling her daughter the truth? She could not watch her daughter's tears, see her heartbreak, and remain silent. Marisol couldn't help but wonder if Lily's pain was a recycling of her own suffering, some cruel, cosmic retribution for leaving her son behind.

And yet, Marisol knew the risk.

She knew her daughter.

As soon as the words slipped out of her mouth, Marisol had known what Lily was going to do. And perhaps somewhere deep down, Marisol had hoped that she would.

Marisol wanted Lily to do with her freedom—with her privilege and her distance—what Marisol could not.

She wanted her to find her baby.

Marisol had resigned herself to the interminable suffering of never seeing her son again.

But what if . . . ?

What if she could get confirmation of his survival? To know what had become of him? That would be enough to live out her days.

Marisol felt a flutter of hope so powerful a smile crept at the corners of her lips.

It was a thought she had not let herself entertain in more than four decades.

And yet here was her daughter—an unexpected heroine in Marisol's own sad saga—injecting hope where there was once only despair.

Marisol wanted confirmation that the despair and sacrifice had borne something—*been* something—and that her decision had not been in vain.

After all, that baby had saved her life.

But by leaving, had she saved his?

Trembling, Marisol reached for the phone, picking up the handle and dialing the numbers on the page.

The line crackled to life. The long dial tone of the international call felt like centuries between pauses, until finally . . .

"¿Dígame?"

Tears sprung to Marisol's eyes.

That voice.

It was him.

"Mateo?"

Silence.

"M . . . Mari?"

Now fifty-seven, her brother's unmistakable, gravelly voice came through the speaker. By now, she knew he had to be *un anciano,* a gray-haired version of the boy she once knew, if he still had hair at all.

"Sí . . ." Mari responded. *"Soy yo."*

Marisol's breath caught. She drew her hand up to her lips, her mouth agape as tears poured down her cheeks.

"Pero . . ." her brother started, in shock.

"Oye," Marisol interrupted. "My daughter is coming, Mateo. Please, protect her."

CHAPTER 42

Lily

Havana, Cuba
August 14, 1999

I looked out the window and saw a sea of green: lush fields of verdant canopy, palm trees with leaves the length of my body.

And the best part?

I could see it all.

There were no towering buildings blocking my view, nothing higher than two or three cement stories. I could see the expanse of the horizon, the earth as it stretched for miles until it touched the sea.

This was Cuba, the land I had dreamed about, the land I had grown up knowing not to ask my mother about.

The wheels of the plane screeched to a halt as the pilot made an announcement in heavily accented English. Roughly three dozen passengers on our small plane from Miami scrambled for their luggage, racing to get down the short set of stairs placed directly on the tarmac.

I grabbed my suitcase and followed them through the narrow hallway until we reached customs, a nearly empty room with marble floors. An old man sat in the center of the room at a splintered wooden desk directing people to one of two lines: *Cubanos o Extranjeros*.

"*¿Cubana?*" he asked brusquely as I approached.

My heart stopped. Was I?

I shook my head, clutching my dark blue passport with a bald eagle on the front.

"*A la derècha,*" he signaled in response, sending me to the back of the line for foreign travelers.

I walked to the right, waiting behind three passengers speaking to one another in what sounded like German.

Finally, it was my turn to approach the counter. The agent, a serious-looking older woman with dyed copper hair, sat behind a glass shield that surrounded her booth. She pointed to the glass and stuck her open palm through a small opening at the bottom.

"*¿Pasaporte?*"

I handed her the passport I'd had for the last eight years, the photo taken at the Eckerd pharmacy in Elk River just before I started college.

The customs agent opened it slowly. She peered at the photo and then looked back at me. She paused. Turning to the computer beside her, a machine that looked just one generation removed from a typewriter, she entered my name into the open field.

I started to sweat.

Isn't this where Mami said secret police stopped you if something wasn't to their liking? Where they whisked you away without further notice, never to be heard from again?

"*¿Qué hace Ud. aquí?*" the agent asked sharply, distracting me from the calamitous scenarios running through my mind.

"*Soy periodista,*" I answered, trying to muster as much confidence as I could. "A journalist."

The woman was silent. She looked at me again.

Suddenly, a whistle erupted from her lips, her hand shooting up in the air.

"¡Alejandro! Ven pa'ca," she shouted. A younger man I hadn't seen standing just beyond the glass emerged from the shadows, jogging over to the agent's booth in his faded brown uniform.

The woman pointed to something at the top of her computer screen.

I tried to angle my body to see the contents of the page, but feeling my eyes upon her, the agent shot me a look that told me I had best consider otherwise.

The male agent grunted, then pointed to something in the bottom left-hand corner of the screen.

The woman looked at him, a question passing between them.

"¿Seguro?" she asked.

The man nodded furtively.

"Dale," she conceded as he turned to walk away.

With a great show of reluctance, the woman stamped my passport and handed it back to me, slowly sliding it through the small opening beneath the glass.

I gathered my suitcase from the floor and slung my backpack over my shoulder.

"*Gracias,*" I muttered, quickly taking back my passport and dashing toward the exit before she changed her mind.

My stomach tightened.

What had she seen? Was this just some fucked-up test? Would there be an armed guard waiting for me once I got to the terminal?

My eyes darted to the sign above the marble hallway: *Llegadas*.

I walked briskly past the luggage arriving at baggage claim, only my roller suitcase in hand, and entered the chaos of the arrivals hall.

As soon as I exited the sliding doors, Chris was standing there beyond the metal barrier, waiting amongst the crowd of Cubans welcoming arriving passengers.

"Lily!" He waved eagerly, like a tourist spotting his safari guide. He was wearing high white socks and long khaki shorts, dressed like he was going on a rare bird expedition.

"Hey there," I answered, embarrassed, my voice low. I didn't want to draw any more attention. "Let's get out of here, okay?"

"Sure," Chris responded, confused and possibly offended. I blew through the double doors and stepped onto the sidewalk, the blast of heat catching me off guard. The humidity was unlike anything I'd ever felt. The air was thick, coating my body with a layer of moisture it hadn't produced.

A swarm of men approached us, shouting a cacophony of commands and questions:

"¿Taxi?"

"¿Máquina?"

"¿Dólares americanos?"

"¡Veinte pesos!"

Chris trailed behind me, his khaki bucket hat nearly falling off in his haste to keep up.

Moving through the crowd, I spotted the small checkered booth of the official taxi stand, and after attempting to haggle, agreed to pay ten C.U.C., which I'd read was the rate in the Cuban currency for foreigners.

Chris and I loaded our bags into the large trunk of the taxi, a light blue Ford from the 1950s. The driver had clearly done his best to keep it in impeccable condition, the paint fresh and silver rims recently polished. I crawled into the back seat, placing my backpack beside me. Chris slid across the white ribbed leather and fumbled with his fanny pack, one of those money wallets old women wore beneath their clothes in fear of pickpockets.

Jesus.

The driver, a paunchy man around my father's age, peered at us through the rearview mirror.

"¿Listos?"

"Sí," I answered, *"a Vedado, por favor—entre las Calles 13 y C—en frente de la Embajada China."*

Chris looked at me in surprise.

"What is it?" I asked.

"I don't know," he answered. "I've just never heard you speak Spanish before."

I leaned my head against the frame of the car door as the driver took off. The windows were rolled down and I could feel the breeze hit my hairline as the car picked up speed. "Yeah," I answered listlessly, already exhausted from the journey. "I guess not."

"Sorry," he added, suddenly self-conscious. "Did I say something wrong? Does that offend you?"

"No," I answered simply, smelling the breeze, the scent of rich earth after a heavy rain. "I guess there was just never anyone to really speak with before, only a few of the cafeteria workers and security guards at school. There weren't a ton of Latino students."

"It's nice," Chris assured. "It's just . . . you sound like a different person. Like I'm meeting you for the first time."

"Well," I said, shifting my body weight as I leaned against the door, "if this trip goes as planned, I'm sure you'll discover lots of things about me for the first time."

"Are you nervous?" he asked, turning from the window to face me.

"Yes," I answered truthfully. "My mom thinks this is a suicide mission. My boss has threatened to fire me if I waste her money on a foolish assignment. And I have no idea who I'm looking for."

"But you do," Chris replied.

"I don't even have my brother's name," I sighed, already feeling somewhat defeated.

"But you have your uncle's. That's the first step. And right now, that's the only one that matters: finding Mateo Soto."

My lips formed a half smile.

Chris had remembered my uncle's name.

"I suppose you're right," I conceded. "Maybe you'll be a decent research assistant after all."

Chris laughed.

We rode the rest of the way in silence.

CHAPTER 43

Our *casa particular,* a small bed-and-breakfast I'd organized after reading several travel guides, was an old, converted dormitory for farm workers. *ANAP,* the sign read, the letter "P" dangling off the concrete façade. The house was owned by the National Association of Small Farmers.

A small *carpeta*, or welcome desk, stood at the entrance, where a woman named Yoanka answered the only phone in the building. A full-figured younger woman with jet-black hair and a gold cap on her incisor tooth, Yoanka swayed back and forth as she walked down the hall to show us our rooms, tiny cells with stark white walls, a twin bed, and a TV. There were plain sheets, no blankets, and a thin pillow on top of each bed. A narrow bathroom sat in the corner with a rusted showerhead bolted low to the ground. I would have to rinse on my knees.

"Gracias, hermana," I smiled, turning to Yoanka. *"Muy amable."*

I accepted the lightweight set of keys from her hand.

"Cualquier cosa, me llamen," she instructed over her shoulder as she disappeared down the hall, eager to continue reading the foreign magazine she was thumbing when we arrived.

I looked at Chris.

"I know it's not much," I said by way of apology, "but when I checked the options with my mom, she agreed we would be safest here since it's run by a worker's union. There's more people and more oversight, which means more safety. And the money goes directly to the farmers. You gonna survive?"

"Are you kidding me?" Chris asked excitedly, placing his suitcase on the floor. "This is so *badass*! A farmer's dorm?" He picked up a copy of the *Granma*, the official paper of the communist party, that had been left on the bed. "Besides, who has ever been to Cuba in the first place?" he said, drawing out the country's two syllables for effect. "I can't wait to tell my parents about this. It actually reminds me a lot of Côte d'Ivoire."

"Really?" I asked.

"Totally. The vegetation, the cows randomly walking along the highway, the women carrying rags in their pockets to wipe away their sweat. Hell, the colors of the place, the colors of the *people,"* he smiled.

"Wow. I never considered that. I've never really seen anything like this before . . ."

I thought back to the ride from the airport. I'd traveled a fair amount for work since college, even to other parts of the Caribbean, but this was something different. Everything felt ancient, like relics from another era. The cars—every color of the rainbow—were all older than me. The buildings were low and built from concrete, save a few taller monuments we passed when the driver said we were in *La Plaza de la Revolución*. But despite all the colors of the people and the vegetation, I couldn't help but notice there was a gray pall over everything "official"—the highways, the roads, the buildings. The whole city felt like photos of St. Petersburg, Russia, if only it had been dropped in the middle of the Caribbean Sea.

I reached for the folded piece of paper in the back pocket of my white jeans. Scribbled on the paper was the phone number my mom had given to me, her only point of contact for my uncle. She wouldn't say how she'd gotten it, or how long she'd had it. She just told me to call the number and speak to my uncle first thing when I landed.

"I think my uncle knows I'm here, or at least, that I was coming," I told Chris, who was standing in the doorway of his new room. "Let's see if Yoanka can part with that phone for a few minutes?"

I left my bags beside the bed and made my way to the front desk.

Yoanka was outside on the porch talking to some friends, which meant the phone was unoccupied. I dialed the six-digit number.

I waited several rings, until an old man's voice answered.

"¿Hola?"

"Buenas tardes, soy yo, Liliana Soto," I cleared my throat. *"Estoy buscando el Señor Mateo Soto . . ."*

"¿Liliana? ¿Estás aquí? ¿Ya llegaste?" the voice answered with a series of questions.

I looked at Chris, who had silently made his way down the hallway to check on me. He stared at me anxiously, trying to piece together bits of information from my reactions.

"I think this is him," I mouthed, my hand covering the receiver. "He's asking if I've arrived."

"¿Aló?" the voice started, wondering if I was still there.

"Sí, sí, que me disculpe," I answered in apology for my silence. *"¿Es Usted? ¿Señor Mateo?"*

"Sí," the voice answered. *"Soy Mateo. Soy tu tío."*

My uncle, he said.

My mother's baby brother.

CHAPTER 44

Chris and I made our way to Mateo's house, the same one his uncle had lived and died in. The house was situated in Vedado, the bustling residential neighborhood just feet from the Malecón, the boardwalk that encased the city. It was a low-slung two-story home, the outer walls painted yellow, tucked away behind a black iron fence with green ivy snaking between the rods.

As I approached the front porch, the door swung open.

A tall, bespectacled man with narrow shoulders and a loose linen shirt appeared at the threshold. He had short, coarse gray hair, its thick waves reminding me of my mother's. And then there was his skin, golden brown, permanently kissed by the sun and sparkling with the thinnest layer of sweat and humidity.

Mateo took one step onto the porch and adjusted his glasses, a small smile spreading across his full lips.

"Liliana?" he asked in disbelief, gripping the railing. His other hand held a carved wooden cane.

"*Sí, soy yo,*" I said, opening the gate and approaching the porch.

He stepped forward, taking a feeble step onto the first stair. Chris lurched forward to help him as I reached out for his hand.

Mateo took my palm in his—thirstily, hungrily—and stared at me longingly. Tears filled his eyes. He looked so much like my mother.

Suddenly, Mateo pulled me into his arms, his cane falling to the ground with a thud. His body shuddered as he gulped back silent sobs, his tears falling into my curls, dark splotches spreading across the bright red cloth of my headband.

"Pero eres igualita a tu mamá," he managed, separating himself to get a better look at me. "You look just like your mother at that age," he repeated in perfect English.

My eyes grew wide with surprise.

"Ah, *sí,"* he said. *"Hablo inglés*. I am a professor at the university."

I smiled, relief spreading through my body, knowing I could communicate in both the languages I loved.

"And who do we have here?" Mateo asked, nodding toward Chris, who was now leaning against the marble column of the porch. *"¿Tu noviecito?"*

"No!" I said, just as Chris shook his head vehemently. How had Chris understood that word?

"Es un amigo," I explained. "He's my best friend's husband. Or, well . . ."

I painfully looked at Chris. What was he to me, now that the only tie that bound us was no more?

"Dale, muchacho. Pasa. Don't lurk by the bushes. I have a *cafecito* waiting for you both."

We followed my uncle inside, his home smelling like warm coffee and sugar. The walls were bare, save for a few framed photos. In one, I saw what must have been his parents—my grandparents. A slender woman with deep brown skin sat demurely behind a table with a lace cloth perched at an angle. Behind her, a man, somewhat gruff, looked sternly at the lens of the camera.

"Tus abuelos," Mateo said, pouring the steaming coffee into a small glass.

"¿Y esa?" I pointed to a square black-and-white picture just beneath it, with two grinning children with matching smiles and lush curls.

"Your mother," he said, taking a seat, groaning with effort. "And me."

I touched the glass of the frame protecting the only image I had ever seen of my mother in her youth. Eyes free and searching, smile wide, she reached toward the sky as her brother looked on.

I turned to face Mateo.

When had the girl in the photo become the woman who became my mother?

"I'm looking for my brother," I blurted out, still standing in the hallway.

"Lily, maybe have a sip of coffee first, no?" Chris suggested gently, pulling out a chair from beneath the kitchen table.

Mateo sighed, looking down at the miniature mug, his feeble hand quivering slightly. He did not seem bothered by my question. Instead, I almost thought I saw a wave of relief.

"I had a feeling you would say that," he said, resting his cane along the edge of the table. "Or rather, I was afraid you would *confirm* that."

"What do you mean?"

"*Ella nunca me dijo nada,*" Mateo answered, his voice rising in exasperation and sadness, heartbreak plainly etched into the deep lines of his face. "Marisol never said exactly what it was, but she mentioned leaving something behind the night she fled. Her parting from the island was painful, but the pain was beyond that of leaving me, leaving my parents. *Ella era diferente,* not just emotionally—but physically. She was vacant, *completamente vacía*. And yet, her body was swollen, heavier. She was bleeding, sure—cuts along her face from the overnight journey and the hellish things she had no doubt suffered at the hands of those monsters. But she was also bleeding from the seat of her pants. My mother had given her some of her old scarves and bloomers for her to board the boat, but she could barely fit into any of them, *pobrecita*."

I winced, hearing my uncle describe my mother's condition.

I wanted to cry, to scream, to run back to her and hug her. How had anyone done that to another person's child? To a woman postpartum?

I thought back to my own swollen middle and aching body. I suffered for weeks after the miscarriage and my baby wasn't nearly full term. What must my mother have suffered, holding the tiny, outstretched hands of her firstborn child, only to be forced to leave him behind, still reaching out for her?

"She never told you?" I asked Mateo. "About the baby?"

"No, but we suspected. My parents and I never talked about it. The truth, whatever it was, was too painful to bear. Marisol obviously didn't have the baby with her, and knowing my sister, she would never have left it behind willingly. Something was wrong with the entire picture, desperately and devastatingly wrong."

"Do you have any suspicions about what happened to the baby?" Chris asked quietly, speaking for the first time. He was sitting across from my uncle and had taken his first real sip of Cuban coffee.

Mateo looked at him.

"To be honest, I tried not to think about it. To do so would have been to acknowledge my own shortcoming. What kind of brother would I have been if I let my own niece or nephew, the blood of my only sister, wallow away in an uncertain future somewhere on the same island?"

Mateo got quiet and stared down at his mug. He was fighting back tears.

"I was only fifteen at the time. As soon as Mari left, I knew I couldn't stay. I blamed my parents in many ways for her leaving. They tried to keep her in Camagüey, which only made the allure of university greater for her. My father didn't believe women should work outside the home—and certainly not get into politics. He had been involved in the labor strikes in the thirties and, based on what he saw, later told me that the underground movement in Havana was too dangerous for women. And look what happened."

Mateo took a sip from his mug.

"I could never make sense of it," he continued, "of my father's unwillingness to let her go, of Marisol's need to get involved so intimately in toppling Batista. But even though I didn't fully understand it, I needed to get away from home—from the guilt, the trauma, the unspoken secrets. And in some sense, I suppose, I wanted to make *her* dream come true, to complete some fraction of what she had started—leaving Camagüey for Havana—so that her journey wasn't all in vain. I came here as soon as I turned eighteen. By then, the Revolution had succeeded and the university had reopened. Years later, in 1976, Castro became president and I became a professor of Cuban history. Somehow, I think, I was privately trying to understand all the events that had shaped, and misshaped, my own life."

"What happened to your parents?" Chris asked again, sensing somehow that I wasn't yet ready to speak.

"They died almost twenty years ago. I went back to bury them, and I swear, they were still waiting for Marisol to come home. They died within months of each other."

"I'm sorry to hear that," Chris said, his genuine care apparent. "Did you ever get any of the answers you were looking for? About what happened back then?"

"Not many," Mateo admitted. "I got polio in the sixties, before the vaccine made it to Cuba." He motioned to his cane. "But I was bookish and kept learning, searching for answers. Once I became a professor, old enough to be the parent of most of my students, I found myself scanning their faces, looking for him. Or her."

"Who?" I asked finally, taking a seat in the wicker chair.

"My niece. Or nephew," Mateo sighed. "I figured the child would have been old enough to be university age by then. But I had no clue whether the child had survived. Still, I began to wonder, obsessively looking for any trace of Mari—or myself—in my pupils."

"Did you see anything?" Chris asked, leaning closer.

"Unfortunately not," Mateo answered, turning toward me.

I looked away, not wanting him to see the tears sliding down my cheeks.

Chris reached across the table and placed his hands near mine. "One step at a time," he whispered softly.

I took a deep breath.

"Maybe you can take a look through *La Biblioteca Nacional*. Or the *Registro Civil*?" Mateo offered. "You'll need a name and a municipality for either of those. Perhaps with whatever details your mother has shared, there'll be something in the records."

"That's a good start," I agreed, rising from the table. "I'll come back to tell you what I find."

"No, *sobrina*. You'll stay for lunch." Mateo tapped the arm of my chair, motioning for me to sit back down. "I am an old man and I live alone. I have just found my sister's only daughter, my only living relative. First, you will eat. Then, you will tell me all there is to know about you. And only after that may you search with my help—and with the power of the ancestors on your side."

CHAPTER 45

I spent the next three weeks in Havana, running out of money and running out of time. I learned in real time how hard it was to be a journalist in Cuba, to do the kinds of research I took for granted back home. I couldn't check police records, access lists of prisoners, or file a request through the Freedom of Information Act. How was I going to locate my brother, an elusive mystery among the sea of struggling Cubans left behind by broken promises?

On each long walk to a new county clerk's office, it was odd to me, seeing the country of my mother's birth, the place where she might still be—where *I* might be—if it weren't for the violence that had forced her away. The entire city was a walking dichotomy: colorful houses, kids playing soccer and drinking fresh fruit, juice that tasted straight from the vine. And then there was the Malecón, the enchanting boardwalk that stretched the length of the city. It came alive at night, young teenagers exploring forbidden love under the warm breeze of nightfall, families with young children running along the cracked concrete, their giggles escaping in the wind.

And yet, there was an invisible dome of disappointment that covered the city, trapping dreams that floated like kites toward the night sky. There were too few jobs, very little industry, and too many young people without employment. There was no place to go. The schools were free, but the opportunities weren't there.

Doctors drove tourists in taxis the shape of coconuts, taking home more money than they would making rounds with their patients. It was a city of enigmas, the resilience of a colorful, dynamic people bound by the invisible rope of unchecked power.

I couldn't make sense of it.

But while my heart was scrambled, my purpose was clear.

I spent hours at the Civil Registrar's Office between dusty card catalogues, opening the alphabetical drawers and their assigned numbers. I checked out stacks of documents—birth records and death certificates—bound by colored tape. All the while, Chris sat beside me, quietly scanning the pages for any reference of my mother's name or babies found between 1957 and 1958, after the attack on the palace. We also searched for any mention of military officers named "Silva," the man who harmed my mother.

Chris had become an unexpectedly promising travel companion. I'd come to rely heavily on his steadfast belief in the righteousness of what I was doing, in the history I was trying to rescue and the family I was fighting to make whole.

Practically speaking, his companionship granted me access to places I couldn't otherwise enter alone. He was the first to open my door, to silently signal to men who leered at me from street corners that I was protected—that he was *there*, and watching. He told officials at the library and in government buildings who wouldn't make eye contact with me to look me in the eye. "She is the boss," he instructed, firmly and unequivocally. He demanded that the world treat me with the respect that he felt I deserved.

And he listened.

At the end of a long day or the start of a new one, Chris sat still and self-possessed, taking notes as I laid out our plans, animated in my telling and retelling of the leads I'd picked up. He quietly helped me piece together the seemingly random mosaic of information we were collecting, until finally, that information began to make sense.

On our fourth week I came across something unusual. An article in *Diario de la Marina*, dated July 11, 1961, showed a photo of a crumbling building in Havana with seven nuns standing in front of its double doors. *"Girls School to be Demolished at End of Month,"* the caption read. The paragraph below said the building was owned and operated by a specific order of Ursuline nuns.

I thought back to my mother sitting on our couch in Elk River, her tears flowing freely as she shook like a child in my arms, finally telling me the details of her story. Something she'd said that night, a small mention that I'd almost forgotten, was that the nurse at the hospital who had convinced her to leave was also a nun.

"Have you ever heard of Ursuline nuns?" I turned to Chris, who was looking at a pre-revolution map of the eastern parts of the island. "Apparently, they ran a girls' school in Havana."

Chris placed his map down gently on the large metal table and walked over to where I was seated. He peered over my shoulder at the sepia-colored photo nestled between the pages.

"Is that them?" he asked, pointing to another picture just below the fold where the same group of seven sat along a bench bearing the school's name. One nun seated in front held a large rosary. The group of women stared at the camera, serious and unsmiling.

"Sister María Inés Zayas runs the Merici Academy, an all-girls school in Havana," Chris read aloud. *"The academy was founded in 1941 to provide English-language schooling and social services for young women. The building will close at the end of July on order from the government."*

"Very interesting," Chris marveled. "Social services specifically for young women."

"Exactly," I agreed. "It only caught my attention because my mom mentioned that a nurse had helped her, but she also said she wore some sort of religious habit. Like a nun."

"Judging from the description of the school"—Chris ran his fingers along the caption—"it seems like if there *was* a young woman in need—say, who had a baby under duress—that this particular group would have been inclined to help her, no?"

"Maybe we've spent too much time looking for the man who made the baby—this Silva character—and not enough time looking for the woman who saved him?" I asked aloud.

"Should we investigate the school?" Chris asked. "Let's write down the nun's name and when we find some internet, we can have a look. This is a pretty strong lead, Lily." Chris wrote down the details in his notepad.

"I mean, we still don't have confirmation that *this* particular nun was a nurse, or that she was anywhere near the prison at the time, or . . ." I started spiraling, the fear of failure rising in my chest.

"Lily," Chris interrupted me, placing his hand on my shoulder. "This is something. This is more than we had before."

"It's just . . . I feel further and closer at the same time. Like we're almost on the cusp of something, and yet, further than we were when we arrived."

"We just need one thing to break our way, Lily. We'll find him. I can feel it."

CHAPTER 46

Chris and I returned to our *casa particular*, bodies soaked in sweat from the long walk. Too tired to make it inside, we sat on the porch in a pair of wooden rocking chairs situated behind two large marble columns. Yoanka made a particularly strong blend of coffee and placed two small glass mugs on the round table between us.

I could tell something was on Chris's mind.

"She would have loved this," he whispered quietly, finally speaking after a long silence. He pushed backward in his rocker, swaying gently.

"She would have been enchanted," I agreed, nodding as I watched schoolboys in their blue and white uniforms kick a deflated soccer ball down the sidewalk. "She'd have loved the Malecón, particularly. The warm breeze at night. The dancing. But . . ."

I paused.

"Is there Diet Coke here?" I imitated in Hana's deep, resonant voice, drawing out the vowels as only girls from the Valley did.

We immediately started laughing, Chris spitting out the water he had just taken from his backpack. We laughed until our stomachs hurt, laughed until we cried.

"The ban on Coke products would have leveled her," Chris admitted, his laughter fading to a faint smile.

"*Ciego Montero* wouldn't have cut it," I smiled, shaking my head as I imagined Hana's horror at the raw Cuban sugar floating in the bottom of the can.

We both smiled.

"She was the best friend I've ever known," I said, tears in my eyes.

"Me too," Chris said, staring down at the chipping green paint of the porch. "I feel stuck, Lily. I wake up every morning thinking about the distance between the life we'd planned and the life I have. Shattered dreams and strangled potential. All I see is blank space. Terrifyingly empty, blank space. I just don't know how to move forward, and I can't tell if it's because I don't want to—or I don't know *how* to."

"You don't have to move anywhere, Chris," I said, folding my legs beneath me as I leaned back in the chair. "Grief is a process, not an act. You can't will it away and you can't speed it up. I think you just have to let it dissolve into you. It becomes part of you."

I shifted in my chair, my hand gently resting on my stomach.

"Not only will you survive this grief, but it will grant you vision. You will see the miracle of humanity that you didn't even notice before: a baby's smile, a fresh tulip, an unbroken horizon. That's where God lives. That's what's holy."

Chris nodded, quickly wiping away the tear that had just fallen.

"It just feels like betrayal to live this life without her. And yet, it feels like betrayal not to. She explicitly asked me to 'find home' again."

"What do you mean?"

"She left me a letter. She told me to 'find home' again—to recreate it. To find a place and people where my soul can find rest."

I nodded, thinking of my own letter from Hana.

"It doesn't have to make sense now, Chris. None of it does. But what she asked of you was perhaps the most generous gift." I pointed to the colorful, crumbling houses around us, the neglected sidewalks and peeling paint. "Love, we know now, is freedom. It is allowing the ones you love most to be swept along with the tide of progress, to ride the current of time, not keeping them trapped inside it. Honor your love by loving yourself enough to experience the joys of this life again."

Chris looked away from me, hoping to hide his emotion.

"Let's go," I said, sensing he needed a distraction. "It's time to get back to work."

Just as we stood to get up, a breaking news bulletin flashed on the TV screen mounted in the corner of the lobby. Yoanka rushed in from the kitchen, hearing the alert.

As soon as the animated graphic of a Cuban flag whirled across the screen, the camera panned to a wooden desk flanked by two taller podiums. At the center, there he was: Fidel Castro in his signature eighties sweatsuit, a military cap situated squarely on his head. "*Compañeros . . .*" he began, his voice weaker than before. "*El bloqueo sigue, pero venceremos . . .*"

The embargo continues, but we will be victorious.

This was the second government announcement I'd witnessed since being here, seemingly random press conferences that generally started the same way: government grievances against the United States, which it blamed for crippling the Cuban economy with a "malicious and unnecessary" trade embargo. There was even a kids' cartoon that aired on Saturday mornings on one of the three state-run television channels where the villain was a wiry gray-haired man in a top hat wearing red, white, and blue. His name was "Uncle Sam."

Castro held this conference with two other men behind him. There was an older gentleman in a suit and dyed black hair that appeared to be an advisor of some sort. To his left stood a young, handsome man with thin glasses and a head of thick, curly blond hair. Seemingly in his early forties, he had a boyish haircut and a clean, chiseled jawline with tawny skin and green eyes. He was wearing the dark green fatigues of the Cuban military, adorned with two downward facing gold arrows sewn into the shoulder board of his lapel. That meant he was a lieutenant, or *teniente*.

Castro continued his announcement, a string of proclamations I didn't fully understand, something about a new counter to the embargo. He then asked the younger man to step forward, his presence clearly meant to show a passing of the torch, an energized, reinvigorated Cuban army with an unwavering stance against the American government's "sabotage and subterfuge."

As soon as the lieutenant approached the microphone, something in his mannerism caught my eye. He gave a quick, furtive glance away from the camera, almost appearing shy, like he didn't want to be there. I noticed a small, silver charm tucked inside the crisp, white collar of his uniform. It was a round pendant with three gold coins at the center, a saint holding the small hands of a child.

Much like my mother's.

"Chris," I nudged the side of his ribs with my elbow. "Look."

Chris peered up from the *Juventud Rebelde* newspaper he was holding, trying to sound out the words in Spanish.

"What is it?" he asked.

"See that guy? The younger one? Beside the president?"

"Yeah," he answered, his eyes scanning to the left of the podium. "The one who looks like—"

He gasped.

"Holy shit. The one who looks like . . . *you*."

"Can you see his name?" I asked, squinting to see the engraved bronze placard on his lapel.

"Z-A-Y-A- . . ." Chris read aloud, moving closer to the television. "I can't see the rest."

Just then, a lower third flashed on the screen, bearing the titles of everyone at the podium:

Fidel Castro, *Primer Secretario del Partido Comunista*
Ricardo Alarcón de Quesada, *Presidente de la Asamblea Nacional del Poder Popular*
Osvaldo Vidal Zayas, Jr., *Teniente*

Zayas.

I had seen that name before.

"Let's go," I said, standing up, slinging my backpack over my shoulder.

"Where? Don't you want to hear the rest of the conference?" Chris asked.

"We've seen all that we need. We've got a name."

CHAPTER 47

Chris and I ran the near half mile to Meliá Cohiba, the newest international hotel in Vedado. We flashed our passports to enter as I pushed past a group of European tourists, cutting the line to purchase one hour of internet access from the front desk.

I waited for several excruciating seconds as the hotel dial-up sputtered to life, Chris seated beside me on a square leather couch in the modest business center. The plastic keyboard squeaked as I typed the young lieutenant's name into the search engine: Osvaldo Vidal Zayas, Jr. I waited anxiously as his photo began to load. Pixel by pixel, the same face I'd seen only an hour earlier came into sharper focus, those striking eyes and high cheekbones, framed by thick curls tucked under a military cap. I scrolled to the bottom of the page and pressed the first hyperlink listed. It led me to an article in *Granma* that said Zayas was forty-one years old and had graduated from the University of Havana with a degree in Economics.

But there was little else.

My thumb hesitated over the space bar. I typed *parents* in the box for related searches.

A stunning amount of data suddenly populated the page.

Dr. Osvaldo Vidal Morales, the elder Vidal, was Castro's right-hand man during the Revolution, his personal physician and the leader of the Ministry of Health.

My mind spun.

I stared at his photo, searching his face for similarities, for clues. Was this his father? The man who raised him? Or the man who raped my mother?

The next link loaded another article in *Granma* from November 1971. It said that Vidal never had biological children of his own. He and his wife raised one boy they claimed was rescued during the Revolution—Vidal's sole heir.

The wife's name was Emilia Lorena Zayas.

Zayas.

The same last name as the nun who ran the school for girls.

There was a death certificate for Emilia Zayas from 1988.

Chris reached across and held out his hand, signaling for me to pass him the keyboard, its wire stretching as he leaned forward.

"Let's see something," he said, quickly tapping out another name. "If María Inés Zayas was the nun who ran the Merici Academy . . ."

The digital hourglass blinked as the page loaded.

"There!" Chris exclaimed. "*La Casa de la Beneficencia*, a historical institution for 'unwanted children,' founded in the late seventeen hundreds. It was the unofficial partner of the Merici Academy, a girls' school run by María Inés Zayas, a nurse at Calixto García hospital and the Reverend Mother of the Havana's Ursuline order."

My eyes grew wide.

"So she *was* a nurse . . ."

"It appears so," Chris marveled.

"Is there any information on where she's from? If she's still alive?"

"It says here she died in 1982 just outside of Havana."

"But then is there any relation to the *other* Zayas?" I wondered aloud. "The lieutenant's mother?"

We pulled up the search results for Emilia Zayas, and a photo from her obituary filled the page.

We scanned the words in silence, her resemblance to the nun uncanny.

"This is some sort of triangle," Chris said quietly, almost to himself. "They have to be related."

I nodded.

"But what about Osvaldo? If my mother is his mother . . . who is the woman who raised him?"

"Let's print this and take it to your uncle. Maybe he can help connect the dots."

An hour later, we were back at my uncle's kitchen table, passing him the stack of printed papers.

Mateo stared at the photo of Osvaldo, his eyes piercing even in black and white.

"It is remarkable what you have uncovered," he whispered, turning the documents over, "and in such a short amount of time."

"Do you think . . ." I was too afraid to finish the question.

"I do," Mateo answered, saving me from myself. "I do."

We fell silent, the three of us looking down at the tabletop covered in loose pages, my notes scribbled in ink on the margins.

"It is difficult not to imagine he could have been one of my students," Mateo said, still staring at the photo of the young lieutenant. "He got his degree in Economics in eighty-two. I was an assistant professor in the History department by then. The economics students have to take a mandatory course on Cuban history, which I teach."

"And what about this, *Tío* Mateo? Have you heard of *La Casa de la Beneficencia*?"

I looked down with a half-smile. Even in the haste of getting answers, I appreciated the way Chris called Mateo "uncle." He, too, was the son of an immigrant and understood the way that titles could restore dignity otherwise denied.

"*La Beneficencia* was an orphanage here in Havana," Mateo confirmed, taking the page from Chris's outstretched hand. Then, he grabbed his cane from where it rested on the edge of the table and, with great effort, walked over to the credenza that held his aging television set.

He rifled through a stack of old newspapers in the drawer below.

"I remember seeing an article in that lifestyle magazine, *Bohemia,* about the orphanage. It made a big splash at the time because no one really talked about formal adoption back then. In the early sixties, right when the regime first took power, they publicly thanked the Catholic charities that had helped them 'rescue' the next generation of Cuban children. It was notable, since Castro was already beginning the slow process of nationalizing church properties. I couldn't figure out why he would pause to recognize churches during his effort to *silence* religion. But apparently, there was a network of nuns that ran a school in Havana, along with the orphanage, and they sheltered a lot of the babies at the beginning of the Revolution: babies of widowed mothers and unwed farm girls who were collateral damage in the areas where some of the battles had played out. For that, Fidel recognized their power in saving thousands of children who would, eventually, become more conscripts for his Communist Party. That's why I took note of it; it was unusual from a historical perspective. I could have sworn I saved that article here somewhere . . ."

Chris walked over to the polished display cabinet and crouched down on his haunches, helping Mateo sort through the old papers. He lifted up a glossy booklet from the pile of torn black-and-white clippings.

"Is this it?" Chris asked.

"*¡Eso!*" Mateo exclaimed, grabbing the magazine from Chris's hands.

I walked over to where both men were huddled and sat down on the oval carpet, the knotted navy and red spirals fraying at the seams.

Mateo handed me the magazine.

"Emilia Lorena Zayas, wife of Osvaldo Vidal Morales, adopts baby boy," I read aloud, translating for Chris.

The thin hairs on my arm stood up.

"She really does look *exactly* like the nun," Chris gasped.

"Which nun?" Mateo asked.

"There was a nun who ran a girls' English-language school—"

"The Merici Academy?" Mateo interrupted. "Why is that significant?"

"Because my mom said a nun—who was also a nurse—kept the baby after she delivered him. He was too weak, too small, to travel."

Mateo's eyes grew wide.

"You think this . . . ?"

"Yes," Chris answered. "My guess is they're related. Maybe she gave the baby to her sister? Or to her cousin? Perhaps that's why they have the same maternal last name."

"Well, there's only one person who can tell us," I whispered, dejected as I looked down at the nun's photo. "And she's dead."

"Pero tu mama está viva," Mateo exclaimed, wrapping his arm around my shoulder. "Your mother is alive, and she can tell us if this is the same woman."

"You have to show your mother the photo, Lily," Chris agreed, gently placing the papers on the table. "That's the only way we'll know if any of this makes sense."

"But what if we're wrong?" I asked. "I don't have the heart to get her hopes up."

"Perhaps don't show her a photo of Osvaldo just yet. Just show her a photo of the nun. We need to know if we're even headed in the right direction."

"Así sabremos," Mateo added.

I stared at the pixilated photos in front of me.

Who were these women?

And who were they . . . to *me*?

CHAPTER 48

Marisol

Elk River, North Carolina
September 3, 1999

Marisol stared at the desktop screen in front of her.

The Elk River Public Library had a row of six donated computers, each with free internet for up to an hour. Marisol sat stiffly in the hard plastic seat.

No one else was in the vestibule this early in the morning . . . except for Kem.

Her husband twisted his plaid newsboy cap between his hands, his elbows resting on his knees as he sat by the window.

He was worried for her.

Kem knew there was an answer Marisol desperately needed that had forced her to take a morning away from the Mitchells, something she hadn't done in nearly forty years. Kem could sense her fear, her unspoken anxiety. He didn't know specifically what had caused it, but was sure that he wanted to be there to catch her if she fell.

Lily had called last night to say that she had found a name.

"I think we have a lead, Mami," she'd said over the phone, a faint clicking in the background.

Marisol wrapped her finger around the coiled cord of the receiver.

"There's a nun," Lily said. "I sent you a photo. *Se murió, ya,* but I found an obituary. Can you see if you recognize her?"

"*¿La monja?*" Marisol said in disbelief, a lump forming in her throat.

"*Sí,* Mami."

Marisol fought back tears.

Had she mentioned the nun to Lily when she recounted what happened? Marisol had thought about the nun over the years, seen her bright blue eyes framed by the thick white stripe of her habit, the silver medallion around her neck framed by three gold coins that dangled as she reached forward for Marisol's baby. The same necklace Marisol wore on her neck now. Marisol assumed the nun had been a mere agent in the misfortune of Marisol's rape, shuttling the malnourished baby to his early grave or to an uncertain future. But had she had a hand in his survival? Did she know where he was?

Marisol stared at the clunky white machine in front of her. She thought she had prepared herself for what Lily might find, but now, trembling as she gripped the computer mouse, she wasn't so sure.

Marisol took a deep breath and opened the attachment in her inbox. She waited for the image to download.

Within seconds, a grainy black-and-white photo filled the screen: a young nun wearing a black-and-white habit, her hand around three small children, standing in front of a school. A black medical bag rested at her feet; a pendant with three gold coins at her neck.

St. Nicholas. The Patron Saint of Children.

Marisol clutched her stomach.

Tears streamed down her face.

How had Lily found her?

After so many years, Marisol had begun to wonder if the nun was an apparition, a figment of her dehydration and despair the night of her labor.

But there she was, staring back at her, those same calm, piercing eyes that had pierced her heart so many decades ago.

Marisol placed her hand on the scuffed desk in front of her, steadying herself against the corner.

The nun was the only person in Marisol's sordid tale who knew whether her baby had lived or died.

Did the truth die with her?

But if Lily had found *her*, did that mean she had also found *him*?

Kem rushed to Marisol's side and reached for her elbow when he saw her struggle to stand. He wiped her cheek and walked her to the sunken couch in the corner of the small vestibule.

"Are you okay, Mari?"

He only wanted to know that she was well, that she was whole. Even after all these years, he granted her space for her own story.

Her own secrets.

But now, Marisol needed to share. She needed to feel the weightlessness of hope.

She knew with a certainty that she couldn't explain, the same instinct to trust the man who had escorted her off that boat so many lifetimes ago, that he would carry her forward once again.

With tears in her eyes, Marisol reached for her husband's hand. His veins now protruded with age.

"Kem," she whispered, "there's something I need to tell you."

CHAPTER 49

Lily

Havana, Cuba
September 5, 1999

The building looked like it was crumbling from the outside. Cracks ran up the edges of the yellow façade, stopping just short of the broad windows encased by ornate wrought-iron grills. We approached the entrance on the left, an open doorframe exposing a steep granite staircase.

I scaled the steps two at a time, feeling my thighs burn as I reached the top. Chris trailed behind me until we reached the roof of the building, a second-story patio with open-air seating. Servers in white aprons scurried past us shouting to men working in the kitchen. The restaurant was bustling with green potted plants everywhere and white café lights strung like clotheslines suspended above our heads. Colorful paintings adorned the walls, images of the Cuban flag re-created on distressed wood.

It was breathtaking: the vibrant décor, the attention to detail, the care that so many owners took to enhance what little space they had. This was a *paladar* my uncle had told me about, a privately owned restaurant above a home that still had to report its earnings to the government. Like so many things in this enigmatic city, it was a hidden gem.

"*¡Bienvenidos a ChaChá, Casa Caribeña!*" A woman holding two steaming plates paused as she passed by. "Take any open seat you can find."

"Shall we?" Chris said, pointing to a table by the balcony. We walked over to the concrete edge and peered over the railing, the side streets of Old Havana, alive and chaotic.

Chris pulled out my chair.

"*Gracias,*" I said, sliding beneath the small bistro table, the white tablecloth grazing my knees.

"*De nada,*" he answered, a sly smile at his attempt to learn Spanish. He unfolded the cloth napkin in front of him and put it in his lap. "So, are you ready for tomorrow?"

I let out a heavy sigh, the air from my lips sending the small flyaways on my forehead shooting up toward the sky. I rarely wore my hair in a bun, but the heat was so strong, the humidity so suffocating, I had to do anything to lighten my load.

"I'm not sure," I answered honestly. "But it's now or never."

My return flight was in two days and tomorrow I was set to meet Osvaldo. After finding out where he worked—the government building in Old Havana that housed the Ministry of the Interior—I staked it out like I did during the early days of the Simpson trial. I went old school, channeling all the tactics dramatized in the movies, ones I'd sheepishly employed when I was a freelance stringer trying to get my start. I put on my sunglasses and pulled out an issue of that day's *Juventud Rebelde,* sitting on a bench that faced the entrance of the government building, hoping to look inconspicuous.

I spent hours in the hot sun, only the shade of a tree to keep me cool, my once cold bottle of *Ciego Montero* warm to the touch.

There, I waited.

And waited.

Until finally, I saw him.

Osvaldo Vidal Zayas, Jr., the man I'd spotted standing behind the president at the government briefing, the man who was hard to find, and the man who had very little about him written in the papers.

The man I believed was my brother.

As soon as he exited the building, I sprung from the bench and tried not to draw attention to myself. I tossed the paper into the waste bin and shielded my eyes from the sun as I crossed the street. Osvaldo stepped out onto the sidewalk and ruffled through the papers in his briefcase, searching for something.

Just as he looked up, I bumped into him.

"*Ay, perdón*," I said, taking off my glasses.

He looked startled and tried to regain his composure.

"*No pasa nada*," he mumbled, adjusting his bag over his shoulder.

Just as he started to turn, I grabbed his arm. Forcefully. With my free hand, I placed a note inside his open palm.

His eyes grew wide.

We looked at each other.

Then, I jogged away, heading down the sidewalk toward the *Capitolio*, disappearing into the throngs of tourists crowding the main square.

Now, I just had to wait.

"Did the handoff go well?" Chris asked, bringing me back to the present.

"We'll see tomorrow," I smiled nervously. "Hopefully I dropped anyone on my tail. Otherwise, he'll never come."

It was well-documented that tourists and journalists on special travel licenses were followed by plainclothes officers. The phones in their hotels and *casas particulares* were often tapped, their letters opened and scanned. That's why we had to turn over our passports upon checking into any bed-and-breakfast—including to Yoanka—so the employees could send details of our lodging, activities, and departure dates to the government.

As if they didn't have it already.

I had heard the clicking on the phone when I tried to call my mother, which is why I started calling from a small café with black market internet in the San Isidro artist's district that my uncle recommended. He said this particular café was designed for people "searching for discretion," something he said he knew intimately given his own "lifestyle."

Still, that privacy wasn't enough. I saw men—sometimes the same ones—casually lingering outside our guest house when Chris and I were having our morning coffee. They'd stand against the light post, leaning and smoking a cigarette, pretending not to look in my direction.

Who knew for sure if they were sent there to watch me, but what I *did* know, was that the Cuban government closely monitored foreign journalists, and more specifically, the people with whom those journalists spoke. I legally had to record the names of each interviewee and keep a copy of my notes, just in case I was asked for them upon departure.

And that was just for the Cuban government.

For the U.S. government, I was required to keep a record of every dollar I spent to prove that I was supporting privately owned restaurants, not establishments directly funded by the Cuban government. By law, I had to keep those notes for up to ten years should the U.S. government ever ask to see them.

Which meant, who knew who was following *me*—and as a military official, who knew who was following *Osvaldo*.

With all these thoughts swirling in my head, I had asked Chris to take a tour of the *Museo Nacional de Bellas Artes* while I went to meet Osvaldo, hoping Chris would be a distraction to whoever was on my trail.

Divide and conquer.

"I think he'll show up tomorrow," Chris reassured. "The universe wouldn't let us come all this way and do all this digging just to have nothing come of it. Plus," he said, scanning the plastic menu in front of him, "we both need a win right about now."

There it was: the unspoken sadness that had catapulted us on this journey, the thing we had both avoided discussing since that afternoon on the porch.

"Listen, Chris . . ."

"Please don't," he interrupted.

"Don't what?"

"Don't finish that statement."

"How do you know what I was going to say?"

"I don't. But I have a feeling it is some caveat—some disclaimer—about the time we've spent here together. Whatever it is, please just let me live in this moment. I need it. I am forty-eight hours away from returning to an empty home, a cruel twist of fate after these past several weeks, just as I've finally begun to feel myself reinflate, to resurface, to come up for air."

I looked down, clutching the mojito that had arrived at our table, its beads of condensation dripping down the sides of the glass.

Chris struggled to finish his thoughts.

"For a few brief moments—walking along the Malecón at night, finding a name in an obscure newspaper, seeing your uncle's eyes light up when you appear at his gate—I've felt like I had a purpose, like I had a mission. Like I was somewhere that felt like . . . home."

I knew exactly what he meant. The truth was, I had felt at home, too: sweating beside strangers in the back of a *maquina*, sandwiched between bodies jostling over potholed streets on our way to rifle through dusty pages in the national library; the taste of fresh guava juice on my lips, the familiar horns of *timba* floating through open windows, wet shirts strung between patios, dangling in the breeze.

All of it felt like home, even though I had never been here before.

And then, there was Chris.

This once mysterious college acquaintance—quiet and sarcastic—turned husband of my best friend. The man who silently watched soccer games in busy bars, who left Hana and I two Tylenol and a cold glass of water after long nights at the pub. I had never really gotten to know him before. Or, had I simply just "known" him all along?

When I looked up, Chris was staring back at me.

"Me too," was all I could manage to say.

Suddenly, the small quartet that had been tuning its instruments began to play, the first three chords of Mirta Silva's "*El Que De Mas Se Muere*." The familiar melody made me smile. My mother always played La Soñora Matancera when she cleaned.

"Everything comes to an end, I suppose," Chris added with a sad smile. "At least this time, I'm confident the ending will be good."

Chris drained the last of his mojito, the bright green mint leaves curling inward as the ice cubes shifted to the bottom.

"We'll get what you came for, Lily. I promise."

CHAPTER 50

Osvaldo Jr.

Havana, Cuba
September 7, 1999

I sat in the back of the dusty tobacco shop, not sure why I was there. Did I believe her? This woman who claimed she knew me? Knew *of* me?

The note simply read: "Your mother has been searching for you. *Prado Puros,* 7 p.m. Come alone."

Two days ago I was leaving my office, daydreaming of a new life just ninety miles away. I had just loosened my collar, the stiff lapels they forced us to wear pinching the skin around my neck, skin that I'd recently noticed had become more slack with age.

Forty-one.

That's the age when they stop sending suitors and start asking questions.

I had just stepped onto the sidewalk in front of the Ministry of the Interior building, posters of Ché, Martí, and Fidel nailed to the outer wall. I reached deep inside my briefcase searching for my key, hoping I hadn't left it inside my desk.

That's when I felt her.

A stranger slammed into me, almost knocking me to the ground.

A woman.

As soon as I stumbled back she steadied me, placing one hand on my shoulder, the other pressing a folded letter into the center of my palm. For one expectant moment, we looked at each other. Then, as suddenly as she'd appeared, she jogged away.

A chill ran down my spine.

Had I seen her before?

I caught the back of her faded gray T-shirt as she turned the corner behind a colonial brick building. She looked taller than most women here, almost like a foreigner.

Had anyone witnessed her handoff? There must have been a reason she gave it to me the way that she did. I quickly slipped the letter inside my pocket so as not to draw attention, just like they had taught us in training. I never knew when the higher-ups were watching; they always sent *palacio* reports from the field, detailed logs of their most valued personnel.

Unfortunately, I was one of them.

I walked the seven blocks back to my apartment in *Centro Habana,* leaving the chaos of downtown behind me. The door creaked as I opened it, my cat Gonzo scurrying between my legs. His purring got louder as I placed my keys in the shallow dish in the shape of a shell that I kept at the entrance.

My mother had given it to me.

At least, the only mother I had known.

Safely tucked inside, I leaned against the back of the door and pulled my hand out of my pocket, the letter coming with it. On the front of plain white notepad paper, almost like the paper torn from the notebooks we were forced to use in school, the woman had written the name of a tobacco shop and a time to meet her. I knew the shop well, it was nestled inside San Isidro—the artists' district—with a private room in the back. I had been there before, seeking anonymity.

I turned the paper over in my hand.

How had she found me? And how could she possibly know the truth about my mother?

I dabbed at the skin just above my brow with a silk handkerchief, trying to calm my nerves. My mind started racing. Was this a trap? Was one of my father's old comrades tapping my line? Could the man I recently spent a night with have shared our secret with the wrong people? Or worse, had someone found out about my failed plans to leave for Miami?

If so, it was over for me.

I would disappear without a trace, locked inside the bowels of the infamous *Combinado del Este* prison I have never seen but have always known existed.

Which is why I wasn't sure what finally made me gather enough courage or curiosity to meet the mystery woman two days later. Perhaps it was recklessness. Or hope?

I showed up early and sat quietly in the corner of the shop to see if anyone had followed me. After nervously watching the slow drip of customers make their way inside, I stood to leave, having decided the risk was simply too great.

Just then, the same tall woman with curly hair walked into the shop.

"Hola, Osvaldo. ¿Como te va?" she asked, immediately pulling out the chair across from me. "Thanks for coming."

My name on her tongue stopped me in my tracks. Why did it sound so . . . familiar?

I lowered my body once again, taking my seat.

"Sin problema," I replied. "I read your note." Switching to English, I took a look around, checking to make sure no one else was seated nearby.

"Dale, pues, gracias por venir," she replied, returning to Spanish. *"Soy Liliana."*

Where was she from? Her Spanish was strong but unfamiliar, as though she might have grown up around someone Cuban but wasn't native to the island herself.

I watched as she swiped the loose curls away from her face, tucking them behind her ear. She shifted uncomfortably in her seat.

"*Bueno*. I've certainly never done this before and I'm not quite sure where to start." She paused. "But," she resumed, taking a deep breath, "I think you are my brother."

I stared at her.

"*¿Tu hermano?*" I repeated, making sure I heard her correctly.

"*Sí*," she said evenly, looking me directly in the eye.

My heart pounded inside my chest. I could feel the thick vein throbbing in my neck.

"*Pero* . . . how?" I managed.

"My mother. Well, our mother. I think she left you behind—was forced to leave you behind—when she fled."

"Fled," I repeated. "When?"

She looked up at me hesitantly.

"Nineteen fifty-seven," she replied.

She was waiting to see if the year registered with me. Of course it did, but I wasn't ready to give anything away.

"I think she gave birth to you in captivity. She was a political prisoner in *El Príncipe* prison in 1957 after the attack on *Radio Reloj* and the presidential palace."

My stomach dropped.

A political prisoner.

Sensing my shock—or perhaps, recognition—she pounced.

"May I ask," she proceeded politely, "who your mother was?"

"She died," I answered simply.

"From what?" she asked again quickly, all pretenses of gentility gone. Her urgency gave her away.

She needed this.

"A brain tumor," I answered. "But you already knew that. You were able to find me outside of my office. Which means if you found me, you already know who I am . . . and who my mother was." I paused, looking up at her.

She leaned forward and folded her hands on the granite tabletop between us.

"That's correct," she conceded. "But that's not what I asked."

I looked up at her, surprised. Who was this girl? Direct. Perhaps a bit rude.

"Was she your biological mother?" she continued. "The woman who raised you?"

"I don't believe so," I admitted, staring at my freshly shined shoes. She had me cornered. Any good military man knew the first rule of battle was knowing when to admit defeat.

"What *do* you know?" she asked.

I blinked. I had never spoken the words aloud, never said what my mother told me that night on the balcony, staring at the palace from the second story of our now-empty apartment. But something about this girl, something about her desperation, told me this was different.

Something was about to change.

"My mother said that her sister found me, that she had rescued me from a woman who was too sick to carry me," I started, the words trying to find their way out.

"Who was her sister?"

"A nun. A nurse. She worked at a girls' school and ran an orphanage on the side for girls who got . . . in trouble."

"The Merici Academy?"

How did she know all of this?

"Yes," I conceded. "But she kept me off the books."

"Why?"

"Because the girl was escaping something. If the man who had put her in that position found me, he would have taken me."

"Do you know who he was?"

"I don't. Not personally, at least. He worked for Batista. My aunt told my mother that he ran the prison at *El Príncipe* and it was clear to her that he had fathered the child of a prisoner. Of *that* prisoner."

Hearing this, the woman looked like she was about to cry.

"When did you find out?"

"What do you mean?" I asked.

"*¿Quién te explicó todo esto?* Who told you all this?"

"Actually, it was my father."

She leaned back in her chair, confused.

"My father told me the story days before he died, too drunk to know what he was saying. He did a lot of things during the Revolution—bad things, complicated things—for both Castro and for himself. Those acts alone cost him his dignity and his conscience. Through it all, I don't think he could ever quite swallow the fact that he had to raise a baby that wasn't his own. He had no legitimate heir, as he saw it, to make all his sacrifice worth it."

I paused, making sure the girl was still paying attention, that she was able to follow the details of a story that had taken me almost two decades to comprehend, and even longer to believe.

"When I was seventeen, the day before I was headed out for military service, he and my mother got into an argument. She had come to my father begging, asking him to re-establish the school where her sister had worked. It was the only girls' school in the city and Castro had closed it, part of the wave of religious organizations being nationalized under the new government. But that school was my aunt's life, it was all she knew. So when my mother screamed at him, telling my father he had to help, *se volvió loco*. It was the final straw. He told my mother he wouldn't do one more thing for *esa solterona* who had saddled him with a traitor's baby. My mother wept, but that didn't stop the bullets flying from his mouth."

I shifted uncomfortably, the truth of that night still hurting to think about.

"It was her fault, my father told my mother, that she couldn't fulfill the only thing she was put on this earth to do: give him a child of his own."

The girl stared at me, her eyes wide and stunned.

"Was it true? They never had a baby of their own?"

"*Sí,*" I whispered. "After my father stormed out, I went to where my mother sat on the balcony, weeping. She was tired of hiding, too tortured seeing what secrets could do when kept inside. She told me that I was never hers—and I was never his—biologically, anyway. And perhaps not legally."

"What do you mean?" the girl asked, leaning forward in her chair, her elbows resting against the cramped café table.

"*Pues, me confirmó todo.* She said it was all true: her sister was a nun and a nurse here in Havana. She enrolled in nursing school at Calixto García hospital and began doing rounds at the prison. One night, she ended up delivering the baby of one of the women she had treated. The birth mother had obviously been raped. The baby was weak and malnourished. The woman had to escape and, knowing that her sister could not have children and that the baby had no home, my aunt gave the baby to my mother after she nursed it back to health. My mother, in turn, kept the 'adoption' mostly a secret, save for an article in *Bohemia*. She felt fine speaking about adoption generally, because she never said *where* she had gotten the baby from and never implicated her sister. Plus, she assumed she would also have her own biological children one day. But she and my father tried everything to conceive, to no avail. My father, feeling increasingly helpless as a doctor himself, took out their misfortune on her."

A tear rolled slowly down the woman's cheek. Was this the answer she had been looking for? The confirmation she sought?

"To make matters worse, after years of hiding and a lifetime of lying, my father decided the baby—this baby—wasn't worth the hassle."

"You?" she asked.

I nodded.

I thought back to the night my father died, seeing my mother weep over his cold, stiff body. She was conflicted in some sense, unsure how to feel.

But I wasn't.

I knew that when he died, so did my dreams of escape.

Men like me don't live freely in Cuba.

We hide in the shadows until we are outed or killed.

My father knew it, too.

By then, I'd been working in the Ministry of the Interior since he had forced me there after graduation. I spent my days in a run-down office, toiling in the department that Castro reimagined in 1961 to ensure security and "public order." I was responsible for implementing the ideals of the revolution in all our domestic enterprises—from schools and hospitals to the military. I had already been fast-tracked, the high-ranking son of a favored doctor.

Which meant once my father died, all eyes turned to me. They were waiting to see what I did next, how I was going to fulfill the expectations of my new role. Worse, I worked directly with the people who, if I made a genuine attempt to flee, would hunt me down. I had become too close to the nucleus of power.

It was then that I realized that even in death, my father had trapped me with his expectations. The man who hadn't even given me life had suddenly taken it away.

I had accepted this, resigned myself to the monotony of a predestined life until this girl with the perfect posture sitting across from me had handed me a cryptic note. Now, she was slumped in her chair, the truth of my words puncturing her once-inscrutable demeanor.

"En pocas palabras," I concluded. "I was not the son my father wanted. I was just the one who fulfilled his duty."

The girl looked like she was about to cry again.

"But she does," she whispered quietly.

"Who?" I asked.

"My mother. She wants you. She has never been whole since she boarded that boat, since she left you behind."

Now, tears filled my own eyes.

I swallowed hard, trying to catch my breath.

I looked up to meet the woman's gaze.

"¿Cómo se llama?" I asked, hoping not to show the gaping wound that was my heart, the worms of painful truth that her words had just pulled out of me. "What is your mother's name?"

"Marisol," the woman answered. "Mari."

"Well, Liliana." I took a deep breath. "Tell Marisol she has already forgotten the first rule of being Cuban: we never regret the things we must do to survive. Marisol did the only thing she *could* do to stay alive—and to save me."

I gathered my briefcase and stood to leave.

My head was spinning.

I couldn't handle more truth, more tears.

"Tell your mother I am sorry for the horrors she suffered. My life is her absolution."

I looked again at the young woman sitting across from me, perhaps fifteen years my junior. Taking her in on the other side of her revelation felt like seeing her for the first time. Her curls were strong and bountiful, her eyes deep and penetrating. Her skin was copper-colored, darker than mine. And while my own hair was more blond than brown, my eyes a deep shade of green—the girl did look familiar.

Not unlike me.

"May I?" she asked, reaching for my hand.

I stood beside the small bistro table, frozen.

"I would like to start over," she smiled through glassy eyes. "*Soy Liliana*, your sister."

A single tear rolled down her cheek.

"And I would like for you to meet our mother."

PART FOUR

TWO YEARS LATER

CHAPTER 51

Lily

London, England
May 25, 2001

"Please fasten your seatbelts as we prepare for landing," the flight attendant announced as the plane jolted forward. "There is unexpected turbulence in our approach to Heathrow."

Heathrow Airport.

It had been two years since I last made my way to London.

What a difference those years had made.

I looked down at the thick book in front of me, grabbing it just before it slid off the tray table. A black-and-white picture of Rodney King's jailhouse booking photo stared back from the cover. A billowing American flag was splashed beneath the title: *We Hold These Truths: The Complicated Legacy of Freedom and Equal Protection Across the Americas*.

I turned the book over and stared at the author's photo on the back: smile bright, wild curls framing a slender face with thin glasses.

Liliana Soto Walker.

I had finally published my first book, a compilation of interviews, photojournalism, and historical research on the Civil Rights

Movement and the complicated myths and unlikely heroes that emerged. It was academic catnip. Francie had pushed me to collect all my published stories into a single work (her, of course, taking twenty percent of the publishing proceeds).

And I'll be damned, it worked.

My book was a niche, scholastic success sold in universities across the country. Professors purchased copies by the hundreds, hoping to showcase the post–Civil Rights Movement through the eyes of firsthand witnesses. Because of the book's broader focus on the Americas, no one was more surprised than me when HarperCollins asked for the U.K. rights for its scholastic publications, hoping to use it as a tool to teach—and rework—the international curriculum on American history.

Which is why I was seated in seat 1F headed to London. I was holding a talk at the London School of Economics about the racial reckoning of the nineties and what civil rights looked like in this new millennium. Would there be more moments like the 1992 Los Angeles riots—moments of injustice that set the world on fire? That reminded people why the populations that had been left behind were still fighting?

As much as this book was a win for me professionally, it was, more notably, a personal triumph.

It was closure.

I looked out the window as the gray London skyline approached. The leaves had changed colors, the snow had come and gone.

And I still thought of him every day.

I couldn't believe that so much time had passed since I'd last said goodbye.

To him, to her . . . to all of it.

I played the scene over in my mind every time I closed my eyes: my mother meeting her only son, her lost child. There, on the shores of Miami, I watched her become whole again: whole in a way I had never seen my mother, whole in a way I wasn't sure she could be repaired.

Maybe that's what redemption does.

Nine months after I returned from Havana, I held my mother's hand as our plane descended at Miami International Airport, her second time flying since my graduation. She was nervous the entire flight, kissing her rosary beads and whispering prayers to a God she had long questioned and whose volition she rarely trusted. Her nerves got worse as she sat in the lobby of the Fontainebleau Hotel, spinning the bracelets on her arm and repinning the stray curls that had fallen into her face. She stared out of the floor-to-ceiling windows that overlooked the Atlantic Ocean, waiting. Anticipating.

That's when he walked in.

Osvaldo strode toward us, a smile spreading across his face as he tried to hide the tears that slid down his cheek. He looked tall and svelte, darker than I remembered, the deep cinnamon of his cheeks tanned from fresh sun, setting off the cool green of his eyes.

My mother stood up from the linoleum banquette where we were seated, her own eyes wide and disbelieving. Her birdlike shoulders folded in on themselves as tears erupted from her small frame. Reflexively, she reached for my hand to steady her.

Osvaldo closed the final distance between them, enveloping her in his arms.

"Mi hijo" was all my mother could manage to say, repeating the words again and again, a blessing and a summoning. She touched the sides of his face, felt the ringlets of his thick hair, unsure if she could trust the sight in front of her. He was a dream she had no longer dared to have.

Osvaldo dropped his heavy briefcase, his shoulders shaking with silent sobs.

This moment, I knew, standing on the white marble floor of the hotel, was as precious as it was fleeting. Osvaldo had managed to get to Miami for three days on a temporary work visa, promising his bosses in Havana several "high stakes" meetings with operators in Miami. He knew, as well as I did, that he would be watched and, most importantly, that he had to return.

I could tell from our calls—the several we had when I dialed the phone in the back of the tobacco shop—that Osvaldo desperately wanted to leave. He dreamt of Miami like every other Cuban with a dream and a dollar. But he also knew the reality: the regime would never let him out of its crosshairs. Osvaldo was too valuable. He was what Castro needed to inject a vision of youth and the promise of vigor into the dying battle cry of the Revolution. Without Castro's support, Osvaldo had no work visa, no job, and—at least on the international market—would be sullied by his high rank within a communist regime.

Which meant that he was stuck, like so many Cubans who had relinquished the dangling promise of freedom. It also meant that Osvaldo was forced to bear witness to the slow decay of the country he was promised, each dying layer revealing the cruelty of its limitations: compromised access to the internet, the denial of basic goods and services, fresh food the average Cuban couldn't afford. Osvaldo had come of age when the dream of what Cuba was—and of what it could be—was still being crafted; he saw both its intention and what greed had kept it from becoming.

Standing there in the center of that lobby wrapped in his mother's arms, Osvaldo knew—as well as I did—that this was the first, and likely the last time, he would see his mother. The officials who paid his bills would sooner see him dead than living free on the shores of Miami.

I wiped my eyes, the bitterness of that truth settling like a rock in my stomach.

But Mami didn't know that.

At least not yet.

Our only job was to protect her in those few precious moments, allow her to delight in the impossible becoming possible.

My mother pulled away from Osvaldo's arms, grabbing both sides of his face, squeezing his cheeks with her open palms.

She touched the silver medallion around his neck, the three gold coins at the bottom, matching her own.

"He kept his promise," she whispered, still staring at Osvaldo in disbelief.

"*¿Cuál promesa?*" Osvaldo asked, a tear falling from his eye.

I watched them quizzically.

My mother just kept staring at Osvaldo, her eyes sweeping over his curly blond hair, round nose and full lips, landing finally upon his eyes.

Those big, green eyes.

"He said he'd never leave," she whispered. "And look at you," she murmured, running her fingers along his jaw, where a tiny scar in the shape of a "v" sat just below his ear. "He kept his promise. He didn't leave."

"Who?" I asked.

But as soon as the question left my lips, I felt the truth of the answer before she even spoke.

Why hadn't I seen it before?

"*Tu papá,*" my mother smiled, looking directly at Osvaldo. "José Antonio Echeverría."

The calm that came over my mother that day stretched into the days and months that followed. I watched silently as she found pieces of herself, collecting them slowly and steadily.

She and Osvaldo spoke every week without fail. Sundays were their night to call, just like they had been when she called me in college.

And they began writing letters.

My mother told me on the plane when we returned from Miami that she was grateful she hadn't known all those years that Osvaldo was José's son. If Batista's men had found out, they would have had no incentive to keep her alive, she explained, and if *she* had known, it would have made their years apart that much more unbearable, knowing the child born of her first love was in the world, unmoored, without either of his parents.

Now, as I listened to her musings—stories about her childhood and homeland that flowed with greater ease—I saw a different version of my mother emerge: wistful, contemplative. Content, even. With each story she recounted, she reconnected with a piece of herself.

And, if I'm honest, with me.

I saw myself, for perhaps the first time, in her reflection. I saw the woman she had wanted to become—free and curious, fierce and tender, open and expressive—but couldn't, trapped by circumstances not of her doing: a government that oppressed her expression, a revolution that stole her freedom, and a violation that shattered her innocence.

But in me—and perhaps through me—she had somehow found redemption.

Through Osvaldo, she had found absolution.

And so had I.

When the plane engine roared to a start as we departed from Miami that day, there was only one person I wanted to call.

I pulled out my brand-new Treo, the two miniature bars in the corner showing my wobbly cell phone reception. This was the corporate phone Francie had gifted me, the one perk she had conceded when I decided to keep my full-time job at NPR despite the independent success of my book.

My mother sat solemnly beside me, staring out the window, no doubt still processing everything that had just happened.

But I couldn't wait.

The phone rang twice before he answered.

"Hello?" his baritone voice resonated through the receiver.

"It was José," I blurted out without pause or preamble.

"Lily?" I could hear him smiling through the line. "What was that about José?"

"He is Osvaldo's father. My mother knew as soon as she saw him. It was never her rapist."

Chris inhaled sharply.

"My God." I could hear his wheels turning even through the phone—the implications of silence, of grief, of a decades-old assumption—shattered.

"I need to see you," I said plainly.

"I would quite like that," he answered.

CHAPTER 52

Chris agreed to pick me up from the airport when I arrived for my speech.

Since our return from Havana two years prior, we had talked almost every week, catching up on work, reminiscing about our trip, planning another time when we might find ourselves in the same city. He had resumed his job with the professional Chelsea Ladies Football Club and was recently promoted to head coach.

Over the phone he sounded happy and settled, more like the Chris I had met in college and more like the Chris who began to re-emerge in Havana. The players had been ecstatic when he returned from his bereavement leave, even renting a storage truck to help him move out of the house he'd shared with Hana and into a flat of his own in Westminster. He was enjoying his new bachelor life and, I suspected, perhaps even beginning to date.

The cabin speaker chimed overhead as the pilot welcomed us to London.

I still couldn't believe my fortune.

Here I was, a girl who had taken her first plane ride in college, now sitting in business class, invited to speak about her expertise in journalism, a "hobby" she had never dreamed could become a profession.

I gathered the briefcase I had purchased in the JFK departures terminal, hoping to look more professional, and stuffed the notes for my speech in its outer pocket. I squeezed between the disembarking passengers and maneuvered into the aisle, making my way down the familiar jet bridge.

As soon as I exited customs, there he was.

"Is that you, Miss Walker?" Chris shouted from the sea of expectant faces, standing a full head above the crowd. "May I have your autograph?" he asked, louder this time, happily registering my embarrassment.

"The one and only!" I echoed back, laughing as my unwieldy briefcase slowed my pace.

Chris leaned against the metal barricade that separated arriving passengers from their waiting loved ones. He held a bouquet of tulips in one hand.

My favorites.

Had I mentioned that before?

Chris stood serenely, wearing a wool, double-breasted coat the color of caramel. He had a silk cream scarf wrapped loosely around his neck, looking like a European version of his former self. Tailored, assured, posh.

He extended his arms to welcome me into a hug, smelling like fresh pine and Old Spice. It was the same smell I had always noticed whenever we left our *casa particular* in Havana, a reminder that beneath the new silk threads and buttoned collar, he was the same guy I remembered.

The one I still thought of daily.

"Long time no see," I said, blushing. Why was I suddenly struggling to make eye contact?

"May I?" he asked, reaching for the briefcase that hung on my shoulder.

I jumped slightly at his touch.

"Yes, of course." I smiled as he tucked my bag beneath his arm.

"These are for you," he said, handing me the tulips. "I figured every debut author deserves her favorite flower."

I curtseyed in jest and accepted the bouquet.

"Let's grab a bite to eat, shall we? I know just the place."

Chris held the door as we walked into a tiny restaurant on High Street. As soon as we entered, I was transported to 1920s Havana, horns blaring, a live band playing in the corner. Thick cigar smoke billowed from the tiny patio attached to the back of the restaurant, the door cracked open as waiters zipped between the tables, speaking the fast, round Spanish that reminded me of my mother.

It was heaven.

"How did you find this place?" I asked, marveling at the miniature potted palm trees stretching from all four corners.

"A little luck and a lot of searching," he smiled. "Plus, someone once told me I was a pretty good research assistant."

I laughed.

"*Bienvenidos,*" an older gentleman in a white guayabera beamed, appearing with two menus.

Just as I was about to answer, Chris put his hand on my shoulder.

"*Buenas tardes, compadre. ¿Una mesa para dos, por favor?*"

My jaw dropped in surprise.

"Right this way," the waiter responded.

My mouth was still open as we made our way to the table.

Chris pulled out my chair, and as soon as I sat down and the waiter departed, he burst into laughter.

"*¿Qué?*" he asked in an exaggerated shock. "You didn't know I could speak Spanish?"

I shook my head in disbelief. "I leave you alone for two years and you learn my mother tongue?" I reached across the table and playfully hit his shoulder. "When did that happen?"

"*Bueeeeeeeno,*" he answered with a perfect Cuban accent. "It's amazing what lots of Rosetta Stone and the will to impress a beautiful girl can do."

I nearly spilled the ice water in front of me.

Impress a girl? Was I the girl?

"Are you coming to my talk tonight to show off your perfect Spanish?" I asked, trying to divert the attention.

"I wish I could," he answered. "But we have a preseason dinner with the team at the owner's house. Otherwise you know I wouldn't miss it."

Sensing my disappointment, Chris reached across the table and touched my cheek, tilting my face up to meet his. "But how about I pick you up first thing in the morning and we hit the town? Visit the old haunts?"

His hand felt nice against my cheek.

The offer was even more enticing. Hours with him alone to just . . . *be?*

It sounded perfect.

"Can't wait," I answered.

Chris held the menu in his hands, making a big show of reading the items.

"So"—he paused—"how does it feel to be back where it all fell apart?"

I had missed the way Chris always cut straight to the heart of things.

Straight to the heart of me.

I fidgeted with the white cloth napkin in my lap, staring at the colorful paintings on the wall. I was feeling anxious about my talk and sad about revisiting the sites that would inevitably remind me of Hana.

And Chris.

The truth was, I couldn't make sense of the feelings that had been tugging at my heart since I landed.

Or more honestly, since Havana.

With each conversation Chris and I had on the phone, my feelings became inescapable: I looked forward to our calls, found myself feeling giddy when I saw his number on my caller ID, cleared my schedule whenever I knew he could talk.

Still, I felt conflicted, unsure of what all this meant—what all of this *could* mean.

Was it fair to want him?

I felt guilty and confused, drawn and attracted.

And yet, every time I was with him, I felt at peace. Our relationship guided me, it settled me. I relied on him.

Chris seemed to sense every thought running through my mind.

"Lily, all of this is unexpected. The confusion. The excitement. Hell, the guilt. None of this is easy. None of this is chartered territory. And yet, it makes complete sense."

Tears filled my eyes.

"How so?" I answered. "I'm pretty sure falling in love with your dead best friend's husband isn't how children's fairytales start . . ."

Chris reached across the table and put his hand on top of mine.

"No," he answered softly. "It is how adult stories—for those of us who have lived real lives with the scars to prove it—begin. It is where those of us who have the courage to start over and to love again, find hope."

I reached for my napkin and dabbed at the corner of my eye.

Had he felt this way all along?

Chris squeezed my hand.

"I have been waiting for six months to see you. Ever since you said you were coming back, I knew this was our chance. We have this thing—this ease—that flows between us. Perhaps it was always there and we just didn't know it. But maybe now, we take this shitty hand that we've been dealt—losing someone who meant more than either of us can put into words—and allow that love, that magic that she brought us, to repurpose itself."

At the mention of Hana, I lost all pretense of composure.

Tears streamed down my cheeks.

"Would she hate us?" I whispered, as the tears fell onto my empty plate.

"Lily," Chris murmured, stroking my cheek. "Deep down, you know the answer to that."

"Love is freedom," he said softly. "And love is finding home. Again."

CHAPTER 53

Ladies and gentlemen," the moderator began, "welcome to the symposium on postcolonial racial dynamics with our featured speaker, award-winning journalist Liliana Soto Walker, author of *We Hold These Truths*."

The crowd erupted into applause. I stared into the sea of faces, blinded by the studio lights reflecting off the glossy wood of the stage. This was a much bigger crowd than I had expected.

"Joining her to help us contextualize this history, we have two celebrated members of our own beloved faculty, our tenured professors of Western Economics and African-British studies."

Another round of applause.

I smiled, shifting my body to face the moderator.

He began with a series of questions about my most recent work, a look at the recent days of Fidel Castro's regime amidst rumors of his failing health. Specifically, he asked about Castro's emergence as a flawed and unlikely hero amongst corners of the Black diaspora.

"He was two things to two people," I began. "The myth of his heroism for race relations was borne from the truth of his actions outside the island—staying at Hotel Theresa in Harlem during his visit to the United Nations, meeting with Malcom X. But back home, on the island, he allowed inequality in his administration and throughout the country."

I continued my talk, pointing to slides of my interviews in Camagüey, older Cubans who called Castro the grandfather of Cuba. I flipped to the next page, a colorful photo of a young Cuban boy sitting against a tree. He pointed toward the State Council building that sheltered government officials who kept the fruits of the country's labor away from him.

Officials, like my brother.

I tried my best to stay focused, flipping through the slides as I told the stories of resistance gaining ground in Cuba's artistic community, some figures in the back standing to applaud from the shadows. I spoke for nearly half an hour, leaving another ten minutes for questions.

After several queries on the future of the island, the ongoing embargo and race relations in the United States, the moderator brought the symposium to a close.

"We can take one final question from the audience," he announced, moving to the edge of the stage. A shadow in the back of the room emerged, walking toward the microphone placed at the center of the aisle.

I raised my hand toward my brow to block the stage light, hoping to get a better view of the speaker. Still, I couldn't see anything.

I listened as the participant adjusted the height of the microphone stand.

"Now then," a familiar voice echoed through the auditorium. "This is a question for Miss Walker."

My stomach dropped.

The speaker stepped out of the shadow and into the beam of light that fell directly onto the microphone.

"Have you seen progress, say, since the nineties?" he smiled, pulling the microphone closer to his lips. "A chance, perhaps, for redemption?"

CHAPTER 54

I rushed off the stage as soon as the forum ended. A crowd was already forming by the podium, hoping for signed copies of my book. I quickly stuffed my notes back into my briefcase and snuck behind the thick velvet curtain, making my way down the dark corridor toward the exit. As soon as I reached the door, I heard him.

"I hope I didn't scare you," he whispered.

I froze.

Slowly, I turned around.

Vikram stepped forward, emerging from the shadow of the rafters.

He looked taller than I'd remembered; older, of course. Flakes of salt and pepper doused his hair. He wore a dark green tailored suit with a white shirt, his father's gold pendant hanging at the center of his open collar.

"What are you doing here?" I stammered.

The room felt like it was spinning.

"That's not quite the reaction I was hoping for," Vikram laughed nervously, "but perhaps the one that I deserve."

He took a step closer.

I could smell his cologne, the same mix of oud and aftershave.

The memories came rushing back:

The bed.

The dancing.

The phone call.

The baby.

"It's been . . ."

"Four years," Vikram answered.

I adjusted the strap of my briefcase over my shoulder.

"I saw you were giving a talk here and had to see you," he swallowed.

Silence.

"May I take you for coffee? Dinner perhaps?"

I could hear the nervousness in his voice.

"I don't know, Vikram . . ." I looked around, searching for an excuse to leave. "It's getting late, I just arrived today, the jet lag . . ."

"One drink," he insisted. "And if it's not as good as the Cambridge 'T' Shop, then you can leave. Immediately."

Memories of dirty snow and warm yellow streetlights flooded my mind.

I smiled weakly.

"One drink," I relented.

"One drink," he promised.

CHAPTER 55

My heart skipped a beat.

It was racing, really.

Vikram and I walked in near silence along Farringdon Road until we stopped at a bright burgundy sign with white block lettering swinging from an ornate iron rod: Bouchon Racine.

A French restaurant.

Vikram held the door open as I slipped past him into the foyer. The restaurant was charming, a cozy French bistro with enough activity to know the food was good, quiet enough to be intimate.

"Good evening, *monsieur,*" the *maître d'hôtel* greeted us. "Do you have a reservation?"

"Yes," Vikram answered. "Desai. Party of two."

My eyes grew wide.

Had he booked a reservation? Did he just assume I'd say yes? How long had he planned this little ambush?

"Right this way, *s'il vous plaît,*" the host said warmly as he ushered us toward a corner table in the back of the restaurant nestled between a fireplace and an exposed brick wall.

I counted the steps as I followed, trying to calm my nerves. Was I really about to break bread with the man who had stolen my heart and left me crying alone in a bathtub so many moons ago?

Vikram pulled out my chair as we arrived at our table. I waited for him to take his seat while the waiter started to pour two glasses of water.

Vikram held out his hand. "Sparkling, please," he said with a smile. "And a plate of limes on the side."

He remembered my order.

"*Oui monsieur*, right away." The waiter nodded, scurrying back to the kitchen.

Alone at last, Vikram leaned forward, resting both elbows on the edge of the table.

He stared at me for what felt like an eternity.

Neither of us said a word, locked in a tug of unspoken thoughts, the teeming silence saying more than we ever could.

And, perhaps, more than we ever did.

"Now then, Miss Walker," Vikram finally said with a heavy sigh. "Where shall we start?"

"I'd say at the beginning," I answered, trying not to let my bitterness betray me. I could feel the hurt welling inside, shards of memories crashing into me after so many years of stillness.

Of silence.

"How did you know I was here?" I asked.

"The Harvard Club," Vikram said simply, already anticipating my first question. "They have a partnership with the London School of Economics. Each month they send a list of featured guest speakers on the alumni listserv. Needless to say, I was surprised when I saw your name."

"Why were you surprised?" I asked defensively.

"Perhaps 'pleased' would be a more fitting word," he corrected, reaching for the glass of sparkling water. "I was surprised to see you this side of the Pond, but wholly unsurprised by your success."

Vikram ran his fingers along the embroidered tablecloth.

"You did it, Lily. You did everything you said you would."

Vikram smiled, looking at me with a tenderness—a knowing—that could only be described as pride. He knew more than anyone how badly I had wanted this future.

This present.

Vikram's eyes swept over me.

I leaned back in my chair and let him stare. I wanted him to see what I had become, what he had lost. My signature curls were swept back into a low chignon, loose tendrils framing my face. I hadn't straightened my hair since Hana's funeral, deciding that the world would have to reckon with the sign of the wild, free spirit that I carried inside. Small pearl earrings adorned my ears, ones I had purchased on my first trip to Fifth Avenue with my advance. I had lost significant weight since college, the toll of adulthood stripping me of the baby fat that once defined my hips and cheeks, now leaving a tall, willowy frame in its wake. I wore a black crepe-knit dress with a gold belt looped around my waist.

I could tell Vikram liked what he saw.

Tonight, I decided, I would set the pace.

"A glass of prosecco?" I ordered from the waiter who had appeared at my side.

"Let's make it a bottle," Vikram said with an assurance I immediately resented feeling attracted to. "We have half a decade to catch up on."

Peering at me over the pages of the wine list, Vikram ordered from the waiter in a smooth French that would have made Madame Carole proud. While he asked the waiter about the two highest-priced bottles and their origins, I quickly stole a glance in his direction.

He was even more handsome than before.

It was startling, really.

I had expected time to be unkind, turning him into one of those middle-aged men with pre-pattern balding and a slightly deflated tire around his waist.

But that, much to my surprise, could not have been further from the truth.

This Vikram seemed newer and fresher, a modern take on a familiar classic. His hair was longer, tapered subtly at the sides in the way that men who still cared about their vanity managed when they didn't want it to become obvious. His shoulders were broader than I remembered, rounded in a way that could only come from protein, intention, and hours at the gym before work. The muscles pulled at the white shirt beneath his suit, the high-quality sort that doesn't wrinkle when you fold it. His hands were well-kept, manly but clean; a simple gold ring catching the light on his index finger.

"So, Lily . . ." Vikram looked up as the waiter departed, the corner of his mouth turning up in a mischievous smile. "The last few years look like they have treated you well."

I leaned back in my chair.

"Why did you find me tonight, Vikram?" I asked bluntly.

Vikram laughed.

"We can't even wait for the wine?"

"Four years wasn't a long enough wait?" I shot back.

"Touché," he relented. Then, he took a pregnant pause and looked me directly in the eye. "I suppose I didn't think it was a good idea to reach out to the girl I couldn't stop thinking about, even after I was set to be married to someone else."

My heart raced.

Vikram watched me, trying to gauge my reaction.

"After my father died, everything changed," he continued, pouring from the chilled bottle the waiter had placed silently in the small bucket beside our table. "His heart gave out while he was on a site visit and I just couldn't imagine it."

"Imagine what?" I asked.

"That life. *His* life. I had given the pharmacy three years, but I felt like I was dying inside. After he passed, I knew it was my only shot to break free, so I started a small production company."

"Desai Destinations?" I said, half mocking, half in awe, remembering the company name he had dreamed of in college.

"Close," he smiled, twirling his champagne glass on the table. "Patel Productions. Named after my mother's family."

"Poetic," I conceded.

"Perhaps, but it was also more than I anticipated. One chapter opened, another one closed. Radhika couldn't understand why I wanted to change course, why I needed to abandon the stability I'd known, the stability I'd once offered. Here she was, about to walk down the aisle, and the man she was set to marry had just pulled the rug out from under her." Vikram smiled sadly at the absurdity of it all. "To her credit, she had been promised a life that I wasn't fulfilling. She had agreed to an arrangement and I wasn't meeting my end of the bargain."

I wasn't sure what to say.

What I *should* say.

"You didn't get married?" I asked.

"Worse: she said no at the altar."

I gasped.

"On the day of the wedding?"

"On the day of the wedding," Vikram repeated. "It was the scandal of the twenty-first century for the Yorkshire Desi community, and to this day, it is all anyone can talk about when you mention the year 1998."

We both laughed.

"My God, Vikram. Talk about going out with a bang."

"Precisely. Which is why I had to make it count."

"How so?"

"It became my first movie. Several months after the wedding, much to everyone's shock—and mostly to my own—my first film won an award from the British Academy of Film and Television Arts, based entirely on my account of the wedding and the months and years leading up to it."

"*Love Over Marriage . . .*" I whispered.

My mind flashed back to Hana's last visit to New York to see me, her first after I had finally gotten my own apartment. Eric had moved to Spain with Mario and Hana insisted that we go out to celebrate my first night of independence in Hell's Kitchen. She had chosen a movie at the new AMC Theater on 34th Street, one by a British filmmaker who the critics said "took a bold, interpretive look at arranged marriage."

I still remember the dread I felt as I trailed behind her, silently making our way into the dark cinema. I had never told Hana about the baby, or why Vikram and I had broken up. It was still too painful, too fresh, and I felt like I needed to keep the secret inside, afraid it would break me wide open if I let it out into the world.

But I had known about the film.

I, too, had seen the announcement in the alumni bulletin, a shiny, laminated pamphlet with his smiling photo under "New and Notable Alumni."

"I saw the movie with Hana before she died," I admitted to Vikram, who was watching me silently from across the table. "But I had no idea it was based on your real life. I couldn't bring myself to . . ."

My voice trailed off.

"You couldn't bring yourself to search the wedding announcements? Look me up on the world wide web?" Vikram smiled, taking a sip of his champagne. "I get it. Although I must confess, I searched for any mention of your name obsessively. I even invited Hana and Chris to the movie premiere in London just to learn any news about you."

I balked. Why hadn't she told me?

"They never came," Vikram added quickly. "Hana said she was quite busy and politely declined on their behalf. I figured, maybe, she wanted to show her loyalty to you by keeping her distance from me."

It *was* an act of loyalty.

In her own way, I imagined Hana had wanted me to see what became of Vikram, sensing that I was still broken inside. She probably wanted me to see a film that had shown a failed marriage, that proved, in some artistic way, the possibility of his regret. Had she known all along?

"At the time, I didn't realize sending that invitation would be the last time I communicated with her," Vikram continued. "I couldn't believe when I heard the news. I had no idea what she was battling."

"None of us did," I sighed. "But I think that was the point. She didn't want the fuss. It was perhaps the *only* time she didn't want the fuss."

We smiled sadly, staring down at the lace tablecloth between us.

"You know, I slipped into the back of the church during the funeral," Vikram said. "I didn't stay for long. I wanted to pay my respects, but I felt like I was intruding on something I wasn't really meant to be a part of. Plus," he swallowed, "I didn't want to risk seeing you. I wasn't ready."

I remember thinking my mind was playing tricks on me when I watched a slim figure in his likeness slip out the church doors.

He *was* there.

"Whatever happened to Chris?" Vikram continued. "I heard he took it really hard."

"He did. It was a pretty brutal couple of years for him. He worked, he traveled. But I think he might have found love again," I smiled softly.

"That's great!" Vikram exclaimed, reaching for the basket of bread at the center of the table. "A nice young lady from Côte d'Ivoire? Or from Belgium to make Mum happy?"

"From North Carolina, actually. Elk River."

Vikram started to smile, and then suddenly, I saw the realization spread across his face.

"Are you serious?"

The color drained from his cheeks.

"Quite," I said, taking a final sip of my champagne before putting the empty glass back down with more force than I anticipated.

"When . . . how . . ." Vikram stammered. "Was that before . . . I mean . . ." I watched as he fought to form a sentence.

"It just sort of . . . *happened*," I answered. "Chris and I had never gotten to know each other independently. But I suppose grief has a funny way of uniting people. After the sharpness of the shock began to subside and the dust began to clear, what was left standing in front of me was this whole new person, one I'd never actually had the chance to know, or frankly, the opportunity to really see."

"But Lily, how could you—"

"How could I *what*?" I challenged, the defensiveness breaking through my restraint. I knew dating my best friend's ex wasn't the stuff of romance novels. It probably seemed morally reprehensible to someone who didn't know Hana's personal plea to redefine "home," for mutual care, for infinite freedom.

But Vikram knew her.

And he knew me.

"It's just . . ." Vikram struggled to articulate his thoughts.

"Just *what*?!" I demanded, the sharpness in my voice catching me by surprise. "You weren't even there! You *left* me!" I shouted, my open palm hitting the table, the fork and knife rattling against my empty plate.

There it was.

The anger I had kept inside for so long, finally erupting.

Vikram looked down at his lap, his hands folded and still.

Was that a tear I saw forming at the corner of his eye?

"Why didn't you wait?" Vikram murmured, the emotion drained from his voice; exhaustion, pure and deep, left in its wake.

"Wait for what, Vikram?"

"Wait for *me*, Lily." He looked up. "Why didn't you wait for me?"

We sat in silence.

My heart raced, my chest rising with each sharp breath.

The waiter came by to take our order, but after taking one look at our faces, returned to the kitchen. The small appetizers we had ordered an hour ago, gone cold.

"I don't even know where to start . . ." I said. "What do I do with that information now, Vikram?"

"You're why I'm here, Lily. I want to start over. That is what I came here to tell you."

I stared back at him, unable to find words.

"I beg your pardon?" I managed. "Why *now*? That's the part I just don't get, Vikram. What made you look up today and suddenly decide to carpe *fucking* diem?"

"All of it, Lily!" he shouted, raising his voice for the first time. "When my dad died, I knew there was no way I could continue growing older with less happiness, just to keel over at my desk at sixty-five. That's not the life I want. It's not the life I deserve. And it's not the life that I've worked for . . ."

"But *you* made those choices," I seethed. "You chose *her*."

There it was.

My heart pounded. I stared at him, unflinching, waiting for an answer.

"Yes, well, choosing a partner is a bit like choosing a seat on the train, *innit*?" Vikram stared back at me, a deep sadness in his tormented eyes. "Everyone is heading in the same direction, and at some point, you just have to take a seat. You take a seat that's open, hopefully beside the friendliest passenger you see in that moment, in that car. And you commit."

"How romantic," I scoffed.

"Look, what do you want from me, Lily? That's the truth.

And don't forget the only model for marriage I've ever known is arranged. Hell, I didn't even realize I *had* a choice until I was twenty-three. And at that point, I thought there were probably two women I could have spent the rest of my days with: you and Radhika. With her, I could anticipate what life would be like, how she would fit into the structure of my life. She was safe and predictable. But in the end I couldn't do it, because . . ."

"Because *what*, Vikram?"

"Because of *you*!" he shouted.

Vikram let out a deep sigh of frustration, running his fingers through his hair.

"Listen, I can't get you out of my head, Lily Walker. I have never felt more alive than when we were together, taking late night walks from the library, dancing under the stars at Hana's wedding. I didn't have the courage then to imagine a life that was less prescriptive, less choreographed. I was simply too scared. And while I was too chickenshit then, I can't keep living like that now. I can't keep *surviving* like this, worlds apart. I want to take back the story that is rightfully ours and finish writing it. We owe that to ourselves. I have never felt that same magic, that spark, with anyone else ever since. Have you?"

Vikram reached for my hand across the table.

I wanted to move it. I knew that I should.

But I couldn't.

I sat there, frozen, his question hanging in the air between us.

I let his hand find its way inside mine, our fingers gently interlocking.

"What am I supposed to do, Vikram? You're so . . . late. We had a chance nine years ago in school. And then again at the wedding. In fact, we've had every opportunity to change our stars, to reclaim our destiny. And yet here we are, worlds apart, new destinies between us—*choices* between us," I sighed, tears pooling in my eyes. "Why didn't you just say something *then*, Vikram?"

"I did!" he moaned, exasperated. "I tried! Don't you remember me sniffling inside that damn tea shop like a bloody fool?"

"Stop it, Vikram," I said curtly, losing my patience. "It wasn't like I rejected you. I just had the heart to do what you couldn't, and say what you wouldn't. You would never have accepted me."

"Accepted you?" Vikram tore his eyes off our clasped hands and looked up to meet my gaze. "Why would you ever say something like that?"

"Because I'm Black!" I shouted. The couple at the table beside us turned to face me, the woman's face turning red.

I shifted uncomfortably in my chair, only now realizing the volume of my voice.

When I looked up, Vikram was still staring at me.

"My God," he said weakly. "Lily, is that what you thought?"

We were both quiet. I sat there, still, trying to read the look in his eyes.

Was this the first time Vikram had truly thought of this? That he was forced to confront the *fact* of race, and the chasm it left between us?

The shock on his face looked unmistakably genuine, the totality of his surprise catching me off guard.

"Yes, Vikram. All those times you talked about your family? The plans for Akshay's wedding? Your mom's pride at hosting the perfect Indian wedding with the perfect Indian bride? What do you think she was really saying? And what do you think *I* was hearing? I couldn't deliver that dream for her—and certainly not for you."

"But *I* didn't need that dream, Lily!"

"Yes, you did!" I lashed back at him, my eyes ablaze. "You did more than *need* it, Vikram, you *chose* it!"

A dry laugh escaped my lips.

"Isn't that what this is really all about? The fact that you needed it so badly that you fucked up your own life for it? And now you're upset about the price that you paid?"

Vikram pulled his hand away. The tears that had pooled in his eyes, finally falling. He looked shocked at the harshness of my words, punctured by their truth.

"I paid mightily, Lily. No one knows that better than me. But I was twenty-six. Just twenty-six!" he whispered, almost shrill, the side of his forehead throbbing. "Who isn't allowed some grace to grow? Especially when that life is the only one you've known? And to be fair, Lily, I don't think this"—he motioned to the space between us—"was ever about race—at least not for me. It was about culture. My family. Honor. Cohesion. Hell, I chose peace, Lily. I wanted a fucking *peaceful* life. I had already known enough turmoil watching my parents behind closed doors. I didn't want to rock the boat. Having the same culture meant an easier choice, which ultimately meant more peace. For everyone. So if race ever *was* part of the equation, I certainly didn't think of it as a rejection of *your* race, I was simply embracing my *own*."

I blinked, tears filling my eyes.

The truth was, I understood him.

His answer was honest.

"Still, why do all of that for your parents? For their approval?" I asked, this time softening. "Was it worth it? You always talked about the struggle of their dynamic. I'll never forget us sitting on the lawn after class when you called it 'dutiful but joyless.' Why on earth would you want to repeat that?"

"Because it was a dynamic that *worked*, Lily. They finished this life together, didn't they? They built a system, a family, a unit. They didn't have the passion that we grew up seeing in Western movies, but they had stability. And that's something they valued more."

"Well if it worked so well, what's the problem? It sounds like that's what you had with Radhika."

"Because it wasn't enough for *me*, Lily. I've seen the alternative. And now I can't unsee it. My parents never knew what romantic love looked like, what it felt like. They never knew what it was to have my heart stop, simply because your hand grazed mine. They never saw the contagion of your happiness, the way my own feet would move, just watching you dance in the library at midnight. They never knew what it was to be riding atop a goddamn elephant on your wedding day, hoping that if you just closed your eyes, the woman you really wanted to spend the rest of your life with would be there when you opened them. But *I* do. And if you believe in redemption, Lily, then you have to believe in me. In us. Just because we didn't get it right once . . . or even twice . . . doesn't mean our story isn't written in the stars the way it's meant to be. It took us a while to get here, perhaps, but we still have our whole lives in front of us. What if this is just the beginning? *Our* beginning?"

Hot tears streamed down my face. This time, I didn't try to hide them.

My hand found its way back into his, underneath the table, gripping harder with each word as if it were quicksand slipping through my fingers.

"Vikram . . ." I started.

Vikram looked at me pleadingly. He could tell there was something bigger left to say; his instinct for me was still intact.

"There was a baby."

"What baby?" he asked.

"After the wedding. After our night in London," I swallowed. "There was a baby."

Vikram's eyes bulged. "*My* baby?" he repeated in disbelief.

"*Our* baby," I answered with finality.

Vikram began to cry.

"Where is . . ."

He couldn't finish the question.

"I lost it. Shortly after I found out."

"Why didn't you tell me?" he asked, crestfallen.

"Because last you told me, you were building a life. A new one that didn't include me. And I wasn't going to beg to be someone's consolation prize just because circumstances had changed. Love is freedom, Vikram. And I loved you enough to let you be free to make your own choices."

"But you didn't *give* me a choice, Lily," he whispered. "By not telling me, you *took* my choice."

I looked down at my hands, suddenly feeling ashamed.

The *maître d'* came by our table, finally building up the courage to interrupt us after seeing our plates still untouched.

"Respectfully, *messieurs,* if you are not going to dine a full course with us this evening, may we kindly ask that you visit us on another occasion?" He pulled the check swiftly out of his vest pocket.

Vikram placed a handful of cash on the table.

"Vik, let me . . ." I started.

"Please," he said, holding up his hand. "Let's skip this dance, shall we? We both know I would never let you pay, and we also know all your Southern mores would judge me to hell if I did."

I set my napkin on the table and smiled. "Thank you," I said simply.

"Let's get out of here." Vikram wiped his eyes with his napkin and came around the table to pull out my chair.

We left the café, heading north with no direction, the silence between us this time shifting back into something comfortable and familiar. I could feel Vikram leaning into my body, his steps matching my own, our shoulders touching.

Vikram hesitated before letting his hand wander to find mine again.

Together we walked hand in hand, the city lights of London's skyline twinkling behind us.

I needed this moment.

I needed, just this once, to live inside a vacuum without thoughts of Chris, or Hana, or Radhika—or anyone else—penetrating our bubble. The two of us needed to exist on this plane, in this reality, just as we were, just as we had been nine years ago.

"What are we doing, Vikram?" I asked, looking down at our interwoven fingers. "Have we already broken the rules? Are we going back in time?"

"We broke the rules then, Lily. Not now. We broke the rules that conspired across continent and time to bring a young boy from Yorkshire and an exceptional girl from Elk River together at the very best university in the world. We defied the odds. We even created a life . . ."

Vikram paused, tears streaming down his cheeks.

"And we didn't listen. We were filled with our own hubris, the arrogance of youth. And I wasn't courageous. I was too determined to follow the rules of man, instead of the rules of the universe. But I deserved better. You deserved better. And now we can *do* better."

Vikram stopped walking and turned to face me, gathering both of my hands in his.

"Come back with me, Lily. There's so much more to say. I need this . . . and I need you."

Tears ran down my cheeks, my hair curling at the tips where the water slid down my neck.

"I've found you again, Lily. And this time, I won't let you go."

Vikram leaned in to kiss me.

My mind went blank.

PART FIVE

TWO YEARS LATER

CHAPTER 56

Lily

Brooklyn, New York
September 5, 2003

I sat on the small bench of our screened-in porch, my body draped between the curling arms of the tufted cushion. The crisp autumn air sent a slight chill down my spine. The knit blanket I'd bought at the thrift store on Myrtle Avenue sat wrapped around my waist, the golden knots of yarn falling just beyond my knees and leaving the bottoms of my feet exposed.

I reached for the mug resting on the oak coffee table in front of me, the fragrant steam of jasmine tea beckoning me closer.

Seeing my outstretched hand, my husband stood from the wing-backed chair where he was reading the newspaper.

"You musn't overexert yourself," he said, passing me the ceramic mug. "Now is the time to be gentle."

Gentle.

That is what he had always been with me, treating the contours of my heart, and now my body, with care. It was a lesson I was finally learning for myself, this teaching of tenderness.

"Your mother said she would be here next month to help," he

offered, lifting the corner of the blanket and sliding beneath it, his body warm as he nestled beside me. "Are you ready?"

"As ready as I'll ever be," I assured him, a small smile forming across my lips.

My mother and I had spoken every day since we called her with the news. I could hear her crying softly on the other end of the line as she summoned my father into the living room. "*Una nueva hoja*," she whispered, her tiny voice breaking through the silence.

It was, I conceded, a new chapter.

For her—and for all of us.

I adjusted my body as my husband drew closer, his feet finding their way to mine. The curve of my stomach peeked through the blanket.

Chris wrapped his arms across my shoulders.

So much had happened in the years since we'd reconnected.

So much life.

So much loss.

And through it all, so much love.

There are days when I still marvel at how it all unfolded, the madness of it all.

But through it, he emerged as my North Star, the calm amidst the high seas of doubt.

Maybe this wasn't the fairytale love of moats crossed and villains slain, but it was the love of my dreams, dreams bigger than I had dared to imagine. It was a love that delivered lightness amidst the density, standing sturdy and whole against the crippling blows of unforeseen heartbreak.

Chris brought me joy and he bought me time, time for bodies that needed to heal and souls that needed repair. He sees me for the woman I've become, not just the girl I once was.

And he chooses me in return.

His courage is both constant and consistent.

Still, when I sit in my chair by the fire, I often think of her.

What would she say about all of this? What would she think of us finding solace in each other, of this friendship turned romantic, turned infinite?

"Love is freedom," I can almost hear her say, sprawled across the dirty white carpet of our college dorm. "Love is a choice."

And her love, above all, was regenerative.

She was the seed that sparked love in all its forms: a sisterhood borne of fate, a romance borne of patience, a family reunited and rescued.

Hers is the love I hope to one day tell my daughter about, when she is ready to hear it.

I will tell it from the beginning.

I will tell her that love is worth finding and fighting for, if you are courageous enough to rewrite a new ending.

If you are strong enough to survive it.

I will tell her a story of love and of freedom, a tale of serenity and peace.

I will tell her how a soul can find rest in another, of how it can find home once again.

I will pray that she embarks on a journey to find her own answers; to love herself, wholly and firstly.

Most of all, I pray that she finds someone who loves her with their eyes wide open.

TIMELINE

October 10, 1940: Cuban constitution implemented.

March 10, 1952: Fulgencio Batista regains power in coup.

July 26, 1953: Fidel Castro's failed attempt to take Moncada military barracks in Santiago de Cuba. *26 de Julio* movement (M26) begins. Castro spends nineteen months in prison (sentenced to fifteen years) and flees to Mexico to reorganize.

August 30, 1956: Fidel Castro and José Antonio Echeverría meet in Mexico City.

October 28, 1956: Colonel Antonio Blanco Rico, chief of Cuba's military intelligence operations, shot and killed at Montmarte nightclub.

November 30, 1956: University of Havana closes due to protests and government opposition. University does not reopen until 1959 when Castro takes power.

December 2, 1956: *Granma* lands in Santiago de Cuba from Mexico.

March 13, 1957: Attack on *Radio Reloj* and the Presidential Palace.

April 20, 1957: Humboldt Massacre. Four *Directorio Revolucionario* members killed by police in Havana apartment.

October 4, 1957: USSR launches *Sputnik*.

January 1, 1959: Batista flees and Castro's forces sweep into power.

January 3, 1959: Herbert Matthews publishes an article in *The New York Times* detailing the success of Castro's Revolution.

December 2, 1976: Fidel Castro becomes president of Cuba.

March 3, 1991: Rodney King is beaten by police in Los Angeles.

March 5, 1991: Rodney King video and interview released by KTLA.

April 29, 1992: Four officers acquitted after seven days of jury deliberations over Rodney King beating. Protests erupt in Los Angeles lasting six days.

February 4, 1997: O.J. Simpson civil trial verdict.

AUTHOR'S NOTE

This book was a labor of love and research.

The bulk of the Cuban timeline takes place in 1957 during the period leading up to the moment Fidel Castro's forces assumed control of the country in 1959, taking leadership from President Fulgencio Batista.

Prior to Castro assuming power, there were several factions competing to determine the trajectory of Cuba's future. One of the rising stars of the Revolution was a young leader who studied architecture at the University of Havana, José Antonio Echeverría. He led the *Directorio Revolucionario*. I have taken artistic liberties in imagining his love interest; the love story I portray here is purely an act of fiction.

The details of the Cuban Revolution and historical figures contained therein, however, are based on true accounts. Thank you to the scholars who have done incredible work gathering details about the period leading up to the Revolution, and for contributing them to the body of Cuban history and recordkeeping. If it were not for your scholarship, many of these stories would have been lost to time.

The Cuban revolution is—both for historians and members of the diaspora—a period filled with tremendous pain, trauma, and outrage. I hope that readers are encouraged, as I was, to learn more about the factors and undercurrents that existed on the island before the Revolution had a name. I further hope that we learn from history—and its warnings—and understand the complexities of the searching human spirit.

LETTER TO MY DAUGHTER

Adelana,

They say that no parent tells their children the full story of how they came to be, living the second act of their lives trying to make sense of the first. We spend our days making an impossible calculation: how can we give our children the freedom to soar, and the roots to grow? How do we give them the wisdom of our experience, and the space to make their own mistakes?

I know you know the basics: that I met your father and our lives changed beautifully and irreversibly when we had you. I first laid eyes on him in the dim yellow lights of Eliot Dining Hall after the spring dance, under string lights and the floating dreams of soon-to-be graduates. He saw me and understood me—and later became a reflection of the journey I was on, searching for purpose and place. Years later, after reconnecting in London, he confidently and quietly—without fanfare or pretense—offered to hold my hand along the way.

By then, I was ready: I wanted a partner—a twin flame—who saw all that this world had to offer and ran toward it without retreat. I wanted someone to embrace our differences, to celebrate them, and to share the lessons from my small corner of the world while learning the lessons of theirs.

And that is exactly what he became.

He silently, almost imperceptibly, became a fact of my life.

A fact I couldn't live without.

His love did not dishonor others, nor was not self-seeking; it was the ultimate act of selflessness. And yet, it was familiar. Through the steady consistency of his love, your father became my choice: a choice that changed my life in ways that were beyond the foresight of my youth.

Which, perhaps, is why that love was so powerful that it later created a life of its own.

You are the product of a love lost and found, of an internal conversation and an external dialogue.

Together, your father and I embarked on a journey to find the pieces of ourselves that had been lost, the pieces of your own story—and of the family we are building—that still needed to be told.

Now, our lessons are your legacy; our experience, your inheritance.

Watching you, I am reminded of a girl I once knew—many moons ago—who embarked on a journey to leave the piedmont of North Carolina, hoping to change her stars. It was so long ago, that when I look in the mirror, I must work harder to recognize her.

You radiate the same pure light, the same spark, the same feisty spirit that demands that the world reckon with you, not the other way around. You are the child that, in many ways, carries the spirit I had—and that I wish the world had done more to protect, instead of try to extinguish.

Spoiler alert: the spark was inexterminable.

May you know that you, too, belong in any room that you enter.

Which is why, when I reflect on the lessons this life has bestowed upon me, the ones I hope—with humility—that I can share with you, I start here:

Fall in love as quickly and as often as you can.

Thank every soul who is courageous enough to share with you a piece of their heart. Protect it, and them, as you would yourself. Enjoy the sweetness of your youth, the ripe fruits of lust and passion, and the intoxicating freedom of your own choices. May you find a love that is true, a love that is wide, a love that is free—and one that is yours.

But also, my sweet girl, look for the stability of peace: the strength of consistency that this society so gravely undervalues. Look for a love that never makes you question where you stand. Look for sameness in your values, diversity in experience. Love is liberating and grounding, perhaps both in equal measure. It is finding someone who sees your heart, whose soul recognizes your own.

Embrace the beauty of your reality, my daughter. Let go of the delusions of "ever after"—built in fantasy and illusion—that have been manufactured and sold to us since we were children. Why has no one ever taught us how to value—or even see—the sublimeness of what it means to settle into the beauty of our lived lives? To ground ourselves in reality, while celebrating the mundane?

Would that not be a love worth choosing? The sacred intimacy of growing old alongside your soul's twin ember, of seeing someone in the full range of their humanity and committing yourselves to the daily act of living? Together?

The journey to getting there, however, is like anything else worthwhile in this life: the best parts are the parts you cannot plan.

And, at times, the parts you cannot see.

That is why we find love in an "other," reflecting and refracting the fragments of our soul that deserve healing, back to us. The love you seek, and the love you will find, will always be a reflection of your own image at different snapshots in time. Because the journey to finding love is a dance with oneself—the self of "now" and the self of "then"— a constant conversation that has no beginning and no end, a conversation that simply "is." It is an invisible pull between two realities: a life you hoped for—one built on the fantasy of love—and a love grown in the face of the realities of adulthood, its preciousness and precariousness.

Now and then.

So when you look up at the stars, remember that you are part of a story, and a universe, that has conspired to bring you here.

To this moment.

To this place.

And as you grasp your future with both hands, remember that you are rooted in such a love—and that you were made from such a love.

You have a history, and you, too, have a story to tell.

Yours,

Mamá

ACKNOWLEDGMENTS

To all the souls on my journey who have ever given me a piece of their heart, thank you. To love is the ultimate act of bravery.

To those who have made the world a gentler place by approaching difference with compassion and curiosity, you have changed lives and granted a sense of visibility that you likely didn't even realize was a gift.

The biggest thank-you goes to my mother, who taught me the importance of building a dream, not just of having one. Mom, you are the blueprint. Your dreams changed the trajectory of generations; you envisioned a life bigger and more vibrant for our family than any of us could have imagined. You are an alchemist—maximizing the potential of everything you touch—and seeing endless capacity in an empty vacuum. When the world does not see us or honor our talent, you taught us that the ancestors withstood the unthinkable so that we could soar. You taught us to create, to own and to nourish our inalienable gifts, so that we can make good things happen for ourselves. We are—and will always be—because of you.

This work of art is for my Papi, my forever fiction reader, who believed that my dreams would—and could—come true. You made a promise that my life would turn out more beautifully than I could have imagined, and you kept it. You are the voice inside my head, Daddy. Your love has shaped the course of my life, allowing me to find it—and recognize it—when I see it. Because of you, I have a wealthy life: rich with passion, rich with peace. Thank you for making that peace the foundation of the life I've known—and the life I am building.

To Miller, my little brother and life's first soulmate: thank you for always being my first phone call. From backyard cartwheels amongst the honeysuckles to midnight dancefloors and Juice Shop smoothies—there is no one I would rather spend this life with than you.

To Adelana, the conduit by which more good things have, and continue to, come. I delight in your ability to love and be loved, and I pray that you know love in all its forms. You, my sweet child, are healing. My dreams came in Technicolor after I had you. Loving you and being your mother is the most natural thing I have ever done. You are my miracle. No one can take from you your spirit, the marrow of who you are, all the love that has been poured into you, and the experiences you will have. Always know to whom you belong and from whence you came. You are the best part of me, and there is no one like you.

To David, the one love who has made it all worth it. You are the bravest of them all. Thank you for loving me with your eyes wide open. Thank you for being fluent in me. Ours is the real-life story behind the fairytales, the true love that the world's ancient dreamers wrote about. Thank you for waiting.

To DTW, thank you for answering that call in November 2022. You kept your promise: you did not meaning-make, but you did help me make meaning. You are an inspiration to the woman I hope to become, leading with intelligent compassion and tender warmth. I will never be able to express the gift you gave me by truly seeing me and believing me the first day we met. You made me dream broader and brighter, not just higher. *What if . . . ? What else?* These are now the questions that guide me.

To Johanna, this story—my story—is in the world because you saw what it could be. Your smile after I told you the real-life saga behind the real-life Vikram was all the confirmation I needed to put my experience to paper. You are fearless, firm, and compassionate—and most importantly, you live your values. You never waivered. You have restored my faith and shown me the full potential of what a beautiful, healthy agent-client relationship can be. I have never in the entirety of my career met an agent like you. You lead with dignity, fierce professionalism, and expertise. *Eres la más talentosa que hay—y te adoro completamente.*

To Tara, thank you for the dignity you and your incredible team have shown me since our very first meeting. I will never forget how nervous I was walking into your (beautiful!) office, and how immediately you put me at ease and made me feel like I belonged. You told me you "loved" my pages and, at some point during that meeting, you referred to me as an "author." An author. That is what you made me. Thank you for your patience, your vision—and for the foresight and faith to believe that this story was one worth telling. You and Johanna cultivate excellence and allow it to succeed, reminding the world that ambitious women—and ambitious women of color—deserve all the good adjectives, too. You do not shrink from hard work and gave me the space and encouragement to do things as many times as it took to get right. This team of bold, beautiful, brilliant women is proof that iron sharpens iron. You certainly sharpened mine.

To Ada Ferrer, who answered my call out of the blue and guided my research and pointed me in all the right directions, thank you for your scholarship and contribution to the recordkeeping of Cuban history as so many of us trace—and retrace—our own stories to its roots.

To my friends and family—namely Eric Rodriguez, Mónica

Zapata, Aunt Charita Johnson, and Grace Cheng—you have held my dreams in the palm of your hand. From reading my early manuscript and helping me imagine the cover, you have walked beside me and shared my excitement along the way. I am forever grateful.

ABOUT THE AUTHOR

Morgan Radford is an anchor and correspondent for NBC News based in New York City. She is the co-anchor of *NBC News Daily,* winner of the 2025 Gracie Award for "Best National News Program." Morgan has won several awards for her reporting featured across *TODAY, NBC Nightly News,* MSNBC, and in Spanish on Telemundo. A graduate of Harvard University, Columbia Journalism School and a Fulbright Scholar, Radford serves on the Columbia Graduate School of Journalism's Board of Visitors and is a life member of the Council on Foreign Relations. Morgan was raised in Greensboro, North Carolina, and currently lives in Brooklyn, New York with her husband and daughter. *Now Then* is her debut novel.